LADY VIOLET FINDS A BRIDEGROOM

THE LADY VIOLET MYSTERIES—BOOK THREE

GRACE BURROWES

GRACE BURROWES PUBLISHING

DEDICATION

This series is dedicated to my nephew, Jackson.

CHAPTER ONE

The time had come for me to have my way with Monsieur Hugh St. Sevier.

The gentleman was willing, of that I had only a scintilla of doubt. I was even more convinced that St. Sevier *was* a gentleman and that he would make an excellent partner for my first venture into the privileges and freedoms a discreet widow was entitled to.

I reached these conclusions as St. Sevier again served as my escort, this time on a journey that would take us the length of England and into central Scotland. St. Sevier professed a desire to see more of his adopted country, and though many widows traveled without a male companion, I did not yet feel sufficiently independent to undertake that challenge.

My decision to dip a naked toe into the waters of dalliance had come over me slowly, in the course of a long winter spent in London. Entertainments in the coldest months are few in the capital, particularly because Parliament, since Waterloo, had not been opening until well after the Yuletide holidays.

In the previous year, I had been all but dragooned into attending a summer house party and then a gathering at my family seat on the occasion of my brother Felix's nuptials. St. Sevier had joined me on those travels and on the adventures I'd encountered when away from my home. The house party had been victimized by a series of thefts. Felix's bride had been abducted prior to the nuptials.

Both puzzles had been solved to my satisfaction, and those excursions had shaken me free of a lingering malaise. After observing two years of mourning for my late husband, I had grown so familiar with the habit of solitude that venturing forth had become an ordeal to be dreaded. St. Sevier, a physician, had coaxed me into leaving Town, and the changes of air had done me good.

As I'd partaken of country vistas, good books, and the occasional horseback ride, I'd shaken off the torpor of grief—a troubled marriage is a more complicated loss than a happy one, in my opinion—and taken stock of my life.

The inventory I found consisted of a smothering portion of boredom, duty, routine, and loneliness. That last item had been difficult to identify, in part because I had so long claimed ownership of it—or it had claimed ownership of me. As the only girl and youngest of five children, I had been isolated by my gender and my age. My mother had died when I was yet a child, and that further nudged me to the edges of the family circle.

I had become engaged at the age of seventeen to Frederick Belmaine, a handsome, wealthy, bon vivant who had appeared to be my every girlish fantasy come true—by the time my father had finished singing Freddie's praises.

Papa, whom the world knows as Sylvanus, Earl of Derwent, has a talent for embroidering heavily on the facts. After my wedding breakfast, Freddie had offered me a chaste kiss on the cheek and nipped off ostensibly to bid farewell to his friends at the club.

He had, in fact, popped around to his mistress's, there to enlist her sympathy for the tribulations he would endure as a new husband. Freddie had not been intentionally cruel, which had made marriage to him all the more bewildering and painful for a girl raised without meaningful female guidance.

Freddie had died five years after speaking the vows he'd broken the day he'd uttered them, the cause of death food poisoning, as far as anybody would tell me. He had expired at his favorite brothel, in the arms of a woman whom I subsequently came to know and even like.

He was a better husband in death than he had been in life. I was quite well fixed and had no need to remarry. I was also somewhat more worldly than many young widows, for Freddie had delighted in educating me out of my sheltered upbringing. Had I provided him with children, he would doubtless have encouraged me to pursue any number of liaisons with his indulgent blessing.

Thoughts of my marriage could still provoke me to anger, but not to the grinding rage I'd felt in the early years of wifehood. I had reconciled myself to the hope that in time Freddie would have put away his extramarital pleasures, and I would have forgiven him his errant ways.

That theory offered comfort and allowed me to instead focus on the notion that I was but six-and-twenty years old, and while I had no wish to remarry, neither did I wish to become a nun. I had no wish to become a mother without benefit of matrimony either, and St. Sevier, as a physician, would be well versed in methods for preventing conception.

With my grand theory of dalliance firmly in hand, I packed up my trunks, endured the grumbling of my maid, Lucy, and climbed into my traveling coach. I sent Lucy ahead with my luggage and a handsome young footman, while I took for myself the pleasure of St. Sevier's company.

That he did not kill me before we'd reached Peterborough was a testament to his great patience and reserves of chivalry. That I did not kill him resulted from the failure of an English gentlewoman's education to teach young ladies the effective use of violence.

Peterborough sits eighty-five miles from London on the Great North

Road. On dry roads in summer, with sound teams at every change, that distance can easily be covered in one long day. Post coaches, which also ran through the night, could do twice the distance in a twenty-four-hour period.

St. Sevier and I were traveling in spring, however. The roads up from London were muddy, two different horses from two different teams had gone lame, and our vehicle was my very own commodious —and thus lumbering—traveling coach.

On our third day, I was determined that we'd make better time. I gave John Coachman the office to make haste where he could safely do so, and we were off. The resulting rhythmic jostling inside the coach meant St. Sevier did not even try to read his newspaper.

"Tell me about the bride," he said, putting said newspaper into the slot fashioned to hold it on the side of the coach. "I don't believe you mentioned her to me before receiving her invitation."

"Fanetta MacPherson was a schoolmate at Miss Harmon's Academy. We both loved books and thus spent many an hour in the school's library. She was a true scholar, while I was..."

What? Waiting to grow up and marry, as all gently bred English girls were supposed to do?

"While you were genuinely curious," St. Sevier said. "She is Scottish?"

"She's half Scottish. Her English mother was raised in the Borders and married a Scotsman, though he unfortunately passed away while Fanny was still young. I would have thought Fanny long-married, but I gather she hasn't had much opportunity to meet suitable parties in her step-father's social ambit. Her mother was ill for some time before she passed away, and Fanny was her companion and caretaker."

Fanny would have been an excellent choice in those roles. She had the most melodious voice, and her narration improved everything from poetry, to plays, to Walter Scott's grand romances. That she lived so distant from the entertainments of Drury Lane was a grave injustice to her literary nature.

"And now," St. Sevier said, "this woman whom you haven't seen for more than eight years invites you north, and you—who have been the next thing to a recluse—are packed and on your way. I must ask myself why."

He was asking *me* why, and doing it from the opposite bench. I was a widow, and proprieties such as never sharing a bench with a man outside my family or my family's close friends were no longer required of me. I had earned my freedom in one of the two ways generally available to a genteel lady.

The first path to freedom was to cast my good name to the wind; the second was to bury a husband.

There was a third way, though, which required heaps of discretion and more than a little cunning. I suspected most women of good breeding eventually stumbled onto that third path, and their lives were a good deal happier for it. They tippled, they took lovers, they gambled at cards, they smoked the occasional pipe of opium or hashish to settle their nerves.

But they did not *get caught*. If I was to embark on my first post-marital liaison, I did not want to get caught either, and St. Sevier's discretion was equal to that challenge.

"I am attending Fanny's nuptials because she did not merely invite me to travel north, she *demanded* that I come." Had begged me by letter, as only Fanny could. Her correspondence over the years had been sporadic but colorful, sketching for me the beauty of her home shire, the squabbles of the servants in her step-father's household, and her utter frustration with her step-father's lack of social activity.

"You will miss most of the spring Season in London," St. Sevier said. "Does that bother you?"

"Not in the least." The coach hit a smooth patch of road, and I let go of the strap I'd been holding. "The last thing I want to spend my time on is a lot of pointless social gatherings where I dodge the overtures of my late husband's friends."

"They importune you directly? Englishmen are so clumsy."

While Frenchmen could be so dense. Hugh St. Sevier had been my escort of choice over the winter, and no matter how much I pretended to lean on his proffered arm, or how often I invited him in for a late-night cup of tea, he was never anything but perfectly correct with me.

And *that* bothered me. He'd kissed me a time or two when we'd been off on our adventures outside of Town, but since we'd returned from my brother's wedding, Hugh might have numbered among London's confirmed bachelors.

While I, increasingly, felt inclined to spread my wings, as it were.

"Those louts don't even importune me," I replied. "Some of them simply assume I'm willing and..." I waved my hand in a circle. "I had to stomp on Timothy Carstairs's foot to get him to withdraw his hands and his lips from my person."

"Carstairs is the pretty blond fellow with the sweet mouth?"

"The same."

"He likes to swive men," St. Sevier said. "I do not say how I know this, but it is a fact. He assaults you to prove his masculinity, or to at least create enough rumor to obscure his preferences. I care not what manner of assignations he makes with consenting partners, but I will thrash him for you if you like."

Hugh was ever gallant, even if he did fail to notice my direct over-tures. "Thank you, no. The less fuss made the better. Carstairs at least apologized. Henry Newell wasn't half so gracious."

"That one." St. Sevier's features reflected quintessential Gallic disdain. "He believes because God favored him with blond curls, that women should fall at his feet, despite his weak chin and big ears. He is stupid, which he cannot help, but he should be thrashed for arrogance."

St. Sevier was correct: Henry Newell was neither good-looking nor clever. St. Sevier, however, was a handsome devil, with chestnut hair, doe-brown eyes, and enough height and muscle that even without a charming French accent, he would have been a coveted addition to any hostess's guest list. His accent, I noticed, intensified when he was in the grip of strong emotion, and he preferred to curse in his native tongue.

What language would he use in bed?

"Violet, did you spend your social evenings in my company simply to ward off Mayfair's horde of Henry Nincompoops?"

And sometimes, St. Sevier was quite perceptive. "I did not remain at your side entirely to thwart the louts." This was as close to an invitation to be frank as St. Sevier had given me in the past six months. I cast around for a subtle, witty lure, or one that at least wasn't silly.

"I like you, Hugh." Not the cleverest observation I'd ever made. "I like you and…"

He cocked his head. "And?"

"And I like you." A blush crept up my neck and suffused my cheeks. I did not tell him that his kisses stood out in my memory like perfect holidays, or that I speculated about his appearance without clothing, or that I enjoyed touching him.

"I adore you," he replied, reaching for his newspaper. "I hope I have been forthright in that regard."

He shook out his newspaper, and I wondered if he was teasing me.

"Did you know these benches fold out to make a comfortable traveling bed?" I asked, as casually as I could. "The jostling is ever so much more bearable when one reclines."

He folded his newspaper over and peered at the article in the upper righthand corner. "Violet, are you propositioning me? If so, I can acquaint you with two facts that are relevant to your aspirations. First, I desire you madly. When I say madly, I do mean *I desire you madly*. Second, if and when it is my very great honor to become your lover, I will not allow our passions to be consummated in the traveling monstrosity where your late husband casually took his pleasure of you between posting inns."

That Hugh would disdain a chance to make love with me hurt;

that he'd judge my husband for the lusty opportunist he'd been comforted.

"So." St. Sevier snapped the newspaper open and refolded it. "*Were* you propositioning me?"

"You flatter yourself outrageously."

He grinned and saluted with two fingers. "My apologies for presuming. Would you like to read the Society pages?"

I did not give a rotten fig for the Society pages. "Thank you."

He passed them over, and for the next three changes, I dutifully stared at somebody's natterings about a Venetian breakfast. All the while, I was preoccupied with a question: If Hugh St. Sevier would not consummate our passions in my comfy traveling coach, under what circumstances would he consummate them?

St. Sevier and I fell into a routine, reading to each other, dozing on our respective benches, and even—this was *not* the done thing under usual circumstances—taking turns riding up on the box with John Coachman. The scenery as we traveled north appealed to me strongly, for it was more dramatic than the tame rural hills of the south. On our fourth night out, we stopped at an inn that appeared to offer better lodging than most.

Unfortunately, the Stag and Stork was also as raucous as an election-day market. On our fifth morning, I climbed into the coach more fatigued than when I disembarked the previous evening.

We bickered away half the day, and I insisted we break our journey with a midday picnic basket. Our coachman and groom were only too happy to enjoy an extra pint or two in the common of a rural inn, while St. Sevier and I took our lunch on a blanket spread beneath an enormous oak on the village green.

We were in Yorkshire, new territory for me, and I found the brisk air and broad sky invigorating.

"You have an appetite," St. Sevier said as I started on my second sandwich of ham and cheddar. "Only great hunger could coax a refined palette past what passes for mustard in England."

"I do have an appetite," I said, "and I asked that your sandwiches be made with butter instead of mustard because I know your digestion to be delicate."

He sat cross-legged on his half of the blanket, and in the bright early afternoon sunshine, I could see that St. Sevier had had no more sleep the previous night than I had.

"My digestion is equal to the insult of English mustard," he replied. "I was with the military. I would have eaten boiled tree bark at times and been grateful. That does not mean I seek alimentary suffering in times of peace. You are wearing a dab of butter..." He used his smallest finger to trace the corner of my lip. "English butter, I will grant you, is preferable to any I have tasted on the Continent, though Irish butter is better still."

He held forth about various nationalities of butter as I dabbed with my table napkin at the corner of my lip. When I'd completed that bit of tidying, Hugh slowly ran his tongue over his buttery fingertip.

As if an oak had fallen from the limb above and coshed me on the head, I realized he might be flirting with me.

Or he might not. We packed up and climbed back into the monstrosity, and almost at once, my eyes grew heavy.

"You need a nap," Hugh said. "As your traveling companion, I have no wish to endure the sharp tongue a lack of rest can produce in you. I believe you mentioned that the benches fold out?"

"I mentioned that three days ago, St. Sevier."

"Two, and now we are tired, and the afternoon ahead of us is long. Let us rest." He rose and, despite the rocking of the coach, took only a moment to fetch pillows and blankets from the cedar-lined cupboards under the benches, and arrange our seats into a serviceable mattress.

"You seem familiar with the coach's mechanisms," I said, opening a blanket over my legs.

"I have my own vehicles," he replied, passing me a pillow. "Not as commodious as your pleasure barge, but adequate." He sat with his back against the rear wall, while he pulled off his boots and stockings.

I did likewise with my half boots, setting our footwear by the door. That Hugh and I were barefoot together set my imagination rollicking down all manner of idle pathways.

"I will be your pillow," he said, making an offer into a statement of fact. "Put a pillow at your back and rest your head here." He patted his muscular thigh. "You will be asleep before the first change."

St. Sevier had apparently actually slept in moving coaches, as opposed to the recreational activity my husband had got up to with me. I did find that bracing my back against the wall of the coach and curling at something of an angle allowed me to stretch out my legs. The pillow at my back cushioned me from the swaying of the coach, and when I laid my head on St. Sevier's lap, he stroked my hair.

"Lovely. Now close your eyes and go to sleep. If any highwaymen come along, I will wake you up so you can drive them off with your parasol and hatpin. This, I promise, my lady."

His caresses were magically soothing and—alas for me—not the least bit seductive. Still, I enjoyed his touch, enjoyed the sense of caring and affection they conveyed, and I was soon drifting off. I could only wonder again if this scandalous informality wasn't another stealthy approach to flirtation, or even—truly, my imagination had grown fanciful—to seduction.

I woke a good three changes later. When we reached our coaching inn that evening, Hugh escorted me to my room after supper and bowed over my hand with the same mannerly correctness he'd shown me on previous evenings.

"If I invited you in," I asked, "would you join me?"

He kept hold of my hand, his grasp warm. "Of course, for some whist or another chapter of Walter Scott's tales of adventure. If you are asking me whether I would seduce you in an English coaching inn, the noise of the common our music and the scent of the stable yard our perfume, I must wonder if you are not in the grip of a slight fever. So momentous an undertaking deserves every luxury and comfort two lovers can imagine."

"Fortunately," I replied, "I wasn't asking you any such thing. Good night, St. Sevier, and thank you for another day of splendid companionship."

He bowed. "Your servant, my lady."

He moved off down the corridor, and I might have been imagining things—a slight fever indeed—but it appeared to me that St. Sevier was ever so subtly strutting for my benefit. I slept well that night and dreamed lovely naughty dreams, and St. Sevier was in every one of them.

CHAPTER TWO

To keep my mind off strutting Frenchmen, and to better organize my thoughts as we approached the Scottish border, I reread the letters Fanny had sent me over the years. She loved her little corner of Scotland, which she described as in full view of the Highland Line, whatever that meant. I gathered her step-father's property was within sight of some mountains, though situated on arable land.

"You are renewing your epistolary acquaintance with the bride?" St. Sevier asked as I finished one of the more recent letters.

"I am." I tucked Fanny's correspondence into a traveling satchel that I kept in the coach. "She has been an erratic but interesting correspondent. Two themes come through, the first being an abiding love of her homeland."

"The second?"

"She has little patience for her step-father. I do wonder if she isn't marrying simply to leave his authority."

A light rain pattered on the coach roof, and I sent up a prayer that the shower would pass. The coachman and groom suffered when the going was bad, as did the horses. Coachmen were expected to maintain strict sobriety on the job—a rule most often honored in the breach—and cold and damp only gave them more frequent recourse to their flasks. Then too, relentless rain had involved me in a serious coaching mishap the previous year, and I had no wish to repeat that experience.

"Women have married to gain independence from parents since marriage was invented," St. Sevier said. He hadn't suggested any other naps, but he had acceded on a particularly bumpy stretch of road to sit with me on the forward-facing bench. He leaned forward now and extracted one of the heavy wool lap robes from beneath the opposite seat.

"That was certainly part of my motivation," I said as St. Sevier unfolded the blanket over my knees. "Thank you. I was a trifle chilly."

"And you ignored your own discomfort, because you are English and Lady Violet and all that other nonsense. Cuddle up, and you will be more comfortable still." He looped an arm around my shoulders, and I was struck again by how often he couched invitations as statements or commands.

I tucked close and rested my head against his shoulder. "As much as Fanny has gushed about her garden and her views, and as effusively as she insisted that I attend her nuptials, I cannot recall her describing the groom."

I had the oddest urge to stroke St. Sevier's knee and thigh, to simply pet him. I did not yield to such foolishness for fear I'd get a lecture about English ineptitude at seduction, how a man prefers to be caressed, and *the good God in heaven* knew what else. Instead, I turned my face into St. Sevier's muscular arm and took a sniff.

"You always smell good," I said. "If I were marrying you, I might gush to a trusted confidante about how luscious I find your scent."

A subtle change of posture came over my traveling companion, and though it was very bad of me, quite naughty indeed, I further tested my hypothesis.

"If you had become the object of my most secret desires," I went on, "I would venture to describe your excellent physique, how stirring

I found the sight of you in the saddle, the delight I took in your smile. Fanny hasn't described her groom in any of those regards."

"What has she said about him?"

I thought back over the letters and tried mentally to locate Fanny's first mention of her intended. "His name is John. He has recited poetry to her—she likes that—and he makes her laugh. She doesn't say if he's young, old, short, bald... But then, Fanny loves poetry."

"Describe your late spouse to me," St. Sevier said, twitching the blanket up over my shoulder.

The coach swayed around a curve, and I was mashed agreeably closer to his side. "Freddie was a rake," I said. "Handsome, hedonistic, unrepentantly self-indulgent, and while he had exquisite manners, and he wasn't overtly unkind, he was impatient with my traditional views. I failed to give him children, and that is the one task required of a wife, so I daresay he was as disappointed in me as I was in him."

And yet, from time to time, I missed him. Missed having somebody with whom I shared a few private jokes, missed his affectionate nature, missed the envious looks from young women whose husbands weren't half so wealthy or charming.

"You do not tell me if he's short, fat, bald, or American. Only that he was handsome, and he neglected you terribly. This is why French wives are so tolerant. Their husbands might stray, but they do not stray sufficiently to ever leave their ladies feeling neglected, and it is the same with the ladies. They have a discreet frolic, but they remain loyal and attentive to their husbands."

"And would you stray, as a husband?"

The coach righted itself, and still St. Sevier remained silent.

"Hugh?"

He leaned near to murmur in my ear, though nobody could have possibly overheard him. "Do you know why I have not become your lover yet, Violet?"

"*Yet?*"

"I practice restraint because I am mad for you, and I insist that you be equally mad for me. I want you to long desperately for me and for pleasure in my arms, to desire me past reason, past your English dignity, past any memories that haunt you from your marriage. People who are mad for each other do not stray; they cannot even conceive of such a temptation. Does that answer your question?"

I disagreed with him. Freddie would have said, as St. Sevier had said, that he adored me. When Freddie had been with me, I'd felt cherished and desired, and I had, for a time, longed for the pleasures I'd shared with my husband. None of that had stopped Freddie from being liberal with his charms outside the marriage, and his attentions to his inamoratas had doubtless been equally adoring.

But St. Sevier was not Freddie, and it occurred to me that perhaps some lady had served my friend a disloyal turn, and that I was not the only traveler whose journey was weighed down by memories.

"You answered my question," I said, "in so far as you might not stray during the honey month. Fanny also hasn't mentioned a wedding journey."

"Scottish customs are different, and wedding journeys cost money. Perhaps finances limit the happy couple's options."

"They shouldn't. Fanny is an heiress through her mama. That's part of the reason I expected her to marry years ago. Whoever has captured her heart has also added considerably to his own security. Might we fold out the benches again? I could use another nap."

"That is enough, Violet."

I patted Hugh's thigh. "No need to growl."

He said nothing, but I rejoiced to learn he was not nearly so in control of his urges as he'd have me think. I suspected he'd be a ferociously faithful and devoted husband. I, however, had had my fill of being a wife. On that point, I was quite certain.

"Scotland has a wealth of building stone," Mr. Lachlan Leland said, leading me and St. Sevier across a soaring medieval great hall. "Anything built reasonably well here will still be around five centuries later. If we don't like it, we simply add on to it. The library holds maps of Leland House, but I also assign a footman to the family wing when we have visitors. Niall won't let you get lost."

Mr. Leland was a surprisingly youthful redhead, broad of shoulder, and nearly as tall as St. Sevier. Fanny's step-father exuded the brisk graciousness of the Scottish host as he led us through his impressive foyer.

My friend Fanny dwelled in a fanciful castle-cum-stately-home, and it struck me as odd that she'd never described such a splendid dwelling in her letters. Leland House sported turrets and crenellations sufficient for any fairy tale, and the main drive was lined on both sides with lime trees luminous with new leaves. The house itself, whitewashed from its foundation to the topmost flagstaff, looked magical for standing against a backdrop of steep hills and dark, majestic firs.

The medieval hall that served as its vast foyer was bristling with weaponry arranged in oddly artistic patterns. Wheels of knives and swords adorned the walls, firearms with fantastically long barrels hung above them. On either side of the hall's enormous stone fireplace stood a suit of gleaming armor, and not the petite versions I'd seen in the south.

Ferocious-looking pikes and halberds, daggers and targes, and even a star-pattern of what looked to be antique pistols made an interesting first impression on me.

"The point," said Mr. Leland, "was to reassure any who came here that allies of this family were well protected. Foes were warned to tread lightly, if they made it this far." He smiled mischievously. "The lot of it requires a prodigious amount of dusting, if you want to know the truth."

St. Sevier said little, but then, our journey had been long, and we were both likely eager for some solitude and a nap in a real bed.

Mr. Leland led us through his home, beneath fanciful baroque ceilings, across parquet marble floors, and along corridors lined with portraits—"That's Betsy Leland, buried three husbands, each younger than the last,"—and an interesting assortment of *objets d'art*. Cloisonné snuffboxes, gilt-framed miniatures, jeweled music boxes, intricately enameled eggs, and whimsical ivory netsukes were displayed at tastefully distant intervals.

Somebody, maybe generations of somebodies, had loved this house and filled it with treasures, and yet, Fanny was apparently eager to leave this place.

"Our housekeeper has put you in the suite fitted out for the previous owner's parents," Mr. Leland said. "You share a sitting room, and your balcony has a wonderful view of the mountains." He opened a door carved with enormous thistles and some prancing beast I would examine later.

"Lady Violet, your effects will be put in the blue bedroom," he went on, gesturing to a door on the left. "Monsieur St. Sevier, we hope you will be comfortable in the—"

"Violet!" Fanny emerged from the blue bedroom and barreled into my arms. "Violet, you came, you came. I am so glad you came."

My first impression was one of great joy, for Fanny had been a friend at a time when friendships had been few and dear, and she had done her part to maintain the friendship over a great distance. I had been through much since she and I had last embraced. To hug somebody who'd been a familiar before marriage and widowhood had changed me was precious.

My second impression was that Fanny needed a few square meals. She'd been a robust girl, but the woman who hugged me so enthusiastically was a slender little creature of bones and angles. With her strawberry-blond hair and great blue eyes, she looked like an escaped denizen of a fairy mound.

"And this," Fanny said, stepping back and curtseying, "must be Dr. St. Sevier. Monsieur, I cannot thank you enough for safely delivering my dear friend to me. I hope you will enjoy your stay with us and that you and Lady Violet will be in no hurry to leave."

St. Sevier bowed over her hand and offered one of his signature charming smiles. "At present, Miss MacPherson, I am so glad to be free of her ladyship's coach that you will have trouble convincing me to ever sit upon its benches again."

A procession of porters brought up our trunks, and a kilted footman carried in a tray.

"I will send your maid to you when you have had a chance to do justice to the tray," Fanny said. "Come along, Lachlan. Our guests are weary, and we will see them at supper. Violet, we have much to discuss. *Much,* though it will keep until you are feeling more the thing."

Just like that, St. Sevier and I were alone in our shared sitting room.

"Miss MacPherson is not well," St. Sevier said, ambling over to the tray. "Or she has recently been unwell. The shadows beneath her eyes, the lack of luster to her skin and hair. Was she always so petite?"

"No. She was nicely rounded, to use genteel parlance."

If St. Sevier was troubled that we'd been given bedrooms that all but adjoined, he showed no sign of it. He poured a cup of steaming tea, added a drizzle of honey and a dollop of what looked like cream, then put a square of shortbread on the saucer and held it out to me.

"You have shadows beneath your eyes too, Violet. One doesn't drink as much as one should when traveling. Soldiers on the march make the same mistake."

The tea was perfect, and that St. Sevier would fix it for me as opposed to waiting for me to pour out and serve him, was a precious consideration. He made himself a cup—black—and took two pieces of shortbread out to a balcony that ran the length of the sitting room.

"What do you suppose is out there?" I asked, joining him at the railing. No rain fell, but the day was so damp with fog and mist that it might as well have been raining. The back garden fell away down a hill to a stand of tall firs that formed a dark green wall. The hill was contoured such that the garden sloped gently to a high stone wall, and beyond that—judging from the trees—the declivity became much steeper. Despite the damp, the cool air felt refreshing, particularly when I held a hot cup of tea.

"The Highland Line," Hugh said, gesturing with his tea cup, "doubtless runs along that horizon. This house was probably originally fortified to defend against raiders swarming down from the hills to loot the prosperous farms and villages in the valley. Back inside with you, Violet. I can't have you getting an ague on the eve of your friend's wedding."

I trundled into the sitting room, which was somebody's aesthetic tribute to a singular plaid. The pattern managed to be both somber and busy, including dark blue, green, and black with dashes of orange, yellow, and white. The rug, curtains, and sofa pillows were all in the same design, while the furniture itself had been spared, though I recalled that the footman's kilt had been of the same hues.

"What do you suppose is amiss with Fanny?" I felt comfortable asking because she was not Hugh's patient.

"Her hand was quite cold," he said, "and her fingernails looked thin and brittle. At a guess, I'd say she suffers a lack of adequate blood. I do not like this house."

St. Sevier was usually quite the diplomat, unless provoked by another's rudeness. He was tired, though, and far from even his English home.

"Why not?"

"Your friend and her step-father live here, amid all this wealth and tradition, and she is soon to leave this place. This is exactly why the French did away with their aristocracy, or tried to. What is the point of treasuring guns that do not fire and swords gone dull? What is the point of housing two people in an edifice of this size?"

I refilled his empty tea cup and added a square of some blond, sugary confection. "My late husband agreed with you. He thought allowing a bunch of wealthy, self-interested, in-bred toffs to run the country for their own further enrichment was stupid. Freddie believed that greed ultimately destroyed France, and in another sense, Napoleon's greed destroyed her all over again."

St. Sevier bit into the sweet. "You think Frenchmen are greedy?"

The French had restored their monarchy and aristocracy upon the Corsican's defeat, but I was abruptly too tired for philosophy.

"Of course not, but aristocrats as a class might be. My husband was greedy when it came to his pleasures. He was half Welsh and half English. Perhaps covetousness is a nationality of its own. Would you mind undoing my dress?"

Hugh finished his treat and dusted his hands. "Why do I have the sense your question is not an invitation?"

"Because it isn't. Either Fanny forgets how women's clothing works, or she thinks I will wait until Lucy deigns to appear to change my clothes. I am tired now, and I want to be free of this wretched dress."

I could get out of my stays unassisted, because the laces tied in front. The dress, however, was held closed by a row of hooks down the back. St. Sevier was no stranger to women's attire, and I was exhausted.

"Very well," he said, turning me by the shoulders. "I will be your lady's maid. Far be it from me to confine a woman to clothing she does not wish to wear."

His fingers were deft and knowing as he stood immediately behind me, and that this was often a service performed by a husband or lover, made the moment more personal than two travelers exchanging a courtesy.

Something warm brushed against my nape, then St. Sevier gave my bottom a gentle shove. "To bed with you, where you will dream of a handsome, gallant Frenchman who longs to see you as God made you."

"Thank you," I said, without turning. Even my husband had not seen me entirely unclothed. That St. Sevier would tease me with such a notion was enough to make sleep far more elusive than it ought to have been.

∾

"The whole tartan thing is a bunch of recently concocted rot," Miss Eulalie MacKellan observed, holding out her wineglass to her brother. "But it's harmless and fun, and our plaids are ever so pretty. Why shouldn't we plaster them all over the country?"

Miss MacKellan was our host's niece, and while she was petite like Fanny, she was dark-haired. Her uncle called her a throwback to the Picts, though she had the same startling blue eyes as Lachlan and his nephew.

"Is it rot," St. Sevier asked from across the table, "if once-forbidden fashions restore a sense of national pride?"

"I want to argue with you," Mr. Donald MacKellan replied, "and claim that prancing around in a lot of itchy wool will never overcome the shame of Bonnie Prince Charlie's defeat at Culloden, but our footmen certainly seem to stand taller for wearing their Scottish finery."

Donald was a strapping blond with a dimple in his left cheek when he smiled, which was often. He and Eulalie bore a resemblance despite a difference in coloring and physique. They had the same merry laugh, the same way of pausing before making a remark. That mannerism imbued their words with the air of a humorous confidence.

I was not sure how they came to reside with their uncle at Leland House, but the term poor relation did come to mind.

"You will note," Fanny said from St. Sevier's side, "that we made it through the entire main course without mentioning the Forty-five. Are you composing an ode to that wine bottle, Donnie, or might you pass it over this way?"

"Walter Scott has much to answer for," Lachlan proclaimed from the head of the table, launching into a recounting of the author's literary transgressions.

I sat at my host's right, St. Sevier at his left. Donald had taken the place to my right, in the middle of the table, with Fanny across from him. Eulalie had the place to Donald's right, and across from her, another place had been laid.

Perhaps Scottish custom was to lay out place settings in pairs, but no cutlery had been arranged at the foot of the table, opposite Lachlan at the head.

I noticed this curiosity while Lachlan and Eulalie argued over whether Walter Scott's romantic Highlanders and clever Scottish countryfolk were trivializing a troubled past or redeeming it. Fanny pushed her venison around on her plate, and when I caught her eye, she winked at me.

She was apparently accustomed to her step-family's table talk, and as schoolgirls, we had exchanged many a wink. We had also developed a whole language of hand signals, our riposte to the languages of the flowers, glove, fan, and parasol.

What a polyglot a fashionable young woman was expected to be.

"Lady Violet is fatigued," Donnie said, suggesting I had been woolgathering, "or perhaps we bore her with ancient history."

"Your grandfather fought at Culloden," Lachlan retorted, and though his tone was casual, the rebuke was not. "His story is not irrelevant in this house."

"Lachlan is right," Fanny said, speaking up for the first time since the soup had been served. "Culloden was little more than seventy years ago. Compared to all of Scottish history, that is quite recent. Shall we take our guests fishing if the weather is fine tomorrow?"

"Fishing?" St. Sevier asked. "You have good fishing here?"

Oh dear. I knew a man in thrall to a sport when I saw one—or saw three—and thus the rest of the meal—until the ladies withdrew—was spent rhapsodizing about salmon, trout, and the lures necessary to tempt a fish to its death.

"Eulie is quite the angler," Fanny said as we ladies settled around an exquisite porcelain tea set. "I spent too much time being educated in England to develop much of a casting arm, but I can recite the Scottish royal succession back to Kenneth MacAlpin."

This comment, like so many others, reminded me that Scotland was a country separate from England. Queen Elizabeth had not ruled over these people, but her cousin Mary's son, King James VI of Scotland, had become Elizabeth's heir—despite Elizabeth ordering his mama's execution—and he thus was also styled James I of England. The history of the two countries for centuries on either side of that union of thrones was tempestuous and more often unhappy for the Scots.

My husband, whose father had been Welsh, likened the relationship between England and Scotland to an arranged marriage between cousins. The result was quarrelsome, as siblings forced by family bonds into proximity were, and intimate, as spouses forced into proximity by holy vows were, with periods of harmony inevitably ending in acrimony.

"Will you come fishing with us, Lady Violet?" Eulalie asked. "Or perhaps you are fishing for a certain handsome Frenchman?"

"St. Sevier is a friend," I said, "a dear friend, and I do believe once somebody puts a fishing pole in his hand, we could swim naked before his eyes, and he would only be annoyed that we were scaring the fish."

"They are all like that," Eulalie replied, holding her tea cup under her nose. "Donnie will spend hours standing up to his thighs in frigid water, swilling whisky and watching his line. If he was as intent on catching a bride, we'd have had a wedding here years ago."

That would have been the perfect opening for Fanny to mention her upcoming nuptials, but the conversational moment passed, and talk wandered to the weather, the housekeeper's departure for a visit with her sister, and the progress of planting on Leland House's tenant farms.

My eyes were growing heavy, and I was on the point of excusing myself when the men arrived. Donnie and Lachlan were having a boisterous argument about salmon and trout, and the patient humor in St. Sevier's eyes suggested his interest in fishing had also fallen victim to fatigue.

He sent me a glance of subtle, cheerful commiseration over the tea service, and as soon as politely possible, I excused myself. My sense was Donnie and Lachlan could argue all night, abetted by Eulalie, while Fanny, St. Sevier, and I were eager for our beds.

"Fanny, will you light me up?" I asked.

"I would be happy to." She popped to her feet before her step-cousin could put down his figurative fishing pole long enough to assist her, and I saw her steady herself on the back of her chair.

St. Sevier rose and put a hand under her elbow. "Are you well, Miss MacPherson?"

"Just a touch light-headed," she replied. "Fine French vintages can have that effect."

"I will escort the ladies upstairs," St. Sevier said, "and thank my host for a lovely meal." He bowed to Lachlan and Eulalie, took up a carrying candle, and held the door.

When he wanted to, St. Sevier had a way of being utterly independent without giving offense, which fascinated me. I also wondered how that characteristic would manifest between the sheets, which was proof positive that I, too, needed to be careful around the *fine French vintages*.

St. Sevier excused himself in our shared sitting room, and I prevailed on Fanny to help me undress.

As soon as my bedroom door was closed, Fanny dropped into a reading chair beside my hearth. "The fishing expedition will leave early," she said, "and for the duration of the venture, Lachlan will insist that evening is the better time for salmon. I could recite their bickering from memory."

I knelt before her and gave her my back. She seemed so fatigued by the whole evening that even standing up to undo my hooks would be an effort. Her gown was loose on her, and by the limited light of the candles, she looked ethereally pale.

She might have been afflicted with consumption, except I hadn't heard her cough once.

"You call your step-father by his name?" I asked, rising and moving behind the privacy screen.

"I always have. He was our steward, a sixth cousin of some sort on Mama's side. I forget the actual connection, but it's ridiculously distant, traversing in-laws and generations and crossing the border a time or two. That's how it is in rural Scotland. You share a last name with half your congregation, and the elders sit about with their pipes and drams tracing family lines back to the Flood."

I eased off my dress and shimmied out of my stays. "Lachlan was younger than your mother?"

"Twelve years younger, which ought to have been a scandal, but it wasn't. He made her happy, and he remained devoted to her throughout her illness. He's equally devoted to preserving the house and the family legacy, and that is fortunate, because I would rather write poetry and read books."

I stepped from behind the privacy screen, wearing only my shift, and shrugged into a flannel-lined dressing gown.

"Does a woman's day hold any greater pleasure than the moment when she removes her corset and is once again free to move about as she pleases?" I emphasized my question with a good, long stretch, followed by a yawn.

"You were married," Fanny replied, smiling. "I will defer to your judgment on the matter of a woman's pleasure."

And again, the moment would have been right to bring up Fanny's approaching nuptials, but she declined to do so, and I did not feel it appropriate to press.

"I am widowed," I said. "My outlook on life has changed accordingly."

"What is your outlook on the handsome Frenchman?" Fanny asked, rising.

"He is a dear friend." I was growing tired of describing him thus. St. Sevier had saved my life, in more ways than one. He'd physically pulled me from a raging torrent in the midst of a coaching accident, and he'd emotionally pulled me from melancholia and reclusiveness.

"That you can say that, after sharing a coach with him for more than a week, suggests he's also a true friend. I suspect Eulie might try to sample his charms. Lachlan is generous about offering any distant relation a place to stay for however long they need it, but we do not entertain much here, and Eulie grows restless."

I knew that same *restlessness*, at least where St. Sevier was concerned. "I have no claim on St. Sevier's person," I said, which was the truth. "And as far as I know, he is unattached."

Fanny considered me, head cocked. She looked like a bright-eyed little pullet, young in body, old in wisdom.

"Then he is an idiot, but then, all men are idiots, and they make idiots of us too." She rose and caught me in a tight hug. "I am so glad you are here, Violet. I was going mad without you."

I hugged her slight frame, glad I had made the journey. "Will you tell me of your groom?" I asked. "I am dying to meet him."

She pulled away and moved toward the door. "There is time for that later, and I'm sure you will love him as I do. Now, you need your sleep."

She was again using my need for sleep to dodge a discussion of her marital particulars. I allowed it, because I did not want to be rude and because I did want to find my bed.

And yet, I had one more question. "I noticed an empty place at the dinner table. Was somebody missing from the company?"

She made a face reminiscent of her girlhood attitude toward our drawing master, a fussy old martinet who had smelled of lemon drops.

"That place was set for Iain. He has no manners, but he works hard. Some mare was probably demanding his attention in the foaling barn, or a plow horse was lamed breaking sod. You'll meet him, but you'd best stand downwind of him when you do. I love him dearly, but he tends to fit the earthy description of the rural Scotsman."

"He's another sibling to Eulie and Donnie?"

"The eldest, and you know what that means." She grinned, blew me a kiss, and was out the door.

I had four brothers, all older than me. Our eldest, Mitchell, Viscount Ellersby, was a duty-bound stick in the mud who unbent only in the presence of his young daughters.

And he, fortunately, was hundreds of miles to the south. If family squabbles were to overshadow Fanny's nuptials, at least they wouldn't be *my* family squabbles. On that happy thought, I warmed the sheets and climbed beneath the covers.

I dreamed of silvery, nimble fish with French accents, and woke to a glorious dawn, made even more so by the sight of St. Sevier in his dressing gown, greeting the day from the balcony.

CHAPTER THREE

"Who would ever leave this?" I asked, taking the place beside St. Sevier as the first rays of daylight streamed over the western hills. Beyond the garden wall, a doe and two fawns nibbled lush spring grass in the shadow of the pines, and wisps of mountain fog drifted up over the firs.

The scent was glorious, piney and fresh.

"Many Scots had no choice but to leave," St. Sevier said, and I wondered what he saw in the mists and shadows. "They were cleared off the land their families had farmed profitably for centuries, left to hope the cities or a new world would have room for them."

I slipped an arm around his waist, and he passed me the tea cup he'd been holding. "I gather the history lesson continued over the port?" I asked.

"I heard all about the Darien scheme."

The tea was delicious. Hot and strong with a hint of honey and a dash of cream. St. Sevier looped an arm around my shoulders, and I bethought myself that this was the perfect way to start a day.

"What is, or was, the Darien scheme?"

He took back the cup, finished the tea, and set it aside. "In the

1690s, some smart soul got the idea that the Scots could make a tidy sum by setting up a company to haul goods across the Isthmus of Panama. In theory, the idea had merit. The English Navy took exception, the Spanish military equally so. Disease, squabbling, and bad management also took a toll, and in ten years, one-fifth of Scotland's circulating currency disappeared into the tropical jungles."

Somewhere in my barely recollected history lessons, I'd been regaled with a different version of this event, something to do with foolish, greedy Scottish adventures, God's will, and the incompetence of bumpkins.

"But England soon opened her ports to the Scots, if I recall, and Scotland recovered."

St. Sevier was blessedly warm, and he smelled good. A little of honeysuckle or gardenia, and also of something sharp, sweet, and clean. I had rarely encountered Hugh so soon upon waking and never when I was still in my nightgown and robe. He was dressed, in so far as he wore breeches, shirt, and waistcoat, but he hadn't donned a cravat and in place of a morning coat he wore a dressing gown.

I was thus seeing him in semi-undress, a privilege a gentleman usually extended only to intimates.

"England did not *open* her ports," St Sevier said, taking me by the hand and leading me to a wooden bench along the balcony wall. "England demanded that the union of thrones James the I and VI effected in 1603 be followed in 1707 by a union of the English and Scottish parliaments. Wealthy Scots saw the gain to be had accessing English ports, while the rest of Scotland saw only a return of domination and humiliation by England."

He kept hold of my hand when we sat and tucked his arm around my shoulders again. I had missed masculine affection since becoming a widow. With my husband, the little touches and passing caresses had been frequent at first, though at least half the time they'd ended with my skirts rucked up and my décolletage disarranged.

I had soon realized that I was the tame appetizer Freddie enjoyed before indulging in his more risqué pleasures.

"Who was right?" I asked. "Were the English presenting an opportunity or taking advantage of Scotland's bad luck?"

"Some of both. Some Scots certainly benefitted from the union of the parliaments, and whoever did the bargaining ensured Scotland could keep her domestic laws, her own church, and her own schools. But the clearances picked up momentum after the Acts of Union, and Scottish uprisings in 1715 and 1745 created more enmity between the two lands."

My head naturally rested against his muscular shoulder. "You learned all this over a glass of port?"

"I was familiar with most of it, having pursued my medical studies in Edinburgh. I do not always enjoy being French, but I have never longed to be English or Scottish."

The sun rose higher, beaming a gentle warmth onto my closed eyelids.

St. Sevier kissed me, his lips brushing against mine like that warm, welcome sunshine. I kissed him back without opening my eyes. I traced the angle of his freshly shaven jaw and winnowed my fingers through his hair.

He would be a tender and relentless lover. The sweetness was there in his kiss, in the glide of his palm beneath my dressing gown. His hand rested on my ribs, and I longed to place it over my breast. I was learning from Hugh, though, learning patience and the pleasure of anticipation.

I sensed something else in his kiss. Sadness, possibly regret. I drew back, kissed his cheek, and cuddled closer.

"You are homesick," I said.

"France is worth missing. I am also thinking of all those Scottish soldiers, taking the king's shilling simply to have food in their bellies. They were stalwart, uncomplaining, and for the most part as bitter and funny as they were ferocious. They fought for Britain and longed for Scotland."

"I don't suppose a subjugated people will ever truly fight for the enemy who subdued them."

"Many a Scotsmen did, and bravely so. Speaking of Scotsmen, when are we to meet Miss MacPherson's intended?"

I sat up. "Let's have another cup of tea, shall we?"

St. Sevier poured two, though I'd been hoping he'd share with me again. "Has trouble come calling in Miss MacPherson's Highland paradise?"

"I suspect so. I asked her about her intended, and she once again put me off. I find it most strange. Did you notice the empty seat at last night's dinner table?"

St. Sevier sipped his tea, and such was my growing attraction to him—my growing *awareness* of the attraction—that I watched his lips touching the cup, watched his throat as he swallowed. His hands were a contrast to the fragile porcelain, masculine, elegant, and powerful in both their competence and their sheer strength.

"I did notice an empty place setting, Violet, and further noticed that Miss MacPherson does not enjoy a good appetite. Her fiancé has become a topic not to be discussed, and you, my darling, are sensing an intrigue."

I had never been Hugh's *darling* before, and I quite liked the endearment with my morning tea.

"And you, my treasure, do too."

He smiled, which made me all the hungrier to kiss him again. "Being French," he replied, "I am too respectful of others' privacy to meddle. Being Lady Violet, you long to do nothing but."

"Fanny is not well, and nobody seems to be remarking it. Did her groom cry off because she's dying? Is there a groom, or did she need that ruse to draw me to Scotland? If so, why? Who is this Iain who simply ignored dinner with the new houseguests?"

"He's Donald and Eulalie's brother," St. Sevier said, "and I gather that, like his uncle, he's serving as a land steward. Spring is a busy time for those with acres to tend."

"Even a land steward needs to eat."

St. Sevier kissed me again, teasing his tongue along my lips, then gently entering my mouth and inviting me to taste him as well. The kiss turned frankly erotic, which was lovely, until I realized Hugh was distracting me on purpose.

I drew back and took up my tea cup. "A land steward who misses a meal with guests should at least send his excuses."

St. Sevier laughed. "I know that if I am ever lost, I need simply stay where I am, and you will find me. Nobody and nothing inspires you to surrender until you are good and ready to give up your causes. I found your determination most attractive when you sought to overcome grief. I beg you, though, please be careful if you embark on this puzzle. I do not want to pluck you from another angry river, nor see you involved in another family's dangerous quarrels."

I hadn't previously regarded my stubbornness as any sort of asset. St. Sevier was right, though—I could still be cowering behind the black curtains of my house of mourning, but for an animal determination to regain my balance as a widow.

"If you don't want to see me investigating any intrigues, what *do* you want, St. Sevier?"

He rose and stretched like a large cat, then shrugged out of his dressing gown and tucked it over my legs. The warmth was luscious, the thoughtfulness equally so. His touch on my thighs was, alas, fleeting and businesslike.

"What I want, Violet, is to see you happy." He kissed my forehead and straightened to once again face the rising sun. He was also treating me to the sight of his muscular backside, for once not obscured by a morning coat or riding jacket.

"What do you want for yourself, St. Sevier?"

"To catch a lot of big, tasty fish." He'd exaggerated his accent. *Beeg, tast-ee feesh.*

"Hugh?"

He faced me and leaned down, pressing his cheek to mine. "I want to take you in my arms, Violet, and lay you down on my unmade bad. There I would make love with you until you forget that vile specimen you were married to. I would bury myself inside you until the sun no longer rises over these magnificent hills. These selfish pleasures I cannot have—yet—so I will stand in a frigid stream and swill good whisky and talk of bait and hooks and lures."

He'd switched to French, and ye gods, the sheer sound of his words, let alone the intimacies they conjured, should have had me undoing his falls.

I put my mouth close to his ear and rested a hand on his flat belly. "*Bonne chance avec les poissons.*" Good luck with the fishes.

He chuckled and straightened, and I might well have imagined this, but I suspect I did feel a glancing caress to my breast as he stood.

"Your servant, my lady." He left me alone on the balcony, snug under his dressing gown, half a pot of hot tea beside me. The moment was lovely, and I let myself savor it. The little history lesson was not lost on me.

More than a hundred years after the Acts of Union, Scotland and England still carried grudges against each other. They used each other—England's army was full of Scottish soldiers, Scottish merchants prospered as well as their English cousins did—but old wounds had not entirely healed.

I had put off mourning, but was I to spend the rest of my life resenting a dead husband who'd made do with a marriage thrust upon him by his family? Freddie had had fine qualities, many of them, and I enjoyed tremendous financial security exclusively because of his insistence on providing well for me.

As the sun rose higher, I vowed to put the past aside as best I could. I would not succeed easily or quickly, but I could do better than I had been doing.

I poured my unfinished tea into St. Sevier's half-full cup and let my imagination travel back over our early morning tête-à-tête. Why did St. Sevier look out over the beautiful vista with such wistfulness? Why did a man who *adored* me and was *mad* for me choose to go fishing rather than lay me down on his unmade bed?

St. Sevier had been right: I did sense a puzzle in Fanny's situation, but that wasn't the only mystery begging for my attention.

I had declined to join the fishing expedition. To pierce a creature's mouth with a hook and make sport out of the resulting death struggles had no appeal for me.

In the breakfast parlor, a maid speaking in a nigh impenetrable accent indicated that Fanny took a tray in her room, and I thus declared myself at liberty for the morning. I donned my oldest pair of half boots, pilfered some buttered rolls and an orange from the breakfast buffet, and set off across the garden.

On so fine a day, and after being cooped up in the coach for more than a week, I was determined to roam. At breakfast, Donnie had told me of the trails winding through the firs, most of which came out at the river that wound between the high hills. One path led to the estate village.

I stuffed my provisions into my pockets, accepted the loan of a man's shooting jacket, and struck off from the garden gate. The hillside was steep, but the path traversed it in switchbacks, which made the way longer, though less of a challenge.

Once I passed into the forest, the temperature dipped noticeably, and the dense, towering pines turned the sunny morning into medieval gloom. The symphony of birdsong that rang out across the garden wasn't to be heard here. Instead, I enjoyed a profound quiet, my footsteps on the worn path the only sound other than an occasional flit of wings overhead.

Donnie had told me to follow the signs notched into the trees, and I was glad for his guidance. Not the angle of the sun, not the sound of the river, nothing but the slope of the land itself served to orient me to my surroundings. The village was along the river, and by moving downhill and downriver, I would eventually find it.

My travels the previous year, to a summer house party and to my family seat in Surrey, had awakened me to the fact that I needed occasional large doses of fresh air to thrive. London was fine for shopping and socializing, but for sheer animal health, I needed country vistas.

The forest was not such a vista. The longer I walked, the more I began to doubt my direction. I had the sense that beneath the trees—a Scottish fir could grow more than two hundred feet tall—time paused and earthly compass points became meaningless. I might have been wandering in an eternal circle, except that I was gradually working my way down the slope.

I was nearly to the point of wishing for a ball of twine—my buttered rolls were not to be sacrificed to scavenging wildlife—when the light ahead of me promised open land. I reached a more gradual slope, and eventually, I passed into a sunny meadow full of sturdy, woolly sheep.

The river flowed placidly a hundred yards to my right, and the center of the meadow held a curious swell of earth, a little copse of trees rising above the contented sheep. In summer, the sheep probably appreciated the shade to be had on that mound, and in winter, the swell of land would serve as a windbreak.

More relieved to be in sunshine than I ought to be, I enjoyed a pleasant meander through a gathering of tidy stone cottages. Daffodils grew by many a garden gate, and a church of venerable lineage made a picturesque scene by the river.

I found a bench in the churchyard and ate my rolls, sharing the crumbs with a half-dozen cheeky pigeons. I tossed my orange peels into the river and returned to my bench.

What a peaceful, pleasant, soul-soothing way to spend a morning. I tarried on the bench for some time, watching the river and thinking of Fanny's upcoming nuptials. I did not want to remarry, but I well recalled how hopeful I'd been as I'd learned that Freddie had offered for me.

My father, Sylvanus, Earl of Derwent, had informed me that "the young Belmaine rascal" had "come up to scratch," meaning Freddie had requested leave to court me. Papa's characterization had been euphemistic at best.

Freddie's maternal uncles and my father had decided that Papa would donate a significant sum to the marriage portion if the Belmaine family included a certain water meadow in my settlements. By marrying me—an earl's daughter—Freddie would add some aristocratic cachet to his family's mercantile wealth. The offspring of Lord Derwent's daughter and the Belmaine scion would have entrée in both the City and in Mayfair's best ballrooms, and of course, the bride and groom were deemed to suit each other quite well.

Freddie and I, at the time of his death, had declared a ceasefire in our efforts to suit.

I had stopped railing against his incessant infidelities; he had given up trying to tease, shame, cajole, and manipulate me into a more adventurous view of life's pleasures. We had reached the phase of the proceedings characterized by mutual disappointment.

I had told myself that the next phase surely would have been true friendship and acceptance, but I would never know.

Somewhat saddened by my reflections, I made my way back through the village. I saw not a soul, which struck me as odd. Perhaps the village folk were already off in the fields, but on such a lovely morning, why wasn't anybody shelling peas on the front stoop or pegging out the wash?

Not even the sheep looked up from their grazing when I crossed the meadow. A jealous ram could be a difficult fellow, but I didn't see any stalwart patriarch ready to run me off, so I angled my steps toward the curious swell of earth at the center of the meadow. The top of the mound would provide a nice view of the river and the village, one I might try to sketch when I returned to Leland House.

"You'll nae wish to disturb the fairies. They willna tek yer meddlin' so weel."

I whirled around, looking for the source of that warning. A tall, kilted man stood just inside the tree line, though the forest shadows had obscured him from my perception. How long had he been watching me, and why not call out a civil greeting?

"I had hoped to enjoy the view."

"They'll snatch ya doon to their magic hall," he said, ambling forth on long legs. "Twenty years on, you'll stagger back into the land of mortals, a daft old woman telling outlandish tales."

Did he believe this twaddle, was he trying to scare me with it, or in the manner of the dour Scots, was he making a jest?

"I am Lady Violet Belmaine," I said. "I am a guest at Leland House, and I am thoroughly enjoying this magnificent countryside."

His gaze was assessing, not exactly disrespectful. "Iain MacKellan," he said, nodding. "I'd heard wee Fanny had some swell friends to call." He'd moderated his accent, suggesting he was a man of some education—when he wanted to be.

I liked his looks. To carry off a kilt took a sort of casual bravado, and this fellow was utterly unconcerned about exposing his knees to a lady's view. He wore half boots and thick wool stockings. Just below his knee, he'd buckled a sheath that carried a substantial knife. A plain leather sporran hung from his waist at the juncture of his thighs. His short leather jacket had gone shiny at the elbows, and hung open to expose a tartan waistcoat and plain, unstarched linen cravat.

He was dark-haired, muscular, and lean, and I could see no resemblance to either Donnie or Eulalie. Iain wasn't quite Walter Scott's noble Highlander—he lacked a sword and a brace of pistols—but he was all the more formidable for being less romantic.

In his build and coloring, Iain reminded me somewhat of Lachlan.

"Is that,"—I gestured toward the knob of earth in the center of the pasture—"a fairy mound?"

"'Tis. We leave them alone, and no babies go missing."

"Are you having me on?"

"Only an Englishwoman would ask such a question. Can you find your way back to the house, or shall I show you the path?"

Even had I been completely lost, I would not have accepted that grudging offer. "Donnie explained the markings on the trees to me. I can manage."

He nodded but didn't move, so I started toward the trees. I had gone several yards past him when he called out to me.

"Our Fanny won't be marrying anybody."

I turned. "I beg your pardon?"

"The bastard disappeared two weeks ago. She hasna seen hide nor hair of him since, but she won't admit he's scarpered. She's hoping he'll pop out from behind the privet hedge, and the worry is nigh killin' her."

Could I trust anything this surly fellow had to say? "Why tell me Fanny's personal business?"

His expression went from stoic to bleak. "You are her friend. Mayhap you can talk sense into her, for she willna listen to family." He strode off in the direction of the village, without a bow, wave, or by your leave.

I made my way back into the chilly, dark forest and found the uphill going more challenging than the downhill trek had been. My steps were weighted by Iain's allegations, but his words had the ring of truth. They explained Fanny's evasiveness and her poor appetite, and—alas for St. Sevier—they explained my sense that I had landed in the midst of yet another puzzle.

"Not this again." St. Sevier added a few ungentlemanly observations in French, about stubborn women, British weddings, and everything becoming complicated when I was on hand.

As I waited out his muttering and pacing, I realized that even when he was testy and impatient, I cared for Hugh. I liked his version of irascibility. I liked his French profanity and wondered again which language he'd use in bed.

When he was finished airing his reservations, he'd listen to me and assist me should I take a notion to hunt down Fanny's prodigal intended.

"A missing groom is different from a missing bride," I said. My brother Felix's fiancée had disappeared shortly before their planned nuptials. All had ended well in that case, though it had been a very near thing.

"This is exactly the same, Violet." St. Sevier stalked across the sitting room to glower down at me. "You are sticking your pretty little nose into other people's business, and you are doing so at potential risk to your own wellbeing."

I smoothed a hand over the fluffy lace of his cravat. "What is risky about asking Fanny a few questions? She promised me we would discuss her marital situation. I simply propose to broach the topic rather than await her overture."

"Stop petting me when I am trying to talk reason to you."

"Stop trying to spout nonsense at me when I am enjoying proximity to your handsome person."

He threw up his hands in a quintessentially Gallic gesture and stalked away. "You are not in the tame shires of England, you are not among friends and family. You are hundreds of miles from home, and these people are nearly strangers to you. Yet, you must poke your parasol into a hornet's nest."

For a man who'd spent a placid morning contemplating a pretty river while pretending to pursue the angler's sport, St. Sevier was unusually testy.

"Did you not catch any fish, Hugh?"

"I caught my share, but there is discord in this house, Violet. Donnie and Eulalie bicker. Lachlan lets them go at it until he rebukes them both. The gamekeeper doubtless insulted the lot of us in his native tongue, and I am nearly certain one of the items on the morning's agenda was to play a round of dunk the Frenchman."

Hugh was a powerful swimmer. I knew that because his ability in the water had saved my life. Dunking this particular Frenchman would not put him at risk of harm, but it would sorely try his temper.

"Explain yourself," I said, taking a seat on the sofa.

"The gamekeeper came with us to increase the odds of fish being caught," St. Sevier said. "Fish are wily. They know where to lurk so they need not fight the river's current, and where the tiny fish or other prey might be more easily found. They tend to like the shady shallows, where flies are within easy snapping reach, and the current is light."

That St. Sevier actually knew something about fishing fascinated me. What other accomplishments would closer acquaintance with him reveal?

"You went wading?" I asked.

"I was shown a patch of river by the gamekeeper, a handsome, dark-haired, kilted fellow named Septimus MacFarlane, who is from yet another branch on the family bramblebush. He told me that working my way along a particular stretch of the riverbend would yield rich results. I went slowly, and I know enough to read the river as I move about in water. MacFarlane had sent me to a place where deep pools form immediately off the riverbank. He must have thought I was so inebriated by the beauty of the Scottish countryside that I would not notice such a significant change in the color and flow of the water."

"What did you do?"

St. Sevier came to a halt beside the French doors, his gaze on the fir-covered hillside sloping away from the garden.

"I know an example of Scottish humor when I see it. I simply fished from the bank and caught a pair of fine fellows who will probably grace the supper table."

"You didn't say anything to Lachlan or Donnie?"

He turned to face me. "In the military, soldiers often play pranks on one another, the enlisted men in particular. They might face death on the battlefield, but off of it, they faced boredom, loneliness, and homesickness. The officers usually looked the other way and considered a prank between the Scots and their English brothers-in-arms better than a brawl."

I have four brothers. I was not amused. "Such as?"

"Sewing a tent closed while a man sleeps inside it. Telling him a surprise inspection is imminent after you've hidden his boots. If you see a senior officer approaching, such that everybody will be required to stand at attention when the officer enters the room, you deliver an insulting blow to a new recruit for no apparent reason. The arrival of the officer will prevent the new soldier from retaliating in the moment."

"Insulting blow?"

Hugh gestured to his falls. "Here or his derriere, or the back of his head. The point is to rile him and then see the fellow's impulse to strike back frustrated by military protocol. The Scots excelled at that particular prank."

"I suppose it's a wonder Napoleon was vanquished, if that's how soldiers behave."

"Women can be equally devious," St. Sevier said, approaching the sofa. To my surprise, he didn't assist me to rise or take the place beside me.

He instead straddled my lap, which effectively pinned me in place. "I beg you, Violet, do not meddle in Fanny's affairs. Lovers have spats and quarrels all the time. Leave them to sort it out."

He framed my face in the warmth of his palms and kissed me. This kiss had a quality of exhortation, also novelty, because I had never been straddled by a big, annoyed Frenchman. Perhaps Hugh was making a point about my relative helplessness as a female, but I suspect his motive was simpler.

He was determined to have the last word.

I had stopped setting any store by the last word three brothers ago. My father in particular liked to end a discussion with a stirring assertion of his own faultless logic—or confused whim—and then stalk from the room in high dudgeon.

I liked Hugh's method of concluding an argument much more, though I had not the slightest intention of leaving a friend to struggle alone with an engagement that had hit boggy ground. I returned St. Sevier's kiss, reveling in the novelty of his overture, until he stood, turned his back, and very likely arranged his clothing, the better to accommodate inchoate arousal.

Poor lad. "Shall we go down to lunch?" I asked.

"I'll be along presently," he said. "I suspect a fresh spring breeze has disordered my hair."

Or my busy fingers had. "I think Iain would tell me more about Fanny's situation," I said, moving toward the door. "He seemed to care for her, or care that she's been served a disrespectful turn."

"You will not let this go." St. Sevier turned a magnificent scowl on me, half disappointment, half frustration. "Then at least promise me you will be careful, Violet. I did not endure hundreds of miles of sexual frustration to watch you anger a lot of prickly Scots over some romantic intrigue."

I had endured those miles too. "Not frustration, St. Sevier. Anticipation." I gave him a finger-wave farewell and slipped through the door. I could not tell if what I heard in my wake was laughter or cursing.

CHAPTER FOUR

St. Sevier's fishing story stayed with me as I wound through the house in what I hoped was the direction of the breakfast parlor. Had the gamekeeper meant to deliver a soaking to a guest who might have been unable to swim?

Scotland was rife with lochs, rivers, and fresh water, and for most Scots, the sea was never more than a short day's journey away. Perhaps this MacFarlane fellow had assumed Hugh could swim, but in England, one would have generally assumed the opposite.

And who had been on hand to assist St. Sevier if he hadn't been a competent swimmer? Sound around bodies of water behaved oddly, and particularly if a breeze moved along the river, cries for help might have gone unheeded.

Had Lachlan put his gamekeeper up to playing this prank, or had Donnie or Eulalie? Why do such a thing, when I would normally regard Scottish hospitality as the equal of any and better than most, and St Sevier was a charming and polite guest?

Those questions plagued me, even as I took my place at the table. Lunch included both a tasty chowder and the catch of the day. To my delight, Fanny joined us at table, though again, she exhibited little interest in the food.

"Might we take a turn in the garden?" I asked her as we rose from our meal. St. Sevier had accepted Eulalie's offer to show him the Leland House herbal and medicinal garden, and Donnie and Lachlan had left the table arguing about whether a redwood alley should be planted on the lane to the dower house.

"You declined to go fishing?" Fanny asked me when we'd assembled shawls, straw hats, and parasols on the back terrace.

"As did you," I said, linking arms with her. "I went for a ramble to the village and found it all but deserted. What did you do with your morning?"

We toddled down the steps into the geometrically trimmed privet hedges of the formal parterres. Somebody lavished attention on these gardens. Even at this early point in the season, pots of heartsease graced the walks, and daffodils and narcissus bloomed in cream and yellow abundance along the central path.

The scent, mingled with the pungent spice of the nearby pines, was lovely.

The garden's unifying feature was a tiered granite fountain that sat at the intersection of the two main walkways. At the apex of the fountain, a sculpture of an entwined couple added a bit of romance to the landscaped formality. The male half of the pair held a water pitcher high above his head, the water cascading down on the kissing pair.

The whole of the garden was ringed by a high wall, within which an outer path of crushed shells had been laid. The space felt both open and protected and struck me as an ideal venue for exchanging confidences.

"This was a maze once," Fanny said. "Every self-respecting Jacobite family of means had a maze in which to hide from the Crown's soldiers."

"Were the Lelands Catholic?" I asked.

"This was a MacPherson holding," Fanny said, leading me to the perimeter walkway. "Mama changed the name to Leland House on the occasion of her second marriage. As to religion... Many a Scottish family learned to play both sides of the church aisle. They'd send one son to ingratiate himself with the Papists rebelling against the tyranny of Protestant England and send another to curry favor with the Crown ordained by God to rule over us."

"Interesting strategy," I said, "one that guarantees the occasional loss of a son."

"While it assures the preservation of the family. The English don't understand that. The majority of Scots will march for whatever lunatic, spendthrift, or buffoon the English put on the throne. We will pray to this or that expedient version of the Almighty. To protect our families, a Scot will endure any number of sacrifices, else we'd be extinguished as a people and a culture."

Fanny settled onto a bench that faced the central fountain. I had the sense that even daundering along for a few steps had tired her. The vista was lush and peaceful, though, so I took the place beside her.

"You must have been terribly homesick at school," I said, taking off my hat and setting it beside me on the bench.

"As were you. One doesn't have to be Scottish to be homesick. You'll get freckles, Lady Violet." She'd delivered that warning in the high, nasal tone of our old headmistress.

"I am a widow." I closed my eyes and tipped my face to the afternoon sun. "We can do as we please with our complexions. I spent two years barely venturing from my house, Fanny. The sun feels good."

I let the silence stretch, having learned that most people will volunteer to speak if given the opportunity.

"You met Iain," Fanny said, "in the village."

"I did. He cuts a fine figure in his Highland getup." Though when had Fanny and Iain conversed? He'd not joined the family for lunch, and my impression was that Fanny had spent the morning in her apartment.

"He works very hard," Fanny replied. "This estate will swallow whole the efforts of an army, and every grannie and bairn must be fed, clothed, housed, and cared for from the estate's resources. I find it more than a little daunting, but John says..."

Still, I remained quiet, pretending to savor the sensation of sunshine on my closed eyes.

"I'm to have the place," Fanny said. "I don't particularly want it, but Mama's will said what it said, and the whole estate will come to me."

I had assumed Fanny was an heiress, else why subject her to an expensive English finishing school? That she had this much property, though, was impressive.

"Your dwelling is lovely, Fanny. Is John your intended?"

"Yes."

I opened my eyes to peer at her. "Tell me about him."

Several parterres away, a gardener tended a bed of bluebells blooming beneath a stand of young birches. The white of the birch bark and the brilliant blue of the flowers was a lovely touch, but bluebells were notoriously delicate. To create that bed had probably taken years of careful work and not a little luck.

The gardener would not overhear us at this distance, though he seemed to catch Fanny's interest.

"I doubt I can put you off any longer," Fanny said, "but you must listen to the whole tale, my lady, and not leap to conclusions, as my family has."

"From what I've observed, your family has added leaping to conclusions to the local assortment of Highland games."

She smiled fleetingly. "That's what attracted me to John. He is thoughtful, by which I mean not only is he considerate, he's also a *thinking* man. I offer him a conclusion, he parses out the premises and conditions necessary to support that conclusion. He ponders. He is the most articulate person I have ever met though also the most parsimonious with his speech."

Fanny, being enthralled with words and language, would be easily smitten by a fellow who made every utterance count.

"How did you meet?" I asked.

"I've known him for years, Violet. I have many of his letters, and he has an equal store from me. It's not done, I know, to correspond with a young man, but I have been so lonely here, and Lachlan isn't much for entertaining."

Fanny idly twirled her parasol, a lacy confection that probably wasn't doing much to shelter her pale complexion from the brilliant sunshine.

"Lachlan isn't reclusive," she went on, "but his idea of entertaining is to have the neighbors over for a meal, to go fishing with the vicar, to chat on the bridle paths with whomever he meets. He's friendly, and I know he's quite busy, but at my own family seat, I have few friends. I am very grateful that you came."

Fanny had neatly dodged my question regarding her first encounter with her swain. I well recalled my first dance with Freddie and recalled watching him flirt with all the other girls long before he'd stood up with me.

"How does Lachlan feel about your engagement?" I asked.

"He wants me to be happy and says Mama would want me to be happy."

The gardener stood, collected his tools, and pushed his wheelbarrow down the walkway to the south-facing garden wall. I suspected this had been developed as a fruit wall. Fruit trees were planted close to the thick granite and then espaliered to a wooden frame along the wall itself.

The wall released the accumulated heat of the sun through the night, reflected sunlight during the day, and could be fitted with overhanging mats to protect the fruit from hail, high winds, or other severe weather.

The gardener was apparently intent on tying new growth to the wooden frame. He worked with the steady, methodical movements of a man long familiar with his task, and yet, he wasn't an old man. He was a young, muscular specimen with a fine head of dark red hair.

"You don't sound very happy, Fanny," I said. "I wasn't entirely pleased to marry Frederick Belmaine, but I was *excited* to be marrying."

"We were supposed to be excited to marry anybody," Fanny said, gaze on the crushed-shell walk. "Remember when Miranda Ponsenby got the letter from her mama telling her she was engaged to that earl's heir?"

The entire school had swooned with envy, though Miranda had met her intended exactly twice prior to finding herself engaged to him.

"How could I forget? She took out that miniature of him at least eight times a day."

Fanny pushed crushed shells around with the toe of her half-boot. "They have four children now, two boys and two girls, and another one on the way."

That struck me as excessive reproduction for a mere eight or nine years of marriage, particularly when the requisite two sons had already appeared.

"Perhaps Miranda and her viscount are besotted." The more likely scenario was that Miranda's viscount was an inconsiderate, rutting bore, and she would continue to increase at his whim and pleasure until she either died in childbirth or persuaded his lordship to confine his attentions to his mistresses.

I was surprised at the bitterness of my thoughts, but then, I had failed to successfully carry a child for Freddie.

"I am besotted with my John," Fanny said, "and he with me. You cannot know how lovely that is, to have a man *listen* to you. To hear that he looks forward to seeing you again, that he rejoices with your every triumph and longs to kiss away your tears."

What twaddle. And yet, St. Sevier listened to me, even when he did not agree with me. "John sounds quite romantic."

"He is romantic, well-spoken, thoughtful, an excellent correspondent, and the man I would have conjured from my dreams, except he's even more than that."

The gardener paused in his efforts along the fruit wall, crossed to a bed of daffodils, and sliced off half a dozen blooms. He approached our bench, and I noted upon closer inspection that my earlier assessment was vindicated.

This was a braw, bonnie laddie, in the local parlance, with snapping blue eyes and a merry smile set off by his close-cropped red beard.

"Forgive my presumption, Miss Fanny, milady." He passed her the bouquet, offered a jaunty bow, and marched off, kilt swinging about his knees.

"Thank you, Evan," Fanny called, sniffing the daffodils. "He's a canny one, that Evan. He's probably the youngest head gardener in Scotland, also another family connection, but he works as hard as Iain does. Did you know that crushing the leaves of the bluebells can injure the plant for years? The Gaelic name is *fuath-mhuv*, which means 'detested by pigs,' or something like that. The flowers can give livestock a bellyache."

Fanny's literary mind stored all sorts of arcana, but she watched Evan's departure with a particular wistfulness.

"Fanny, what's wrong?"

She sniffed the flowers. "I asked Evan to plant all this heartsease this spring. Love-in-idleness. John said it was his favorite flower, so cheerful and hardy. Like me, he said."

Fanny had been hardy once. She was nearly frail now. I kept that thought to myself.

"I've exchanged letters with John for years," she said. "I answered one of those 'single gentleman seeks to make the acquaintance of' advertisements, though I don't bruit that about. If a man could be perfect for me on paper, John fulfills that description, though I met him only recently. He proposed to me by mail, a beautiful letter that I shall treasure all my days."

"I accepted by return post," she went on, "and we began to meet discreetly. We have discussed our nuptials, planned our wedding trip —we are to go to Paris and Rome, and I would like to see the Greek isles. John wants to take in Venice and Florence, and I must admit to you, Violet, the prospect of such wonderful travels pleases me almost as much as the prospect of becoming John's wife."

To a young woman interned in rural Scotland, those travels would be a powerful lure. For Fanny in particular, the Continental capitals, with their literary wealth and history, would loom as a promised land. The origin of the relationship among the lonely hearts advertisements was unusual for an heiress, but among the less exalted strata of society, not unheard of.

"When is the ceremony?" I asked.

Fanny passed me the bouquet. "The ceremony was to be next week, but since we set that date, I haven't heard a single word from John. He hasn't kept our trysts, hasn't sent me a single flower. Violet, I fear he has come to a bad end."

"The neighbors are coming for dinner," I informed St. Sevier as we took a constitutional around the same garden where Fanny had confided her problem to me earlier that afternoon. "Fanny says there might be dancing afterward, but it won't be the kind of dancing I'm used to."

"Imagine if a lot of Vikings were to take your English country dances with them to war. That is how the Scots dance."

We strolled arm in arm, and I was once again grateful for St. Sevier's company. He was more than familiar, he was *dear*. In this strange and beautiful place, treasuring my friendship with him was easy.

"How did you become familiar with Scottish dances? Were they another cure for medical school boredom?"

"Something like that."

The hard-working gardener, Evan, was nowhere to be seen, and in the later afternoon light, the space within the walls was still and peaceful.

"I must ask a favor of you," St. Sevier said.

"You are uncharacteristically serious about this favor."

"I have allowed myself to be put in an awkward situation, and to best extricate myself, I would appreciate your assistance."

And people claimed the English were a formal lot. I considered the near hauteur of St. Sevier's bearing and Fanny's recitations about how few new faces Leland House hosted.

"Eulalie importuned you in the herbal."

"Violet, the woman all but assaulted me."

And that troubled St. Sevier, who was a gentleman to his bones. He was particularly careful never to create untoward expectations in young women mad to acquire a handsome spouse—or mad to sample some forbidden French fruit.

"She is excessively lonely, Violet, and the fresh spring air has obliterated any claim she has to decorum. I fear for the fellows in their kilts."

From what I'd seen, the kilted fellows were substantial enough to defend themselves against all comers. "And yet, you do not want to offend Eulalie."

"I do not want to *touch* her, for God's sake, but our visit will become very awkward if I start dodging behind the nearest curtain every time she walks into a room."

We passed the patch of bluebells beneath the birches, the air acquiring a hint of sweetness. "Eulalie was persistent?"

"Bold and persistent. My favorite breeches are now missing a button."

"I can sew it back on for you."

He took me by the hand and led me to a bench beside the garden's back gate. The imposing white bulk of Leland House faced us across the sunny formality of the garden, and the deep blue of the Scottish sky set off the vista wonderfully. Leland House was grand, beautiful, and lovingly cared for, but to me, it lacked something.

A quality of home, perhaps?

"Your skills with a needle would be much appreciated," St. Sevier said, coming down beside me, "but that is not the favor I must ask you for."

He kept my hand in his as we sat. I had been embroidering with Fanny for most of the afternoon, and thus I wore no gloves. Why St. Sevier was bare-handed, I did not know.

"I esteem you greatly," St. Sevier said, "and I know you do not seek to remarry. I had hoped to woo you carefully, to entice you with my modest charms, and let you reexamine your distaste for marriage from a new perspective."

Oh feathers. Oh blast and bedamned. "St. Sevier, do not, I beg you, propose marriage to me. I am not a year out of mourning and have hardly found my balance as a widow moving in Society."

I had also yet to take my first lover. St. Sevier was my preferred—and only—candidate for that honor, but not if he meant to muck up the whole business with a marriage proposal.

He kissed my knuckles. "I am sensible of your reservations, and you would be surprised to learn that for many years, I shared them. Marriage is not for everybody. I have seen it ruin happiness and turn friends into sworn foes."

Some unspoken hurt lay behind that admission. Some lesson learned at personal cost. "What is this favor you ask of me?"

"I have been pursuing an affair with you, a discreet dance for two, about which others might speculate, but they would never know. To my very great delight, you have appeared receptive to my advances."

"Of course I am receptive to your advances, you daft man. I'd be receptive to a good bit more than—"

He put a finger to my lips. "I told Eulalie that we have an under-standing," St. Sevier said. "That you expect fidelity from your intended, and I would not stray even if Lilith herself ensorcelled me with her demon magic. I presumed to over-represent our situation, my lady, but I hope you will support the presumption."

I had not foreseen this turn of events, but St. Sevier was hand-some, charming, unattached, and gallant. If I found him wildly desir-able—and I *did*—then other women would as well.

"Put your arm around my shoulders, St. Sevier. Give me a moment to think."

He embraced me with one arm and angled his body as if he were listening closely to whispered endearments. Nobody spying from the house would mistake his posture for that of a man casually lounging on a garden bench with a friend.

"You were pursuing me on your terms, for your ends," I said. "Now you will pursue me on mine."

"I am listening."

"Freddie would notice me when he was in the mood for a domestic romp, then forget he had a wife. I do not want to be teased and tested, nor do I care to play out any sort of mating dance. My confidence, if I ever had any, is at low ebb. What I seek in your arms is reassurance that I am desirable and whole."

Saying the words helped me sort out my feelings and to draw a line between teasing, which was cruel, and flirtation, which I could enjoy.

"What of pleasure, Violet? What of closeness and caring? You make an affair of the heart sound like target practice, a means of sharpening your aim in case worthy game stumbles from the undergrowth."

Exactly as I'd felt in my marriage. As if I were target practice for my husband's lust, and when he was sure his trusty firearm was working accurately—as it invariably was—he'd turn it loose on the women who were equally skilled with their own weapons.

"I am sorry that my insecurities render me less than romantic, St. Sevier. I can offer you passion and friendship, but where that will lead, if anywhere, I do not know. I want very much to go to bed with you. I had hoped you shared that objective."

I offered a silent thanks to Eulalie for creating a situation where St. Sevier and I could have this discussion. Far better to put my cards on the table than to be led a dance the length and breadth of Scotland by a man who wanted what I could not give him.

He spoke with his lips very near my ear. "I never meant to give you cause to doubt yourself. Just the opposite."

I enjoyed his warmth and closeness and enjoyed even more that I had spoken my mind and was content to face the consequences. St. Sevier would become my lover, or he wouldn't, and either outcome was a better bargain for me than more dithering and feinting.

I had suffered my last lecture from him on the proper rituals for embarking on an affair, on that I was very clear.

"I meant to flatter you," he said, "to convince you of my interest."

"Words, St. Sevier. Convince me with your deeds, or consider that Eulalie might make you a fine wife. She's pretty, lively, a good conversationalist, and she fancies you."

"The only woman I fancy is on this bench, scolding me—a *Frenchman*—for my lackadaisical wooing. I will mend my ways, Violet, and you will not have cause to remonstrate with me again."

I doubted that, but I also looked forward to seeing what Hugh St. Sevier's version of mended ways entailed.

"Then let's go in," I said. "If we're to have company for dinner, we must dress accordingly. I had wanted to acquaint you in more detail with Fanny's situation, but I suppose that will have to wait."

"Acquaint me now," St. Sevier said, rising and assisting me to my feet.

"Her engagement has been a largely epistolary undertaking, though she and John have met regularly since plighting their troth. Shortly before you and I left on our journey northward, John ceased all communication with her, and she hasn't seen him since. Iain's comments, about John being least in sight for the past fortnight, confirm Fanny's version of events."

"If she's met with her intended, then he must bide among the neighbors," St. Sevier said, "and you will doubtless take note of anybody at dinner tonight who is behaving the least bit oddly."

Oh, perhaps. I suspected I would instead spend the meal contemplating the looming pleasure of having St Sevier naked in my bed.

As it happened, I was quite, quite wrong.

"What in seven Papist purgatories are you doing here?" Sebastian MacHeath, Marquess of Dunkeld, had waited the duration of the meal to put that question to me. The gentlemen were escorting the ladies to the withdrawing room, and Sebastian had managed to take the place at my side.

St. Sevier was escorting Fanny, who had again misplaced most of her appetite. An errant fiancé would have put me off my feed too.

"I am visiting an old school friend on the occasion of her marriage," I muttered. "Why aren't you in London searching for a bride?" The marquess and I had exchanged perfunctory notes at Yuletide, good wishes to the household and so forth. I had not expected him to be on hand in Perthshire, or I might have notified him of my travel plans.

Though we'd been close friends in our youth, the relationship had become strained by distance, time, war, and misunderstanding. In the past year, we had worked our way back to mostly cordial dealings, but I still wasn't entirely comfortable with Sebastian.

"I tried looking for a bride in London," he retorted. "I have plenty of time yet to head south again if I want to subject myself to the matchmaking marathon. Perthshire is my home, and I've spent too much of my life away from it."

Sebastian's burr was in evidence, but then, it had been all evening. His titled uncle had sent him to England as a boy, there to be groomed to take his place in the British aristocracy. As Sebastian had approached his majority, the uncle had married a sweet young thing, and Sebastian's prospects had been significantly diminished.

"How is your daughter, my lord?"

Sebastian's eyes, so blue and perceptive, looked haunted. "Annis thrives. I will call upon you tomorrow afternoon to take you riding."

We had reached the guest parlor, and the gentlemen were parting from the ladies.

"Why should I ride out with you?"

"Because I'll steal into your room in the dark of night and carry you off to my Highland stronghold if you refuse me, and your pet Frenchman will have nothing to say to it."

Sebastian and St. Sevier had served together on the Peninsula, though St. Sevier had been at war in a medical capacity, while Sebastian had fought and bought his way to a colonel's rank. In his youth, he'd been prone to daydreaming, poetry, and sketching butterflies.

Sebastian had survived the war, but that fanciful youth had apparently come to a quiet end somewhere in the hills of Spain.

"St. Sevier would never presume to tell me what to do," I retorted. "If I don't wish to ride out with you, I shan't."

I was being contrary, but then, Sebastian, who I had considered my dearest friend in our younger years, was being outright surly. We seemed to go through this ritual irascibility with each other upon each reunion.

He picked up my hand. "You love to ride, and I have a bay mare with sweeter gaits than heaven has clouds. Don't come because I asked you to, come because you long to ride the countryside with a knowledgeable escort."

He knew me still. I wasn't sure if that comforted or alarmed me. "Come at two. Bring the mare."

After enduring three hours of his fulminating glances, arched brows—Sebastian's swooping dark brows arched very nicely—and polite small talk, I finally won a slight smile from him.

"Two of the clock, then." He bowed and withdrew, and I confess I did watch his retreat and note what a fine picture he made in his kilted ensemble.

Fanny took me by the arm. "We are all agog," she said. "You never told me your Sebastian was a Perthshire lad in anticipation of a lofty title."

"He wasn't my Sebastian," I said, though that was untrue. He had been *my Sebastian* in those difficult years between girlhood and my come out. The tea dance years, when a young lady was often taller than the boys of her own age and torn between the peace of the schoolroom and the excitement of approaching adulthood.

Sebastian had bided on the estate next to my father's, tended by English tutors and English staff, with only a rare visit from his uncle or some other Scottish relation. He'd eventually been sent off for a few years at public school, then a few more years at university. That my brothers had befriended Sebastian had been inevitable.

"He wasn't our Sebastian either," Eulalie said, pouring three cups of tea. "The previous Lord Dunkeld sent him south, and there was an end to it."

"Except for the letters," Fanny said. "Sebastian wrote to his uncle every month, and the marquess all but posted the letters at the village crossroads. Violet likes cream and a drop of honey in her tea."

A pair of Sebastian's maiden aunties joined us, having made use of the ladies' retiring room. I was taken somewhat aback when Aunt Maighread produced a silver flask and tipped a portion of the contents into her tea. She passed the flask to Aunt Hibernia, whose tipple was even more generous.

They were both venerable, white-haired, and petite, though they had an indomitable quality too.

"A health to your guests, Miss MacPherson," Aunt Maighread said, lifting her tea cup. Aunt Hibernia followed suit and then turned to me.

"Tell us of your family, Lady Violet. The boy has become the most unforthcoming fellow you ever did want to turn over your knee, and we used to hear much about your brothers."

The boy? The boy was about six feet and three inches of strapping marquess. "My youngest brother, Felix, is now married, and he and his wife are in anticipation of a blessed event." That event might well have occurred while I had traveled to Scotland. "Ajax and Hector are the banes of my father's existence, but they will remove to Paris in the autumn for a year's tenure with our man of business there. Viscount Ellersby and his family thrive."

Mitchell, my oldest brother and the heir to the Derwent earldom, didn't quite thrive. He went about his duties with an air of haughty long-suffering, perhaps in part because he and his viscountess had so far produced only daughters.

And perhaps in part because serving as my father's right hand was a thankless and difficult task.

"Tell us about St. Sevier," Eulalie said, sending me an arch smile over her tea cup. "He is *quite* an impressive specimen. I do love a man with brown hair and brown eyes."

Fanny muttered something in Gaelic, and the aunties exchanged a look.

"Hugh St. Sevier has spent much of his life in England, though he still considers France home. He has both family and property there. He supported British forces in a medical capacity on the Peninsula, where his path and Lord Dunkeld's apparently crossed at some point."

"Hugh," Fanny said. "I like that name. It's a bit Scottish."

"You call him Hugh?" Eulalie asked. "I thought the English were always formal."

"With my close friends, I am not formal at all, and Hugh is a very good friend. He was a great comfort to me in my mourning. I owe him much and am very fond of him."

I hoped that little speech gave countenance to St. Sevier's contention that he and I had an understanding, though I felt sorry for Eulalie. Gorgeous rural scenery and tippling elders were not exactly the circumstances a marriageable young lady longed for. St. Sevier's conclusion came back to me, that Eulalie was *lonely*, and I found new reserves of patience for her.

Eulalie sipped her tea, her gaze speculative. "But you don't love Monsieur?"

Fanny winced.

Aunt Hibernia set down her tea cup. "Eulalie MacKellan, for shame. Lady Violet will think we are all barbarians."

"I think Eulalie is forthright," I replied, "and to answer your question, I do love Hugh. He saved my life and my sanity, and I count him my dearest friend."

I spoke nothing less than the truth. Whether the peril facing me was melancholia or a growing dread of leaving my own house, a raging river, or a widow's bitterness, Hugh had been there to intervene.

Of course I loved him. I had simply been confused and bewildered by my husband's version of marital affection. I was thus slow to recognize a gentler and steadier version of a much finer emotion when St. Sevier inspired it in my heart.

"Well, I suppose love must be in the air," Eulalie said with forced brightness. "Fanny has her beau, you have your smitten Frenchman. I ought to set my cap for Dunkeld."

She ought to. Sebastian needed a sturdy young wife who could give him sons. The idea, however practical, did not sit well with me, because Sebastian also ought to be his wife's first choice, not the frolic she turned to when the nearest Frenchman was unobliging.

"Speaking of Fanny's beau," Aunt Maighread said, "when is the happy day, Fanny?"

Fanny rose. "There's been a slight delay. Mr. MacDonald has pressing business to tend to, and we will have to move the nuptials back a bit."

The aunties exchanged another glance.

Eulalie—to her credit—looked displeased. "What business could be more pressing than speaking vows with the love of your life?" she asked. "What presses more acutely than the longings of the heart?"

"John is conscientious about his business affairs," Fanny said, "and that is only one of the many fine qualities I esteem about him."

Fanny's gaunt cheeks were shadowed by the parlor's flickering firelight, and her pallor took on a spectral cast.

"You can hardly esteem a laddie who isn't about," Aunt Hibernia muttered.

"Absence makes the heart grow fonder," Aunt Maighread retorted.

"Perhaps if you're some sentimental old Roman poet," Aunt Hibernia shot back. "If you're a young lassie pining for her mon, and he's been wooed away by the recruitin' sairgeant to take the king's shillin'…" She lapsed into the local tongue at that point, and I began to suspect that bickering was a Scottish means of expressing affection.

"Do you fear your John has scarpered?" Eulalie asked, holding out the shortbread to Fanny.

Fanny took a piece, she did not eat it. "I fear he has come to harm. He would not do this to me. Would not leave me at the altar if he could avoid it."

Eulalie offered me and the aunties the shortbread. I took one piece, each aunt took two, and they both dunked their servings into their spiked tea before eating them.

I could come to like Scottish society very much.

"We should find him," Eulalie said. "You're an heiress, Fan. Even if John isn't exactly arse over ears for you, he's a Scotsman, and he'll not turn his back on all your lovely money."

Plain speaking indeed, though Fanny did not appear either reassured or offended. "You think he's come to a bad end too?"

Eulalie shrugged. "Boats leave the Clyde for Newfoundland every week."

"What does Lachlan say about this?" Aunt Maighread asked, topping up her tea cup with yet more whisky.

"I haven't told him." Fanny nibbled her shortbread. "I don't want his pity."

"He doesn't understand," Eulalie groused. "He had the great love of his life. He's been happily married and is content. He wants to live out his years in sight of the Highlands like some poet harper of old. It's not like that for us. Donald and Iain don't want to die here without having seen something of life either. I dare say even Evan enjoys the occasional jaunt into Glasgow."

"Well, what's to be done?" I asked. "Fanny's beau has gone missing, and she can't very well marry a memory."

"Or a ghost," Fanny said.

"What is his full name?" I asked. "If he's a businessman, he'll have engaged in commerce with somebody, and perhaps we might start there."

"John S. MacDonald," Fanny said. "I don't know what the S stands for, but he gave me a monogrammed handkerchief."

"That should narrow it down," I said, which occasioned laughter from everybody but Fanny.

"My lady, you are in Scotland," Aunt Hibernia said. "Throw a stone, and you'll hit a MacDonald in these parts, every fifth one will be a John Stuart MacDonald. I walked out with two of them in my youth."

Aunt Maighread sniffed. "You did a sight more than walk out with them, Bernie MacIntyre."

"So did you, Sister."

"What else do you know about your fiancé?" I asked Fanny.

Aunt Hibernia passed me a flask. "Best top up, my lady. The gents will soon rejoin us, and we wouldn't want to scandalize them. Delicate sensibilities, you know."

Even Fanny took a wee dollop of the water of life, though by the time Aunt Bernie, as she preferred to be called, had tucked her flask away, the gentlemen did, indeed, rejoin us. The ladies permitted themselves to be regaled with fish stories, nodding gently all the while, but when I accepted St. Sevier's escort abovestairs, both Aunt Bernie and Aunt Maighread winked at me.

And I winked back.

CHAPTER FIVE

"I had forgotten how very hard the head of the average Scotsman is," St. Sevier said, holding the door for me to our private sitting room. "We French enjoy our wines, or the occasional cognac or Armagnac, but these fellows and their whisky... Uncle Archibald is worse than Lachlan, Donnie, and Iain combined."

Archibald was Sebastian's uncle, and I would never underestimate a MacHeath. "The aunties tipple," I said, "as do Fanny and Eulalie."

"And did they extend their corrupting influence to you?" He faced me and draped his arms across my shoulders. We hadn't yet lit any candles in our sitting room, so the fire on the hearth was our only illumination.

"I confess I had a wee drop," I said, wrapping my arms around his waist. "Fanny admitted to the ladies that she has lost her swain. The ladies are inclined to embark on a hunt for him."

St. Sevier considered me. "Do we assign teams as the English do for their scavenger hunts? I claim you for my team, Violet, and we will make a very thorough search of any follies, empty cottages, or belvederes."

I was inclined to make a thorough search of St. Sevier's person, though he looked tired to me. Travel could be like that, taking a day or two to clobber the traveler with the fatigue of the journey. I had told Lucy, my maid, not to wait up for me, and while I could wiggle, twist, and otherwise extricate myself from my dress, I preferred to have assistance.

I turned my back and swept my hair off my nape. "Perhaps you'd be so good as to undo my hooks?"

His fingers were deft, and as soon as he'd executed his task, he looped his arms about my middle. "You're sure, Violet?"

He wasn't asking about missing bridegrooms or tippling aunties.

"Absolutely certain." In fact, I was nervous. Hugh would be considerate and passionate in bed, but marriage to Freddie had left me deeply insecure about both my desirability and my ability to please a lover.

Hugh kissed my nape, then the sensitive place below my ear. Corsetry ensured any attempt to fondle my breasts was doomed, and my body was already unhappy about that limitation.

"Give me thirty minutes," I said, easing away. "Not one minute more."

"Twenty-nine and counting," he said, cupping my cheek against the warmth of his palm.

I walked away, feeling more than a little naughty to be half undone and anticipating a lover's company. That naughty feeling refused to ignite into confidence, though, as I finished undressing and took down my hair.

Only Freddie had seen me with my hair entirely undone. I'd somewhere come across the notion that such was a husband's wedding night privilege. He'd braided my hair right back up again, lest it *get in the way.*

I subsequently learned that some fool had assured Freddie that women liked to have their hair pulled during certain versions of the marital act. I had disabused him of that notion, though I'd needed weeks to marshal the courage to tell him so.

Memories of my late husband were not helpful, given my agenda for the rest of the evening. As I used my toothpowder and ran the warmer over the sheets, I considered Fanny's missing beau instead.

Eulalie had made an excellent point: Fanny was an heiress, also witty, pretty, likable, and from good family. Any man lucky enough to win her favor should be eager to marry her. Heiresses weren't exactly thick on the ground in England, and I suspected they were rarer still in Scotland.

To climb into bed, or to await my lover while I read by the fire?

I chose the latter, my room boasting a selection of Walter Scott's stirring tales of Highland romance. They made for good reading in the midst of Leland House's tartan décor, with the Scottish hills undulating beneath a waxing moon beyond my window.

I had read Waverley before and hadn't found the hero quite so worthy of approbation. A young man is enticed by lust, essentially, to flirt with ideals contrary to those he was raised to value. His rebel cause fails spectacularly at the Battle of Culloden, and by happenstance he can reingratiate himself with the established order. The lovely woman who inspired his attempt at independence consigns herself to a French nunnery, while our hero is rewarded with the hand in marriage of a beautiful Englishwoman.

As a sermon on the evils of thinking for oneself, the book succeeded. As a romanticizing of Scottish history, it reached unprecedented heights. The book was fundamentally dishonest, and as the fire burned down, I stared into the flames, trying to put my finger on the nature of the deception.

When a log fell to the andirons, sending a spray of sparks up the flue, I realized my lover should have long since joined me. St. Sevier had more or less given his word to set aside his daft notions of seduction by intermittent indifference. He would not change his mind.

Therefore—my imagination made this leap before the last spark had been sucked into the darkness of the night sky—he had come to harm.

I stood and rebelted my robe, took up the iron poker from the hearth stand, and crept out into the sitting room. The door to St. Sevier's room was ever so slightly ajar, and I could detect no movement from the room beyond.

I listened for long moments, I sniffed, I stood still and tried to sense any subtle shift in the air of our little apartment. My senses brought me nothing in the way of new information, so I stole forward, poker at the ready, and slowly pushed St. Sevier's door open.

Fanny had agreed to let me read some of the letters her beau had sent her. The relationship had apparently progressed to trysts, and the missives recounting the pleasures of stolen moments were doubtless too personal to be shared.

Nobody had ever sent me any such letters, and I was frankly envious. Fanny was talented with a pen and a formidable poet. Her epistles to John had clearly caught his fancy—she'd kept copies of her missive—while his to her were... almost prosaic.

At least the ones she let me see. I had taken the letters to the library after breakfast, and it was there that St. Sevier found me.

"My lady, on my honor as a Frenchman and lover formerly without equal, I am deeply ashamed."

"You were exhausted last night," I said, putting aside the letter I'd been reading. "When you didn't join me, I went to your room, thinking to find you coshed on the head by reavers or stolen away by banshees."

His smile was bashful. "The water of life and fatigue stole me away, abetted by Uncle Archibald's tall tales. I am abjectly ashamed."

"You don't look ashamed," I said. "You look rested and a little sheepish. Have a seat."

He looked like he'd say more on the subject of having succumbed to sleep despite the siren call of my charms, though I had been oddly relieved by his defection the previous night. I, too, had been tired, and I, too, felt a little sheepish.

A woman in greater thrall to a passionate attraction would have climbed into St. Sevier's bed and made free with his person. Heaven knew, Freddie had taken those liberties with me often enough. I wasn't comfortable presuming on St. Sevier's privacy to that degree.

"You are back to searching for the missing beau," he said. "Did this man sign settlement agreements?"

The library was sunny and pleasantly scented with the fragrance of old books and the tang of countless peat fires. This corner of Scotland had ample wood, but because lumber was valuable and not that easy to harvest, peat was also commonly burned for warmth.

Had the curtains and upholstery not been the ubiquitous plaid and the portraits on the wall Elizabethan burghers rather than kilted ladies, I might have thought myself in an English country house, though no English country house boasted such spectacular scenery.

The library overlooked the formal garden, with a grand view of the wooded hillsides and the silver ribbon of river sparkling far below us in the morning light. I had scheduled an outing on horseback with Sebastian for that afternoon. Otherwise, I would have been once again exploring the woodland paths.

St. Sevier took up a letter I hadn't yet read.

"This man is educated," he said. "Nobody develops such lovely penmanship unless his tutors require it of him."

I had not noticed what St. Sevier had spotted in an instant. "What else do you see?"

He read for a few moments. "He's Scottish. The syntax is not English public school though he might well had attended one. A Scottish public school is more likely. Your man Dunkeld did not write this."

If I'd suspected any such thing, I had not admitted as much to my conscious mind. "My man Dunkeld, who is not my man, is very much in evidence. I believe we can trust Fanny to know her own fiancé when he holds her chair."

"Can we?" St. Sevier set the letter aside. "Has she described his appearance to you?"

"She has met him in person on many occasions, though he proposed by letter. They met through a newspaper advertisement. *Bachelor with farm seeks to meet hardworking woman from good family... A lady of means seeks a spouse of good character and scrupulous personal habits...* You've read them, I'm sure."

Those advertisements had been inordinately cheering during my mourning period. That a romance could have epistolary roots didn't strike me as any more peculiar than marrying a man to gain possession of his family's water meadow.

"But she did not tell you what he looks like," St. Sevier said. "For a young woman in love, one whom you describe as a gifted writer, that is not an oversight, Violet. She either does not know what he looks like, or his looks are quite plain."

"Or Fanny doesn't care about his appearance." I thought more deeply about the six letters I'd read. "I suspect he's a local man, or he was raised in this area. He mentions where he'd like to walk with Fanny, a good spot for a picnic."

"Any curate or alewife could provide him that information."

True, and Scotland was increasingly popular as a holiday destination for hillwalkers, birdwatchers, and amateur landscape enthusiasts.

"There you are." Fanny closed the library door behind her. "Monsieur, good morning. Donnie tells me Uncle Archibald was in excellent form last night. Lachlan can mix you up a cure if your head pains you inordinately."

"A sore head *is* the cure for overindulging," St. Sevier said, rising to hold a chair for her. "And I can only hope Lachlan, Donnie, and Iain are in the throes of a similar exercise in humility."

"Not those three," Fanny replied. "They were surreptitiously watering their glasses to make you think they were keeping up with Archie. Next time, watch them more closely. Archie is a legend in these parts."

"How fortunate," St. Sevier said, "that I was watering my own drink as often as I discreetly could—though not nearly often enough."

Fanny grinned. "I knew Violet wouldn't give her heart to a foolish man. You must not admit that you bested them. They would be crushed."

"My victory shall be a private one," St. Sevier said, smiling back at her. "We are reading your correspondence in an effort to help locate your missing swain, Miss MacPherson, and I must say he sounds like a man of some learning."

Fanny's smile faded. "John considers things. He doesn't pop off with the first notion to catch his fancy."

St. Sevier was being subtly manipulative. He'd noted to me that John had had a public school education, or the Scottish equivalent. That did not make John *a man of some learning*. That degree of education implied university and independent scholarship, perhaps over a period of decades.

St. Sevier flattered Fanny's intended and thus gained her trust.

"He also appreciates the natural world," St. Sevier said. "His diversions include picnics and hikes and pretty vistas."

Also blather about Fanny being prettier than the hillside of blooming heather and twice as dear.

"I like those things too," Fanny said. "And we read many books together, or at the same time. You know what I mean."

St. Sevier cocked his head. "Miss MacPherson, can you describe him for us?"

She stared off into the middle distance. "He's soft-spoken and patient. He has a sweet laugh. He's substantially taller than me and can quote poetry by the quatrain."

Most men would be taller than Fanny. St. Sevier was six feet and two inches, Sebastian six feet and three. My brothers' heights had been a source of great contention growing up, especially when Felix, the youngest, had turned out to be the tallest at six feet and one inch.

"And could you tell us John's age?" St. Sevier asked, all helpful curiosity.

"Youngish. I haven't asked specifically."

"What color is his hair?"

"Dark."

St. Sevier examined the portraits around the room, then he shifted in his chair. He aimed a look of such kindness and understanding at Fanny that had I been her, I would have blurted out any and every secret I'd ever possessed.

Instead, I blurted out the obvious question. "You've never met him, have you, Fanny? Never *seen* him."

She rose and went to the windows that opened onto the terrace. "Sometimes, I wish I hadn't met him. Then I am disgusted with myself for being so faithless. We started meeting after the first of the year. I sneaked out to be with him at least a dozen times."

I joined her at the window, hating how the morning sun accentuated her pallor. Below the terrace, the gardener Evan was back at his tasks, espaliering more new growth to the fruit wall trellises.

"You slipped out at night," I said, "and you did not take a lantern, the better to avoid detection. You met with John in darkness, or the next thing to it."

St. Sevier remained sitting at the table, which was both shrewd of him and a bit unmannerly.

Fanny nodded. "I loved the idea that I had a secret admirer, that somebody risked discovery to spend time with me. We talked for hours, and I would know his voice anywhere."

St. Sevier casually took up a pencil and a sheaf of blank paper from the center of the writing table.

"Can you describe his voice for us?" he asked.

John sounded "like a Scotsman," but Fanny could not place the accent beyond that. He did not speak the Doric dialect of the northeast, nor the softer inflections of the Borders. He sounded local to Fanny's somewhat undiscerning ears.

"And what of the quality of his clothing?" I asked. "Fine wool, cashmere, something in between? Were his hands callused?"

She presented us with a puzzle: The winter weather meant the fellow had worn a woolen cloak, and Fanny pronounced it good quality. Soft wool and thick. His hands were callused, not only in the locations a gentleman equestrian would acquire calluses.

He wore no hat, but he had given Fanny a scarf in the Leland House plaid.

He carried embroidered handkerchiefs, a gentleman's affectation.

I watched the gardener, Evan, going about his task. "Is John clean-shaven or bearded?"

Fanny returned to the table, face flaming, though I could not see why my question would occasion mortification.

St. Sevier, however, apparently sensed currents I could not detect. "Miss MacPherson, I am a physician with experience as both a surgeon and an accoucheur. I have gone to war. I have tended the fallen women who ply their trade in the London stews. Nothing you can say will shock me or cause me to think anything less of you."

I had not heard previously of St. Sevier's charity work, but it fit with what I knew of him.

"Sometimes, John had a bit of a beard. Sometimes, he did not. He..." She bit her lip, glanced at me, and squared her shoulders.

"Fanny?" I could not grasp why this point should occasional equivocation. "Bearded or not?"

"In certain circumstances," Fanny said, "the abrasion of a man's beard can give a lady pleasure."

Oh dear God. I fixed my gaze on the garden as heat crept up my cheeks. I knew in a theoretical sense exactly the pleasure to which she referred, courtesy of my wicked husband's endless offers to take me on various intimate adventures.

Offers I had largely declined.

"This tells us," St. Sevier said, as casually as he'd comment on the weather, "that John had access to regular shaving equipment and could choose whether he wore a beard. He was not a shop clerk, not in service, not a tutor. He was his own man."

Fanny looked at him as if he'd solved the riddle of the Sphinx. "He might be a farm laborer," she said. "Some of them have beards."

"Aren't the bearded ones usually married?" I asked. "I don't know of a farmer's wife who lets the hired help go about looking like ruffians."

"Was he built like a farm laborer?" St. Sevier asked.

"*Is* he built," Fanny muttered. "Not *was*. John is not quite as tall as you, monsieur, but he is muscular and fit. His hair is thick, and dark, as I said, but I don't know if it's sable, auburn, or titian."

"He's right-handed," I said, thinking back to his penmanship, but then, most people were right-handed, particularly if any sort of formal education had come their way. "What of his teeth?"

If Fanny had kissed him, she'd know that.

"Excellent teeth," she said. "This isn't getting us anywhere."

We had made significant progress, and I still had most of the letters to read.

"We have only begun," St. Sevier said, patting Fanny's hand. "How long is his hair?"

"Medium," Fanny said. "About like yours. But your hair is a bit wavy. His is straight and so soft... I love that about him. He's such a sturdy, self-possessed man, but he has angel hair... I'm sorry to be a watering pot. I have been telling myself he'd show up any day, that I would get a note explaining his absence. Sometimes, he would not write to me for weeks, then I'd receive a letter every day for four days."

I hugged Fanny and resumed my seat in the chair beside hers. "Did he ever explain the lapses?"

"No, and I did not ask. He would apologize for neglecting our correspondence, then resume as faithfully as ever."

"Was he trying to break it off?" I asked.

St. Sevier watched Fanny closely.

"No, he wouldn't do that. I know him. What does it matter the color of his eyes when I know his heart?"

I had nothing to say to that. My suspicions regarding John's protracted silences were myriad, and not a one of them flattered the man *at all*.

St. Sevier and I stayed in the library until luncheon, reading the letters and jotting down notes. The actual paper on which the letters were written told us little, because nearly every household of means in Perthshire patronized the same stationer's shop in Perth itself, and that shop was supplied from Edinburgh.

"What if she's making him up?" I said. "What if there was a man and some letters, but Fanny has fabricated the meetings?"

St. Sevier sat back, tossing his pencil onto the paper before him. "You think somebody has toyed with her affections? Somebody with a wife and family—or several wives and several families?"

Bigamy was a common crime and easily committed. "Or John has engaged the affections of an heiress with more wealth than even Fanny has?"

St. Sevier had removed his jacket and turned back his shirt cuffs, a shocking display of dishabille that I hoped was for my benefit.

"Whoever he is," St. Sevier said, "he knows her well, whether or not she's fabricating the meetings."

I thought back to the prosaic letters Fanny treasured so dearly, mostly reflections of the passing seasons, *I miss you*, and snippets of poetry.

"He recommended books to her," I said slowly, "suggesting he has, or at one time had, the leisure and means to read."

St. Sevier perused the list he'd made. "The Scots are fanatic about education, while the English upper classes almost hoard education away from the masses. The Scots have philosophers, inventors, radical theologians, and novelists to show for their love of books. John could be a law clerk, publican, or shepherd and still be very well-read —and surely Fanny would have known an English accent when she heard one?"

"She would, but do I take it you admire the Scottish penchant for literacy?"

He looked around the plaid sanctuary, his gaze falling on a life-size portrait of a couple in traditional Highland attire. They were both red-haired, the lady almost as tall as the man, and a pair of stately, coarse-coated staghounds panted at their feet.

He gave me a crooked smile. "I admire much about the Scots. The medical education offered here is far superior to any available in England. Edinburgh also has a vitality London lacks, a sense of forward momentum rather than stagnant reverence for the tombs of the ancient Romans juxtaposed with a ruling class bent on frivolity. I thrived in Scotland, as I think most young men with ambition and opportunity would. I was happy here."

Meaning St. Sevier was unhappy in England? That question suggested I did not know him nearly so well as Fanny professed to know her John.

"I can understand why a man might entice Fanny into a relationship," I said. "She's wealthy, comely, and good company. I cannot understand why, having gone to all the trouble to court her, to win her hand even, to spend years in correspondence with her, he'd leave her standing virtually at the altar after having been intimate with her."

St. Sevier rolled down his cuffs. "Perhaps he is ashamed. Perhaps he has recently contracted an unmentionable disease. Perhaps, as you suggest, he's married. Sometimes in matters of the heart, hope eclipses common sense, and much sadness results."

"Then why not send her a final letter telling her that urgent business requires that he break it off? Make up a frail uncle, a scandalous legal matter, a vague obligation of honor that suggests he got somebody else with child. Men have a thousand ways of escaping blame for their scurrilous behavior."

St. Sevier slipped the sleeve buttons through his cuffs and shrugged into his morning coat. If I married him, I would see him dress and undress a thousand times, but I doubt the grace and intimacy of such simple gestures would ever fade for me.

"You are angry," he said, coming around to put his hands on my shoulders and lean down to murmur in my ear. "I am glad that you are finally angry. I watched you waste two years trying desperately not to be angry, when I knew Belmaine had broken your heart, and your father had betrayed your trust. When you found your anger, I knew your spirit remained whole."

He kissed the place below my ear that deserved a name of its own for all the shivery, sweet sensations that resulted from a tender press of lips to that location.

"I am abjectly sorry for falling asleep last night, Violet. I will make amends." He straightened. "I must become presentable before the midday meal. How will you spend your afternoon?" He used his fingers in slow circles on my nape, the touch both soothing and arousing.

"I'm to go riding with Dunkeld. Would you care to join us?"

St. Sevier's fingers paused, then disappeared. "I think not, but thank you for the invitation. Until I am fully recovered from Uncle Archibald's mischief, I had best move slowly and imbibe mostly water. Please give the marquess my regards."

The Creator in His dubious wisdom had designed men and women at cross purposes, or so I had concluded within a year of becoming a wife. To me, relationships between women were straightforward. I knew almost instantly if a woman liked me or not, and other ladies were never left guessing with respect to whether they had my regard.

Men, by contrast, seemed unable to conduct themselves with a similar clarity of feeling. Brothers could be absolutely loyal and detest one another; soldiers would die to protect a superior officer whom they loathed. Men frequently put duty above common sense, to the detriment of the man himself. Women, by contrast, generally strove to maintain a simple set of allegiances that sprang from genuine regard and from nothing so arbitrary as a chain of command or arcane code of honor.

I did not, therefore, understand the relationship between St. Sevier and Dunkeld. They had served together on the Peninsula and shared a soldier's ability to cooperate in the interests of securing a shared objective. They could snipe at each other like brothers. They could exchange looks that spoke volumes indecipherable to me and share a joke as true comrades shared private jests.

They never, though, overtly competed with each other and seemed to avoid any near occasion thereof. They avoided archery tournaments, races on horseback, even the quotidian competition of the chessboard from what I could see, though I had no idea why.

In declining my invitation to go riding, I caught a whiff of that odd dynamic between the marquess and the physician that I could not fathom. They liked and respected each other, but they weren't friends. They thought alike, but did not always agree.

I valued them both, though, and was pleased they made the effort to get along in my presence.

Left to my own devices in the library, however, I found I was no longer able to focus on the letters. I gathered up the lot, intending to take them up to my room. By now, I felt I had a general sense of how Leland House was laid out—having that map in my head mattered to me—and thus I sought to make a shortcut by using backstairs down the corridor from the library.

I somehow got turned around and found myself in an unused part of the manor. The quiet was profound, the chill deep. Little light penetrated the corridor, for the sconces were unlit, and the single window at the end of the corridor was draped with heavy curtains.

I surmised that I was either one floor above or one floor below the suite I shared with St. Sevier, and rather than go back the way I'd come, I expected to find another flight of stairs at the far end of the hallway.

I traversed the worn carpet with a growing sense of unease. No portraits adorned the walls, no pretty little *objets d'art* graced sideboards or deal tables. The entire corridor was devoid of decoration. The wallpaper was peeling near the ceiling, and the floor creaked as I made my way through the shadows. I opened one door then another, finding each room empty.

Curtains served many functions, not the least of which was to protect upholstery and wallpaper from the pernicious effects of sunlight. These rooms had not even curtains on their dingy windows. It was as if I'd stepped from a gracious country manor into a neglected ruin. If creditors had come through to loot every salable asset, the rooms could not have been emptier.

I opened the last door and indeed found the maids' stairs. I took them up one floor and, to my relief, was once again in familiar surrounds. By virtue of another corridor and a second set of steps, I was soon in my room and very relieved to be there.

CHAPTER SIX

I had brought my riding habit with me to Scotland on a whim, and when I saw the elegant mare Sebastian had ponied to Leland House for me, I was glad I had.

"She is lovely," I said, petting a glossy bay neck and smoothing my hand over a perfectly angled shoulder. "What is her name?"

"Iona, like the island. On three."

Sebastian had boosted me into the saddle countless times in our youth, and we still had the knack of executing the maneuver smoothly. A ladies' mounting block would have been more dignified, but I sensed Sebastian enjoyed showing off his brawn.

"How fares St. Sevier on this lovely day?" Sebastian asked, swinging into the saddle of a handsome bay gelding. Hannibal stood over seventeen hands, and while Iona was elegant, Hannibal was formidable. He'd been Sebastian's last military mount and apparently meant enough to his owner that Sebastian had shipped him home from France.

"You are asking if St. Sevier survived Uncle Archibald's story-telling." I picked up my reins and positioned my whip. "He realized he needed to discreetly water his drinks if he was to live to see the sunrise, and he's still a somewhat subdued fellow as we speak."

Sebastian led the way out of the stable yard at a sedate walk, the iron horseshoes *clip-clopping* on the cobbled lane.

"And what of you, my lady?" Sebastian asked. "Did you survive Aunt Bernie and Aunt Maighread's tippling?"

"They were merciful, but I suspect when next I meet them, they will interrogate me about more than how my brothers go on. I was spared the worst of the questions by the fact that Fanny's beau—her intended—has disappeared."

Before last night's meal, I had never encountered Sebastian in his homeland. Against a backdrop of steep hills and brilliant blue sky, he seemed more relaxed to me and more robust than ever.

"Lachlan muttered something to that effect," Sebastian said as we turned onto the main drive leading from the house. "He intimated that the romance has been largely conducted by letter, and the mails have been unforthcoming in recent days. That might explain why our Fanny looks like a death's head on a mopstick."

"She doesn't look well to me either. St. Sevier says she's not consumptive, and I suspect if he gets her alone, he will make more pointed inquiries. I have a theory."

Sebastian smiled down at me from atop his taller mount. "You were ever one for theories."

"I think Fanny is carrying a child, and her condition makes her dyspeptic."

"She's not dyspeptic, Violet, she's emaciated. We're headed up there," he said, pointing to a rocky tor crowning the top of a pine-covered hill. "We won't get in much galloping, but you will never forget the view."

"When I conceived the second time," I said, "I couldn't keep anything down. The midwife wasn't sure I'd survive to give birth." I'd had two miscarriages, both in June, and every year since, I became a bit morose as June arrived. "I was sick within days of conceiving."

Sebastian peered over at me. "You know that for a certainty?"

"The second time I got with child, Freddie had spent a few weeks in the country, then he went off on one of his Parisian jaunts. I had to have conceived within a specific one-week window." And I'd been so happy, despite the horrendous nausea and lack of energy.

"So you think Fanny's beau balked at the notion of starting a family?"

"He may not even know she's carrying, *if* she's carrying, but this is gloomy speculation for such a pretty day. Do you ever ride out with your daughter?" I had never met the child, and had learned of her existence only the previous year at my brother's wedding. Sebastian had brought her home with him from Spain, and I assumed her mother was no longer extant.

"Annis is incorrigible. The aunties delight in telling me how like her father she is. Mind the footing here, it's rocky going for a bit."

The terrain was a bit challenging—we were spiraling around the hill on a path that climbed ever upward—but the conversation with Sebastian was as comfortable as if we'd last greeted each other at Sunday services.

I had needed to move, to get away from the worry hanging over Leland House, and Sebastian had probably seen that last night before he'd even bowed over my hand in greeting.

We emerged onto a smoother path, and I again brought Iona even with Hannibal. "How goes the bride hunt, Sebastian? Will you be going south for the Season?"

"Tell me more about Fanny's missing beau," he said, holding back a branch for me. "What do we know of him?"

I explained the peculiar gap in Fanny's experience with her intended. She had corresponded with him at great length on an array of topics from Walter Scott to the symbolism of the colors in the MacPherson plaid, to the proper education for a wealthy young woman, to the best flowers for conveying courting sentiments.

She knew his mind.

She apparently knew him in the biblical sense too.

But she did not know what he looked like. "Other than telling us he stands about six feet and has dark, silky hair, she doesn't know if it's auburn, red, black, or brown. He's not blond, and he's not bald."

"He's probably not a redhead either," Sebastian said. "Truly red hair—the bright, orange kind—tends to be particularly thick, also a trifle coarse on an adult. You can see the village from the next overlook."

Not a redhead was a significant addition to the relevant facts, given the prevalence of ginger hair in Scotland, and Sebastian had picked out that detail easily.

We dismounted at the overlook and loosened the girths, giving the horses a chance to blow. Some considerate soul had carved a bench by hacking out one-quarter of an enormous fallen pine, and I sank onto the perch gratefully.

"How old is this bench?"

"My grandfather's grandfather apparently recalled it being a fixture in his youth," Sebastian said, taking a seat beside me, his gaze on the valley below. "You look splendid, Violet. Scotland agrees with you."

"Scotland is gorgeous. I'm glad I have a chance to admire your home shire, Sebastian." The view was spectacular, with the silvery skein of the river running between the majestic pine-covered hills, and the granite cottages of the village appearing like toy houses. Sheep were mere fluffy dots against the lush spring grass, and the sky was a blue more brilliant than I typically saw in England.

"The aunties will invite you and St. Sevier over to Dunkeld House," Sebastian said. "You are to oblige them and tell your Frenchman that he can't flirt hard enough to suit those two. They are worse than a pair of shepherdesses newly down from winter pasture."

Sebastian was not inviting me over to Dunkeld House, I noted, which was petty of me.

"Who do you think Fanny's beau could be?" I recounted what else we knew of him, which was precious little.

"You claim the correspondence has gaps," Sebastian said when we were once again in the saddle and moving up the path. "When do the gaps fall?"

I thought back over the list of dates I'd made and the longer list Fanny had supplied. "April is a consistent gap, as is September. He usually manages some letters in early May, but the exchange doesn't resume regularly until mid-June."

"He's landed, I'd say," Sebastian said. "Plowing, planting, foaling, calving, sheering... He's run ragged for weeks in spring and then again at harvest."

The breeze was crisp, the woods scented with the tang of pine, and yet, the little chill I felt was not from the fresh Scottish air.

"That makes sense," I said, "particularly if he's not fabulously wealthy. Even my father used to take a turn sleeping in the foaling barn in the spring." But then, Papa loved horses, and a bit of horse madness was nearly an English earl's patriotic duty. Lord Derwent would not have been caught holding a pair of sheep shears in his hand, if he even recognized what they were.

"If John isn't a small holder, he could be a steward," Sebastian observed. "Every large estate has one. My own is a crusty old article who is as bald as a billiard cue."

I made a mental note to ask for a list of the small holders and stewards in the area who were dark-haired and about six feet tall. Lachlan or Fanny could supply those names, and doing so might spark her memory regarding more pertinent details.

"Tell me how your brothers go on," Sebastian said. "Felix's letters are odes to wedded bliss, but not that informative."

I rattled off the particulars as we climbed higher and higher, and we emerged above the tree line into a brisk wind.

"We'll not tarry long," Sebastian said, helping me dismount. "On a clear day, you can see nearly to the Firth of Forth, but those clouds suggest we've weather coming in. Look you there, though." He turned me by the shoulders and faced me toward the northwest. "Dunkeld land, and some of the best fishing in Scotland along that patch of river there."

Beneath the brisk pine-and-peat scent of the land, I caught a note of Sebastian's shaving soap. He favored the delicate notes of cedar, though he wore the fragrance so subtly that it was evident only in close proximity.

He stood immediately at my back, sheltering me from the breeze. He pointed out the surveying oak, the treaty oak, and the trysting oak and mentioned another oak along the River Tay under which the late Neil Gow had composed many a fiddle tune. Sebastian's love for his homeland, and for this corner of it, was clear in every rolled r and knife-sharp t.

I had only a vague idea who Mr. Gow had been, which was a reminder to me that though Sebastian had been a fixture in my girlhood and was familiar with every extant Derwent, vast areas of his life—his homeland, his family, his culture—were unknown to me.

In all of England, I was certain I would find no vista as dearly beloved as this view of Scotland was to Sebastian.

"I'm glad you brought me here," I said, turning slowly to take in the whole panorama. "You must have died a thousand deaths of homesickness in England."

"And a thousand more in Spain and France," he said, watching me twirl. "Would you oblige me in a whim, Violet?"

Sebastian was the least whimsical man I knew. "Of course. For a view like this, I'd oblige you in much more than a whim." I had needed to see this, needed to be reminded that vast, wild nature existed and could take away not only the breath, but also worries, sorrows, and petty conceits.

Believing in an all-powerful unseen hand was much easier from atop a high Scottish hill than from inside a stuffy London parlor. Why on earth did mourning require that women cut themselves off from natural beauty and confine themselves to darkened houses and crepe-covered mirrors?

"You like it here," Sebastian said, cocking his head. "I'd always wondered if you would."

"I spent years shut away as Freddie's wife and more years shut away as his widow. Though Aunt Bernie or Aunt Maighread are proper ladies, I do not think they would allow themselves to be treated thus, and this view is part of the reason why."

"Perhaps." Sebastian took a step closer, and I was reminded again of how much more vibrant he seemed for being in his home surroundings—and he was an imposing man on his most subdued days.

He astonished me witless when he kissed me, though as kisses went, it was a chaste affair. Lip to lip, but neither lingering nor passionate. A simple, sweet kiss such as friends might share—very, very good friends—or a very innocent couple.

His hand lingered on my cheek, and his smile was the saddest expression I had ever seen on a man's face.

"Thank you," he said, stepping away. "Those clouds will be here before you can say Tam O'Shanter. We'd best be trotting back."

We spoke little on the way to Leland House, the wind rising around us, and I was honestly relieved when we cantered into the stable yard. Iona had been a perfect lady, and the outing had been marvelous, but I had no wish to earn Sebastian a soaking.

"Will you make it home before the heavens open up?" I asked, unhooking my knee from the horn and sliding into Sebastian's arms.

"I will be snug and dry before my own fire with a wee dram to ward off the chill before the rain starts—if I gallop most of the way."

"Then I won't ask you to tarry. I am in your debt, Sebastian. Thank you for a lovely outing."

A groom stood a few yards off, holding both horses. Sebastian took me by the arm and led me into the warmth and quiet of the stable.

"St. Sevier's courting you, isn't he?" Sebastian put the question to me quietly, no hint of emotion coloring his voice.

I saw no reason to dissemble. "He has asked permission to court me, and I have granted it."

Sebastian stood directly before me and took both of my hands. "Promise me, Violet, that you will not marry him because he's convenient or charming or of suitable station. Don't even marry him because he'd die to protect you and nearly has."

"Why should I marry him?" Particularly given that I wasn't keen on marriage as an institution, regardless of who was proposing to me.

"Because you adore him, because he makes you happy when nobody else can. You deserve that. Of all women, you deserve that. Belmaine was a disgrace, and you deserved so much better. Don't settle, do you hear me? Please just don't settle."

"I thought you liked St. Sevier."

"I more than like him," Sebastian said, dropping my hands to gaze at Leland House on the rise west of the drive. "I respect the hell out of him, I trust him, and I wish him every happiness, but not at your expense, Violet. Never again at your expense."

Ah, well, then. I had found solid ground in an unexpected conversation. Sebastian was being protective, and for that, I esteemed *him* greatly.

"I will not settle," I said. "You have my word. But, Sebastian?"

He had pulled on his gloves and taken two strides toward the stable yard. "Violet?"

"Promise me you won't settle either."

"Impossible wench." His smile suggested all manner of mischief. He strode back to my side, kissed me a smacker on the mouth, and strode off.

"Get up to the house," he called over his shoulder. "Damned weather is moving in quickly."

Then he was cantering Hannibal down the drive, Iona following obediently on her lead rope.

That evening saw me once again ensconced in the library. I had read a dozen or more of the letters Fanny had provided, and I had asked her to fetch me some older samples.

"How was your ride this afternoon?" St. Sevier asked when

Fanny had left us alone. He sat across the reading table from me, looking a bit tired and rumpled.

"Breathtaking. The countryside hereabouts is more dramatic than any I've seen thus far." I had never left England, and that had begun to bother me. The Corsican had wreaked havoc for nearly twenty years, and in those twenty years, many an English farm boy had taken the king's shilling and seen the world far, far from his mother's dairy.

While I, an earl's daughter, hadn't been even as far as Paris with my late husband. "Would you take me to France, St. Sevier?"

He donned reading glasses, the gold rims glinting in the candle-light. "France is a ruin. If I had to fault Napoleon for one thing, I fault him for plundering his own countryside. The English knew better than to loot their way to victory, for which I must accord them grudging respect."

"Some would say we looted India and other colonies to pay for our victory." My brother Mitchell among them. His views of empire —of fueling England's wealth through military conquest and exploitation of foreign lands—were radical and mostly muttered late at night after several brandies. They would scandalize my father, but they fascinated Ajax and Hector, my middle brothers.

"Some would." St. Sevier said. "What are you learning from the older letters?"

For a man of St. Sevier's polish, the change of subject was abrupt. "I am learning that two people can discuss books with more passion than I can discuss almost anything."

He peered at me over the rims of his spectacles. "Some people use up all their passion in words. Others reserve expressions of ardor for more private moments."

"You are flirting with me."

His smile was slight and naughty. "You might consider flirting back."

"Or I might reserve my expressions of ardor for a more private moment. Fanny will rejoin us soon. I want to compare the hand-writing between the older and newer letters."

"I want to throw you over my shoulder and haul you upstairs to my bed, there to make love with you eight different ways before morning."

I did not know eight different ways to join my body with a man's. I moved a branch of candles closer to the letter I was studying.

"What a delightful prospect, though I am not keen on being hauled around like a sack of laundry, even if the destination is your bed." I was keen on increasing my amatory vocabulary with St. Sevier, but he apparently attributed to me a sophistication I lacked.

"Then, as I carry you through the house, I shall cradle you in my arms like the dearest treasure ever to gaze adoringly into a smitten man's eyes."

I put down the letter. "St. Sevier, have you been at the whisky again?"

"God forbid. I have been contemplating the intoxicating prospect of becoming your lover, while you are absorbed in a lot of musty old literary letters."

What was keeping Fanny? "You speak of lovers. I have never had a lover. You contemplate intimacies I cannot conceive of, unless Freddie described them to me in an attempt to shock me out of my hold on propriety. Perhaps for you, lovemaking is a simple animal pleasure. I do not enjoy the same uncomplicated view of the matter."

He covered my hand with his own. "Lovemaking should be a pleasure for both parties."

"Both parties aren't likely to conceive and bear—or lose—a child."

He came around the table to take the chair beside mine, and I liked that better than sitting across from each other.

"I was also married once upon a time, Violet. The union was ill-advised from every perspective, but let me assure you that if my wife and I had lost a child, both she and I would have mourned."

"Hugh, I am sorry." He grieved for not only that wife to whom he was so ill-suited, but for the dreams and children he would never share with her. "I am so very, very sorry." I took his hand, struck anew by how much St. Sevier and I did not know about one another.

He contemplated marriage to me, and I had selfishly assumed lingering issues with grief were exclusively my burden as we embarked on a courtship. His familiarity with grief was not the clinical expertise of the physician—or not only that—but the fruit of bitter experience.

"We were young, foolish, arrogant, and... *libidineux*, randy. We were not in love, but we tried to make the best of our situation. Following the drum makes for a poor wedding journey."

I could hardly imagine undertaking a marriage in the midst of a military campaign. "Will you tell me more?"

He kissed my knuckles. "Someday. I would rather tell you of my immediate plans for your luscious person." He kissed my cheek, then my lips, a slow progression of intimacies that I was mad to reciprocate. His tongue had just grazed my mouth, and I was contemplating the great boldness of sitting in his lap when the door burst open.

"I just saw him," Fanny said, panting heavily. "John, my John. He was in the garden, and I know it was him."

St. Sevier thought to snatch a lamp from a wall sconce as we bustled into the garden. The wind was still high, and exposed candles would have been snuffed within two steps of the house.

"He was there," Fanny said, pointing to the bench she and I had occupied shortly after my arrival. "He sits with his arms braced on his knees, hunching forward, and he scoops up a handful of pebbles and tosses them one by one in a straight line. He says it's an exercise to help improve an angler's accuracy."

"Then how do you know you weren't seeing another angler?" I asked as we approached the bench. "Lachlan or Iain or Donnie?" Or that gamekeeper fellow—MacFarlane—who'd thought to see St.

Sevier dunked in the river? And why hadn't Fanny run to her beloved? Why had she run to fetch us instead?

"The menfolk all went up to bed," Fanny replied. "They are still recovering from Uncle Archie's visit. I haven't ever seen them toss pebbles like that, but with John, it's a habit when he's in a certain mood."

"What of a gardener?" St. Sevier asked. "This area is the family's personal preserve. A man who works here might be comfortable stealing a few moments at the end of his day where others don't belong."

The rain had moved through earlier in the day, but even within the walls of the garden, the sharp wind was still blowing, snapping at our cloaks and tossing the flowers this way and that. The moonlight came and went as clouds scudded through the night sky, and somewhere in the forest, an owl hooted.

"Who would linger out here on such a night?" I asked, striding over to the bench.

"John would," Fanny said. "Lachlan doesn't normally light torches in the garden unless we're entertaining, and we rarely entertain. John and I spent hours on that bench when everybody else thought I was fast asleep."

St. Sevier held up the lamp, though the bench was bare, and nothing about the crushed-shell walkway or surrounding beds suggested John had helpfully dropped a calling card.

"He was here," Fanny insisted, a note of hysteria creeping into her voice. "I saw him. I know the outline of his shoulders. I know how he bows his head when he's thinking."

"If this was a trysting place," I said, walking off a little way to consider the bench from the approach that led to the fountain, "how did John usually signal you that he was here? On a moonless night, you would not be able to see him easily from the windows."

We had a nearly full moon, and still the bench was cast in deep shadows.

"I'd wait in the library, and he'd fling three pebbles at the windows. One, two, three, not all at once. I was to wait five minutes, and he'd meet me at the foot of the garden. That bench was as close as he'd come to the house."

Lest the light from the windows illuminate his features. What sort of man indulged in such games?

"What is that?" I asked, striding back to the bench. "St. Sevier, the light, please." I knelt down to extract something from beneath the bench that turned out to be a little bouquet done up with a plain white linen ribbon.

"He was here," Fanny said, taking the bouquet from me and holding it beneath her nose. "I knew it! He hasn't abandoned me, and we shall be wed."

St. Sevier lowered the lantern. "Let's put the flowers in water, shall we? I'm sure Lady Violet would like to ask you a few questions, and this cold, damp air is insalubrious."

To preserve her little tuzzy-muzzy, Fanny would likely have hiked to Edinburgh in her bare feet.

"What do the flowers mean, Violet?" she asked as we once again assembled in the library. "Forget-me-nots are obvious, but what about the violets?"

"Eternal faithfulness," I said as Fanny put the flowers into a crystal glass and half filled it with water. "Both violets and forget-me-nots are both blooming in the wild this time of year. They like the same growing conditions and can often be found together." Meaning anybody—any cowherd, groom, boot-boy, or footman—could have picked that bouquet.

"So this is a frequent combination?" St. Sevier asked, slouching into a chair at the reading table and eyeing the flowers balefully.

"The first bouquet I was given was exactly this pairing." I'd found the flowers on my pillow the day my brother Felix had left to take up his commission. At the time, I'd thought Felix was being sweet, and I still had the dried remnants pressed between the pages of an old journal.

As the clock on the mantel ticked away the late-night hour, and the fire roared softly on the hearth, I recalled that Sebastian and Felix had reported for duty together, and the flowers might not have been from Felix after all.

I took a seat at the reading table and gestured for Fanny to do likewise. "What was the man in the garden wearing, Fanny? Was he kilted or in breeches?"

Sebastian had silky dark hair, Sebastian was richly landed, Sebastian was well-read and had a fine hand. Sebastian was more romantic than he wanted to admit, or he had been as a younger man. He was taller than St. Sevier, but Fanny had not been exact in her recollections of her swain's height.

"Kilted," Fanny said. "But that's about all I can tell you."

The head gardener, Evan, had been kilted. "Does John have a particular scent?" I asked, still considering the flowers.

"You mean a shaving soap?"

"Or cologne, Hungary water, pomade."

St. Sevier had taken up his paper and pencil again. He was keeping a list of facts regarding the prodigal groom, though I didn't see how the evening's events added much to that list

"John is fastidious," Fanny said, "at least when he spends time with me. He doesn't smell of livestock or unwashed clothing, if that's what you mean."

"You met him in the dark," I said, marshaling my patience. "What scent did he wear? When you held him close and kissed him, did he savor of lavender? Heather? Roses?"

"What does it matter?" Fanny asked, looking peevish and wan. "He wears a light floral fragrance, but we won't catch him by his scent."

St. Sevier put down his pencil. "If he can afford a custom blend, he has some wealth. If he's fond of heather, he's likely using scents from his own stillroom or that of the nearest herb woman. If the scent is particularly complex and sweet, hinting at an ambergris base, he might even be buying his fragrances in Paris, and travel from Britain might also explain the periodic lapses in his correspondence."

Had I delivered that lecture, Fanny would have turned up mulish. She gazed at St. Sevier as if the philosophers of old should have been vying for a chance to touch the hem of his dinner jacket.

"When you came upon him in the garden tonight," St. Sevier went on, "had he signaled you with pebbles?"

"No. You two have been in the library all evening. He likely avoided the usual signal because of your presence."

"You were here with us," I reminded her, "and we would think nothing of a twig or branch tossed against the windows on such an unsettled night. He ran from you, didn't he, Fanny? He saw you emerge onto the terrace, and when you called his name, he scarpered."

She began to weep, and St. Sevier passed over a handkerchief. "Violet, perhaps a glass of water for Miss MacPherson."

I went to the sideboard and poured a drink, feeling equal parts exasperation and remorse. I ought not to have pressed Fanny, but she wasn't being exactly helpful.

St. Sevier crossed the room to take the glass from my hand. "You will please excuse yourself," he whispered. "I believe Miss MacPherson has been poisoning herself, and I would speak with her privately."

Dear God. "I'll wait up for you," I murmured.

"Best not," he said. "The topic wants much patience." He kissed my cheek, and I had no choice but to leave, though I took a final sniff of the delicate purple flowers already wilting in their whisky glass.

CHAPTER SEVEN

Hugh joined me the next morning as I enjoyed my first cup of tea on the balcony. I was in my dressing gown and slippers and sat swaddled in a soft wool blanket as the sun rose over the high hill across the valley.

He was dressed for the day, his hair still damp and neatly combed back. What a lovely sight he was early in the morning, the sun turning his hair to a fiery copper, his elegant length lounging in the opposite chair.

I passed him the cup. "You had a late night."

"Another late night." He finished my tea and made us up a second cup. "To profane such a glorious morning with talk of misery and mischief is a violation of the natural order, but my suspicions were correct."

"Fanny is poisoning herself?"

He handed me the cup, the steam rising from the tea like the mists rising over the pines adorning the hillsides.

"I did manage to notice one or two details about the Leland House herbal as I was dodging Miss Eulalie's friendly overtures. I went back there yesterday afternoon and did a more thorough inspection, locking the door lest I be accosted."

He'd fixed the tea exactly as I liked it. "What did you find?"

"A predictable abundance of the usual items—lavender, heather, various mints and herbs, but the late Mrs. Leland's illness also required that somebody get in the habit of storing a quantity of medicinals. I came upon a number of exotic preparations, some of the supplies too old to be of much value, and I also found a relatively fresh supply of rue."

"How can you tell it's fresh?"

"By the scent, the texture, the color. Rue is used sometimes to bring on menses, but it is dangerous, and responsible practitioners don't recommend it."

I set down the tea cup. "Fanny has been dosing herself?"

"She and John were—are?—betrothed, and an engaged couple is expected to enjoy a certain license. Fanny yet preserved enough caution, or uncertainty, to take measures to prevent conception."

"Did she succeed?"

"In that vast Leland House library, she could not find an up-to-date herbal. She dared not ask the midwife, given that nobody knew she and John were engaged. She got hold of some old English pamphlet that advised rue tea, the better to space pregnancies, and she has done serious mischief to her internal organs as a result."

"Has she conceived?"

"I cannot be sure." Coming from a physician who'd also practiced as a surgeon, that uncertainty was disturbing.

"Hugh, I knew when I was pregnant, both times, within days of conceiving. I was physically miserable. I could not keep down a cup of tea until afternoon, and then I craved barberry ices." Freddie had arranged with Gunter's to have them delivered every evening.

St. Sevier cocked his head at me. "You lost two children?"

I selected a piece of shortbread from the tea tray. "I wasn't very far along the first time. The second was a boy. He did not survive a very premature birth. I have hated June, because June took both of my children from me."

"And then your husband died in June, did he not?"

A prickling at the back of my neck accompanied a nod. "And I was expected to put off mourning in June. No wonder the month fills me with dread."

He brought my hand to his mouth and took a bite of my short-bread. "This June, you will be a happier lady, if I have anything to say to it."

I popped the rest of the treat into my mouth. "Tonight, I would like to be a happier lady." Though the discussion regarding Fanny's situation brought up a potential worry: What if *I* conceived? St. Sevier was courting me, but we were not engaged, nor did I want us to be... not so soon, maybe not ever.

"Your wish is my most fervent dream, my lady. This day cannot pass quickly enough for me."

"Tell me about Fanny. How can she not know if she's carrying a child?"

"She has none of the secondary symptoms usually associated with early pregnancy—her breasts are not tender, she is not unusually prone to sleepiness, she is not making water with particular frequency."

My gracious, a physician learned to be blunt. "But?"

"But the monthly inconvenience has not fully visited her for weeks. She has only the lightest of evidence in this regard at irregular intervals. Her appetite is most unreliable, which is both a symptom of pregnancy and the herb. She is listless, which can again be a symptom of both, also of nervous exhaustion."

I drew my blanket more closely around me. "You are saying she might be carrying, or she might be fading from poison, or she might be losing ground due to the strain of a missing fiancé?" Or all three, the poor woman.

"I suspect she is mostly feeling the ill effects from the rue, which I directed her to cease using immediately. The later in pregnancy one takes such measures, the more dangerous they are. If the tea were to be effective, she'd have lost the baby by now."

"I hate that Fanny has been so miserable and so alone with her troubles."

St. Sevier helped himself to more shortbread. "She summoned you, a true friend, and you are determined to get to the bottom of her troubles. You doubtless aired the situation with Lord Dunkeld. What insights did he have to offer?"

Whatever else was true, my friendship with Sebastian did not make St. Sevier even the least little bit jealous. That was fortunate, because I would never again allow myself to lose touch with the man who had been such a good friend to me in my girlhood. We might drift apart, eventually exchanging only holiday greetings, but if so, that would be our choice.

"His lordship made two observations. First, Fanny's beau is unlikely to have bright red hair, because a silky texture and that color are an unusual combination."

"But not impossible."

"I suppose not. Second, he suggested John has landed interests, given when the gaps in the correspondence occur."

St. Sevier gazed out across the beautiful landscape, and though we were simply starting our day with a cup of tea, discussing other people's business, I would long remember the moment. Hugh would be handsome into old age, patrician features aging into distinguished attractiveness, his brown eyes always holding a hint of mischief.

Not every love manifests as an initial excess of girlish glee. Some loves were deep and steady, marked by both friendship and desire.

"Dunkeld's theory has merit," St. Sevier said. "Did you ask him to make a list of such fellows in the area?"

"I thought I'd ask Fanny."

"She will bring to mind only the men she might find attractive, and we must entertain the possibility that John is not such a man."

"You believe he might be scarred?"

"Physical scars are usually obvious to the touch. He might be tainted by scandal, obligated to another woman, in service, plagued by creditors... The possibilities are endless."

Not endless, but I felt compelled to add another to his list. "He might also be quite well known to her and unscrupulous enough to dally with her while promising a marriage he has no intention of allowing to happen."

St. Sevier regarded me in that assessing way of his. "What or whom do you suspect?"

I had pointedly asked Sebastian how his bride hunt progressed, and he had pointedly dodged the question.

"Dunkeld is tall, Scottish, landed, has silky dark hair, and travels periodically. He is well educated, loves books, lives a fifteen-minute ride away, and has long known Fanny. He needs a wife who can bear him children, and he wears a light fragrance." Though not a *floral* fragrance.

I disliked raising this line of inquiry, not only because Sebastian would never jilt a fiancée, but also because to do so felt disloyal to my friend.

St. Sevier picked up the tea cup and lifted it so we could both watch the steam wafting skyward. "Interesting list, Violet, but you forget one significant factor."

"And that is?"

"Dunkeld has no motive for sneaking about. He needs a wife, as you say, and Fanny is an heiress. Why not court her openly and be done with it? Moreover, he is temperamentally unsuited to subterfuge. He will take a confidence to his grave, but his version of honor does not permit dishonesty where the ladies are concerned."

"And yet," I said, "he fits the pattern otherwise. You must admit that." I had to admit that—grudgingly.

St. Sevier took a sip of tea and passed me the cup. He was quiet, and I was content to sit beside him and watch sunlight steal over the land. I wanted to watch more sunrises with him, and moonrises too.

"Shall I help you to dress?" he asked when we'd finished our tea.

"Lucy will be along shortly, and if I allow you to play lady's maid, we might miss breakfast altogether."

"The day will be the longest of my life, Violet." He rose, kissed my cheek, and went on his way.

While St. Sevier investigated the herb garden and conservatory further, I closeted myself in the ladies' sitting room, an interesting space over the medieval part of the hall. Because needlework requires copious light, the sunniest space available in any dwelling is a good place to work at embroidery. At Leland House, what had once been a solar was now an airy parlor with a wide balcony.

Though the fresh air on the balcony beckoned, I did not want an errant breeze to make off with any of Fanny's precious correspondence. I was thus sitting by the window after luncheon, reading through older letters, when the butler announced Sebastian, Marquess of Dunkeld.

"This is a pleasant surprise," I said, rising to offer him my hand. He made quite a fetching picture in his kilt, one I would miss when I returned to England. Sebastian seemed happier in his homeland than he could ever be in the south. I could understand why, now that I'd seen the beauty of his native surrounds.

"I won't take up much of your time, my lady, but I could not sleep last night. I busied myself making a list. Shall we sit?"

"Of course." Though it was ungracious of me, I nonetheless wondered if his restlessness had been the result of an aborted attempt to meet Fanny in the garden. But then, why leave? Fanny had been hurrying to the side of her beloved, and he'd bolted.

Sebastian would not bolt.

Sebastian would not conduct intimate correspondence under an alias.

Sebastian would not abandon a woman who could be carrying his child.

I hoped. I had barely recognized my girlhood friend in the man who'd come home from war, though Sebastian had had reasons for his distant treatment of me. Then too, I had to wonder at my motivations for trying to wedge Sebastian onto the list of potential John S. MacDonalds. Did I want him paired off because I was pairing myself with St. Sevier?

"Should I ring for tea?" I asked as I took a seat at the writing table. Sebastian held my chair for me, and I was reminded again of his faint cedary fragrance. After the scent lingered for a while, would the finish turn more flowery?

"No tea, thank you." He took the place at my elbow. "I made a list of men who fit the description you gave me of Fanny's missing beau." He passed over a folded piece of paper, which—I noted—bore the same watermark as the paper John used for his letters.

"There are fifteen names on this list," I said. "Surely you don't think Lachlan, Iain, or Donnie could be Fanny's swain?" I studied the list more closely. "Your name isn't on here, and you fit the descriptors quite closely."

Sebastian was too tall, but not by much.

He smiled slightly, though I found nothing humorous in the situation. "Add me to the list, Violet. I like Fanny very much, though she'd be miserable as my marchioness. I would not inflict misery on a woman I cared for."

That was the answer of an innocent man. "Why would she be miserable?" Why would any woman be miserable married to such a handsome, vigorous, wealthy, and well-educated man? Sebastian could appear toweringly arrogant, but he could also laugh at himself and at life, a quality at variance with true arrogance.

And he would be loyal and faithful to his wife. Of that, I had no doubt.

"Fanny was even more unhappy in England than I was," Sebastian said. "She's retiring, preferring the company of books to that of people, and she does not enjoy travel. I am a marquess and, as such, am already under consideration for Scotland's parliamentary delegation. I will spend long periods of time in England, and my wife would be expected to accompany me south and manage a significant number of fancy entertainments."

I hadn't considered any of that, though it explained why Sebastian had begun his bride hunt in London.

"Mind you," he went on, "I believe Fanny and I could rub along well enough personally. She's beyond smart, has a good sense of humor, and understands Scottishness. Lately, though, she has grown frail. I had hoped the good doctor might take an interest in restoring her to better health."

I was not beyond smart, neither did I possess notable wit, and I barely fathomed *Scottishness*. Moreover, I was apparently unable to produce healthy children, another requirement for any marchioness.

All of which was irrelevant to the instant discussion.

"St. Sevier has consulted with Fanny informally," I said, "and I believe Fanny's health will improve soon." She hadn't exactly attacked her midday meal, but she'd made an effort with the beef and barley soup, buttered bread, and cranachan.

"Was she sickening, then?" Sebastian asked, gaze on the portrait over the mantel. If ever a member of the Leland family was tempted to forget his or her heritage, the abundance of kilted laddies, plaid-bedecked lassies, and dramatic landscapes on the walls would provide abundant reminders.

"She is at risk for nervous exhaustion." Quite true.

Sebastian regarded me closely. "'Tis none of my affair. Let's have a look at that list, and I'll tell you what I know of each man."

Of the fifteen, three were easily dismissed as family whom Sebastian had included for the sake of thoroughness. Donnie and Iain weren't even strictly landowners, though I did pause at Lachlan's name.

"Is it legal in Scotland for a man to marry a step-daughter after her mother's passing?"

Sebastian wrinkled his splendid beak. "I should think not. I don't sense any such interest on Lachlan's part, but Fanny looks very like her mother and has some of her mother's ways. Lachlan's regard for his late wife was considerable, and—unusual for a Scotsman of means—he hasn't remarried."

"Why would Lachlan spend years on an epistolary charade?" I mused. "Why invest all that time and effort on a doomed relationship?"

Sebastian took up the goose quill pen and twirled it between his palms. "We aren't all gifted with your English pragmatism, Violet. If Lachlan were smitten, he might engage in foolishness."

"But he has no need to be subtle. He can brace Fanny over supper about Walter Scott's romanticism, or debate the Irish question with her at breakfast. Enjoy commerce with her lively mind firsthand and leave the impossible longings out of it."

Sebastian was quiet for a time, twiddling his feather. "I think we can agree, for many reasons, that Lachlan is an unlikely suspect. I'm not as convinced when it comes to some of the others. Rudyard MacKinnon is a handsome devil who cuts a wide swath, and he's the despair of his lady wife. Daniel Brewster is widowed, but his wife took ever so long to expire, and he might have started up a correspondence out of loneliness."

I stared at the list, trying to put myself in the frame of mind of a young woman trysting late at night with a man whom I knew only through letters. I'd drink in every detail of his physicality, every scrap of information personal to him to hoard up and treasure...

"Does either man smoke?" I asked.

"MacKinnon favors a pipe," Sebastian said. "Brewster indulges in cheroots—the Havana variety, which tells you he loves them, for they are deuced dear, and he's seldom without one."

"Then we can strike them from the list. As much wool as is worn in these parts over the winter months, the stink of tobacco would be impossible to hide. Fanny noted only a light floral fragrance about her swain."

Sebastian took back the list and used the pen to put an X beside eight more of the names, for they all partook regularly of the tobacco habit. If we discarded family for want of any evidence implicating them, we were left with only four names.

"We can cross off MacMillan," Sebastian said. "He burns only peat and reeks of it accordingly. Even his hat smells of peat."

"Are any of the remaining three left-handed?" I asked, taking up the letter I'd been reading. "I know right-handed penmanship can be beaten into a child who is naturally left-handed, but some adults do write with the left hand."

"Croft is left-handed, at least when fishing, shooting, and eating. He might be able to write with either hand. I have a note from him about a boundary survey. I'll send it along to you."

Handwriting could be disguised, but maintaining that disguise consistently over a period of years would be difficult. "Do you have any handwriting from the other two?"

"I might, if I look back far enough. Louis Deardorff's sister is his hostess, and I suspect she might be his amanuensis as well. George Ballard is wealthy enough to employ clerks to handle his penmanship."

"But wouldn't those men append their signatures personally to social correspondence? We could compare their signatures with John MacDonald's."

Sebastian set aside his feather. "Show me some of the letters. I might recognize the hand. I keep a pair of secretaries busy at Dunkeld House, but I read all the mail myself."

A *pair* of secretaries. Even my father employed only the one secretary, a fresh-faced young fellow who literally walked three paces behind the earl at all times and addressed any remarks to Papa's watch chain.

I passed Sebastian one of the more recent letters and one of the oldest Fanny had given me. He studied them with the singular focus he'd always had, an eye for detail that had doubtless stood him in good stead riding dispatch for Wellington.

"He changed how he makes his ones and sevens," Sebastian said.

"Picked up the Continental habit of crossing his sevens to distinguish them from his ones."

Never in a decade of trying would I have spotted that difference. "Who on your list has traveled to the Continent?"

Sebastian passed me the letters and sat back. "I don't know, but let's assume we're focused on George Ballard and Louis Deardorff. Ask Fanny about them and have her take you on a social call on their households. She might pick up some detail that eliminates one or both, and you can concoct a reason to inquire into their Continental excursions. Now, are you up for a turn in the garden, or do I leave you here, solving another woman's problems while you ignore a beautiful Scottish day?"

Sebastian's focus on the handwriting in the letters had tickled a realization lurking beneath my mind's notice—a comforting realization. I'd received many notes from Sebastian as a girl. The usual *Meet me at the river. Bring your fishing pole,* scribblings, and then later, *Found this, thought you'd enjoy it,* when he'd copied whole poems for me.

Neither Fanny's early nor late letters bore a close resemblance to Sebastian's penmanship, at least as I'd known it years ago.

"A turn in the garden sounds delightful," I said. "Let me fetch my shawl, and I'll join you on the terrace."

When I met him out of doors, he was deep in discussion with St. Sevier, as both men apparently shared an interest in falconry. I let them prattle on, while wishing Fanny would join us so I might order her to take me calling on our two suspects.

"A lot of birds flying around, as birds do," Donnie said, waving his hand in circles.

"You are jealous," Eulalie retorted, pointing with her fork. "We haven't a mews at Leland House anymore, and you haven't a clue how to fly a falcon."

Iain alone of the three siblings seemed more intent on his supper than on bickering. He had arrived for the meal only as we were sitting down, made his excuses to Fanny and Lachlan for being late, and then tucked into his soup without another word.

I spent supper observing Lachlan and Fanny and wondering if they made any sort of couple. They were nominally the host and hostess of Leland House, and had they been so inclined, they could have maintained a discreet liaison, no one the wiser.

That notion disturbed me, but it bore consideration.

I saw no odd glances, no casual brushes of the fingers, nothing that would overtly suggest Lachlan regarded Fanny as anything other than a dear step-daughter. But then, if I were Lachlan, I would be exceedingly careful not to give myself away.

"I have no idea how to fly a falcon," St. Sevier said, "but my grandfather kept several raptors, and they were dear to him. Some species of owl in particular, I believe, bond with a keeper if raised in captivity."

"I have always wanted to try falconry," Fanny said, considering a bite of buttered potatoes. "It seems so noble, something knights and ladies of old did, and the birds are stunning."

"I would not want to be that bird," Donnie retorted. "My life spent in the dark tied to a perch, my only freedom at the whim of another. No, thank you."

In a sense, Donnie, as a poor relation, was very like a domesticated falcon. He flew no farther than his allowance took him, if he even received an allowance. His socializing was limited to the few informal entertainments Lachlan hosted for the neighbors, and his only hope of freedom was to marry a woman of means.

Oh dear. Perhaps Sebastian hadn't been so foolish to include members of Fanny's step-family on the list of suspects.

I ate enough to be polite, while trying not to cast repeated glances at the clock on the mantel. I had ambled around the garden with Sebastian and St. Sevier as they'd discussed breeds of raptor and a few common acquaintances from their military days. St. Sevier would occasionally bend to sniff a flower, or pause to watch a hawk wheeling overhead.

He was an exceedingly attractive man, and when he'd used a penknife to cut me a bouquet of irises, he added a few words of French flirtation that I'd hoped Sebastian hadn't overheard.

Jusqu'à ce soir, ma chère. Irises symbolized faith, hope, and courage, among other things. St. Sevier's gesture had disconcerted me out of all proportion to the moment, though it was the only time I could think of that a man had picked flowers just for me—excepting the violets and forget-me-nots that might have been from Sebastian.

I'd carried the irises inside, and they now graced my bedside table. Nonetheless, *ce soir* was taking forever to arrive.

We finally reached the fruit and cheese plate, an interesting combination of *chèvre* and candied citrus. Fanny, I noted, took none of either, but did allow herself a piece of shortbread when the ladies retired to gather around the teapot.

"I vow, Donnie grows moodier with each season," Eulalie said, pouring out for us. "Lachlan needs to find him a sweetheart, before I do him an injury."

"We could find him a sweetheart," Fanny replied, accepting her cup of tea. "If Aunt Bernie and Aunt Maighread put their minds to it, they could find him somebody."

"What of the settlements?" I would not have asked such a personal question if I'd felt my Scottish friends would take offense.

"I'll dower him from my inheritance," Fanny said. "Eulalie, too, and even Iain, though I doubt Iain will ever bother with a wife."

"He'd have to smile every once in a while," Eulalie said, "and arrive at dinner in time to actually socialize. Your Frenchman is such a gentleman, Lady Violet. I love simply hearing him speak. He has the ability to make a lady feel that her words are the center of his universe and her every sigh and glance the source of endless fascination."

Fanny smacked Eulalie's arm. "You could set your cap for Dunkeld. He's worth a sigh or two."

He was, and Eulalie, unlike Fanny, was far from retiring. The notion bore further consideration, though my instinctive reaction to that pairing was unfavorable. Eulalie was a bit impetuous and frivolous and more than a little self-centered. She had a quality of bored restlessness that I didn't think marriage would cure.

But then, maybe Sebastian needed some frivolity, and a woman who demanded that he take some notice of her. Eulalie excused herself after one cup of tea, declaring that she simply wasn't up to the challenge of more time spent in the company of a grumpy sibling.

"She's in a mood," Fanny muttered. "Donnie hasn't been any worse than usual lately. I think he picks fights so there's at least some conversation at the table. Iain is usually too tired and famished to bother with more than 'please pass the butter' or 'may I have the salt,' and Lachlan mostly concerns himself with the ledgers and tenants."

"You've been very lonely here, haven't you, Fanny?"

She poured herself a second cup. "I sometimes think I was born lonely, my lady, and I don't mean that to be dramatic. Mama was consumed with my father's illness, then with Lachlan's courtship, then with her own bad health. I was shuffled away to England—Edinburgh wasn't far enough—and you know what school was like. Then I came home to this rambling old pile, and John's letters were like a beacon of light in a subterranean darkness."

"Speaking of John…" I apprised her of the day's developments, showing her Sebastian's list.

"I never once caught a hint of tobacco on John's person," Fanny said, studying the names. "Dunkeld was thorough, though I see he did not include himself."

"I noticed that too."

Fanny stared off at the peat fire tossing desultory heat from the drawing-room hearth. "Dunkeld could simply court me outright. I'm an heiress, he has a title. It's done all the time. I don't think John is as tall as Dunkeld, but I haven't examined the heels on John's boots when we're together. John might be disguising his height, or lack thereof."

"I know Dunkeld's penmanship," I said, "and his hand is much less elegant than the script in your letters."

"Handwriting can be disguised, but Dunkeld was also out of the country when my correspondence began. He'd have had no reason to place an advertisement for a lady, and retrieving my letters from the posting inn in Glenbennach would have been quite difficult. John does not dwell far from here, at least some of the time."

An element of dispassion had come into her use of John's name. "What do you think of George Ballard and Louis Deardorff?"

Fanny made a face and set down her tea cup. "Mr. Ballard wears a corset because he has a bit of a paunch. I've danced with him at enough assemblies to know that much, while John is exceptionally trim and fit. Mr. Deardorff has notably crooked teeth. I am in a position to tell you that John has excellent teeth."

I had had as much tea as I could stand. "I don't know whether to be relieved that the local husbands and bachelors don't qualify for the post, or frustrated because I can see few other avenues to investigate from here."

Fanny rose to poke at the fire. "I don't see any other avenues."

"The posting inn, Fanny. We must make inquiries at the Glenbennach posting inn. Even without a sender's direction, we can learn on what stage route John's letters arrive, and we might eventually determine who picks them up on his end." Though if John were bent on subterfuge, he'd be sending the letters from any number of locations other than the one posting inn he used for household purposes.

"Postmasters aren't supposed to give out that information."

Meaning Fanny had considered this aspect of the situation already. "Bridegrooms aren't supposed to disappear. We must make the effort, and who knows what we might find?"

Fanny set aside her poker and replaced the fire screen. "Monsieur had a very frank talk with me last night, in the manner of a physician with a patient. Without once transgressing good manners, St. Sevier was most severe with me, Violet. I must tell you, it was a relief for a man to take an interest in my welfare. I was poisoning myself and didn't know it."

"You can recover from that." I hoped. I hadn't asked St. Sevier about lasting damage from abusing rue.

"I can, but, Violet, I understand why Eulalie is as bold and heedless as she is. If I am not to marry John, then what will I do? Spend another decade stitching samplers and sketching scenery? Promise me you will not give up until you find him."

I was not prepared to spend the foreseeable future in Scotland, but neither could I disappoint my friend.

"We will find him, and if we don't, you will visit me in London come spring. I will introduce you to my brothers and all their handsome friends. A Scottish heiress will be a novelty, and all the matchmakers will want to see you packed off to the church so the field is left clear for the English contenders."

Fanny stared at the fire. "I don't want to do the pretty in Mayfair, though I thank you for the thought. I want to know what became of my John and why he'd abandon me this way. I'll bid you good night, and thank you again for coming—and for bringing Monsieur with you. He truly is a gem of a gentleman."

He truly was, and if the clock would ever see fit to advance at a pace faster than that of a glacier in winter, St. Sevier might become not simply a gem of a gentleman, but my own personal gem of a lover too.

CHAPTER EIGHT

The glorious morning sunshine beaming down as we rode to the village of Glenbennach suited my mood. I had for the first time in my life awoken in the arms of a lover. Not a husband, a lover, and what a lover St. Sevier was.

Freddie's lovemaking had been considerate as far as it went. He'd taken the time to establish a mood, though not much time. If I'd been out of sorts or indisposed, he'd kiss my forehead and take himself off— to his mistresses, as it turned out. He hadn't *ever* physically hurt me. On the rare occasions when I'd initiated marital intimacies, he'd obliged me with something like brisk good humor, taking as much as thirty minutes from his schedule to see to my request.

But he hadn't *cherished* me. Hadn't made me feel as if his greatest privilege was to take me in his arms and learn all my favorite caresses and kisses. He hadn't held me tenderly and whispered shocking French indecencies that he then demonstrated with equally shocking French competence.

I gained a new insight into Fanny's comment about a gentleman's beard affording a lady pleasure.

I gained new insights, too, into myself. Freddie had implied that I was something of a nun—standoffish and not particularly warm. St. Sevier, by contrast, turned cuddling into a high art, as much about affection as passion, and I gloried in his brand of attention. He was as friendly about his lovemaking as he was inventive, and his sheer fondness for me—my person, my mind, my conversation—was balm to my soul.

That, I thought, as my mare cantered along, was how a lady ought to go about her intimate liaisons. With fellows who conducted themselves with élan and humor—St. Sevier had tickled me—and unrelenting consideration for the lady's needs.

St. Sevier had spent breakfast gently flirting with Eulalie and Fanny, which I suspected was his way of both making me feel less self-conscious and expressing his own high spirits.

Fanny and Eulalie had chosen to drive a gig to Glenbennach, while St. Sevier and I went ahead on horseback. The road paralleled the river for much of the distance, occasionally rising to scale a hillside when the riverbank became too steep.

St. Sevier slowed his horse to the walk, and I did likewise with my mare, falling in step beside his gelding.

"Such beautiful country," I said, "and such a beautiful day."

"Appropriate, after such a beautiful night. Any regrets, *mon coeur*?"

I had never been anybody's heart before, particularly not in that caressing tone. "I might say I regret not having my way with you sooner, except that's inaccurate. I wasn't ready. Something about being in this more wild place, away from all that's familiar, and spending time with you en route, has given me the courage to meet you on my own terms. I regret nothing, St. Sevier."

"Then I am the happiest of men, until tonight, when I might be even happier still. Where do you suppose Donnie got off to this morning?"

I appreciated the change of subject—joy could be diminished for being analyzed too closely—and I'd wondered the same thing. "He was nearly sullen at breakfast and none too cheerful at dinner last night. Do you suppose your flirtations with Fanny are making him resentful of his place in the household?"

"I am careful to flirt with all the ladies, you will notice, though I agree that Donnie is in a taking over something. You should find a moment to speak with him privately about Fanny's situation."

"Should we chat with Iain as well? He told me plainly that Fanny's intended had decamped, and that was my first conversation with him."

"A quick word can't hurt, though Iain has perfected the role of dour Scotsman."

The gig tooled over the rise, and because we didn't want to eat its dust, we got our horses moving again. Glenbennach turned out to be more picturesque than the humble gathering of cottages that made up the Leland House estate village. The posting inn was a charming Tudor whimsy that nonetheless had the extensive stables such establishments required.

The high street formed a gradual arc away from the bend of the river. On the outside of that arc, shops ranged between the posting inn and a venerable stone kirk. The inside of the arc was taken up with a village green that extended down to the water.

The buildings were whitewashed and half timbered, most of the roofs thatched, though the inn and the church boasted slate shingles. In the little touches—pots of forget-me-nots and heartsease, sparkling mullioned windows, pristine wash flapping in the morning breeze— the village had an air of quiet prosperity.

And yet, this could never have been an English village. The accents of the folk we passed on the way to the inn were indecipherably Scottish. The high hills across the river equally so, and the blue of the sky more intense than any I saw in the south. The azure hue continued from the apex of the celestial vault right down to the horizon without paling or fading toward white.

I loved this village at sight, but perhaps I was predisposed to love everything I encountered at sight, given how delightfully I'd spent much of my night.

"Charming," St. Sevier said as we turned our horses into the inn's stable yard. "Absolutely Scottish. An English village can be sleepy, but it's never so with a Scottish village. Something about granite cottages and heather on the breeze."

"You like Scotland too," I said, somewhat surprised, for I sensed no particular fondness from St. Sevier for his adopted English homeland.

"I learned much here," he said, "and early adulthood is an impressionable time." He swung down and assisted me to dismount, stealing the barest hint of a liberty in aid of ensuring I had my balance. The hostlers who came to take our horses were instructed to loosen girths and offer hay and water.

When the gig rattled to a halt on the cobbles, St. Sevier assisted Eulalie and Fanny to climb from the bench. We next inquired of the innkeeper's wife about a tea tray and some comestibles. That lady directed us to a sunny table off to one side in the common, a somewhat novel experience for me.

This rural inn probably had a cellar beneath the common where the drovers, domestics, and farm labor could do serious justice to the summer ale. The common was exceptionally clean and tidy, and yet, I looked about for a ladies' parlor, a private dining room, even an inglenook that might afford some privacy.

What caught my eye was a shelf running around the whole room at the height of the tops of the windows. Empty bottles sat side by side, some brown, some blue, green, clear or amber, most bearing labels and a few in distinctive shapes.

"Is that the bar menu?" I asked, nodding to the display of bottles, most of which appeared to contain whisky.

"Something like that," Fanny murmured. "You're in Scotland. We pride ourselves on being ourselves." She slid into a seat at the table before St. Sevier had a chance to hold her chair. I did likewise, leaving Eulalie to do the pretty with St. Sevier.

St. Sevier took the place beside me. "I suspect Madame Innkeeper hails from Provence. She has the accent."

"She is French," Eulalie replied. "Lachlan said it caused quite the raised eyebrow when Hamish MacDuie married a foreigner rather than a local lass, but,"—Eulalie dropped her voice to imitate Lachlan —"at least she wasna English."

"Are the English really so hated here?" I asked.

Fanny and Eulalie exchanged a look. "The antipathy is worse," Fanny said, "out to the west and north, where Butcher Cumberland made a name for himself. Lallan Scots was never suppressed the way the Erse has been, and Lowlanders didn't miss the pipes and plaid the same way the Highlanders did. There's still bitterness, and it would have been worse still twenty years ago. Wherever England inflicts its definition of civilization on the unwilling, there's bitterness."

Exactly my brother Mitchell's point about the evils of colonial dominion rather than simply building trade alliances.

"We're having our revenge," Eulalie added. "Our lads are making good money in the shipyards and foundries now, and we trade all over the world. The Scottish regiments are known to be the fiercest fighters too. If this village prospers, it's because Scotland prospers."

"We prosper—at last," Fannie added. "I might as well have a word with Mrs. MacDuie about the letters." She rose, and St. Sevier was on his feet as well.

"I will accompany you, *non*? The better to admire this fine establishment and inquire of Madame regarding our homeland."

"That man," Eulalie said, accepting a lady's pint from a serving maid. "He flirts simply by opening his mouth, and then he's so mannerly. I think that's what has Donnie in a pet. A real gentleman shows up, and Donnie's smiles and small talk pale by comparison."

"Do you think Donnie could be Fanny's beau?"

Eulalie sipped her ale. "Donnie likes books. He needs to marry money if he's to marry at all. He certainly has time to write all the letters in the world, but why bother? Why not simply approach Fanny with an offer of marriage? They are fond of each other, not related by blood, and he knows Leland House well enough to help her with it when Lachlan grows too old to take a hand in matters."

Which would not be for quite some time.

"Maybe Lachlan forbade him to court her? Threatened to issue a writ of ejectment if Donnie tried to press his suit?"

Eulalie shook her head. "Lachlan isn't like that. His branch of the family hasn't two feathers to fly with, and he's forever inviting this or that poor relation to bide at Leland House for a season or two. He's dowered more than one cousin to preserve her from the dread fate of spinsterhood. He claims he's providing company for Fanny when our relations bide with us, and he is—what am I, but an unpaid lady's companion?—but he's also looking after his own, as Scots have always done. He'd not begrudge Donnie a match with Fanny. Just the opposite."

Eulalie spoke without bitterness, though I hadn't seen her perform at all in the capacity of a lady's companion, paid or otherwise.

"Iain earns his keep looking after the property," I said. "You provide female companionship for Fanny. What function does Donnie serve?"

"He's decorative," Eulalie said, grinning. "The local lasses love to stand up with him, and I find him ever so much better at bickering than old Iain. If we didn't make Iain come in for meals, he'd sleep in a shieling nine months of the year."

"A hut," Fanny translated as she returned to the table, "such as shepherds use in warmer weather. Mrs. MacDuie staunchly defended the privacy of postal patrons throughout Scotland. She claims to handle hundreds of letters each week and has no idea where mine might come from."

Fanny slid back into her seat, leaving me to suspect St. Sevier had stepped around to the jakes. "That is a lot of postage for a small village," I said.

"Not so small," Eulalie said. "The nearest major crossroads will take you to Stirling or Perth in one direction and north to Inverness or east to Aberdeen in the other. The river flows indirectly into Loch Tay, which connects by water with Crianlarich, and from there you're a hop and a half from the Highlands and the Western Isles."

"In Scotland," Fanny added, "you are never more than forty miles from the sea. We aren't as tied to one place as you English tend to be. We haven't been allowed that luxury, particularly since the Clearances gained momentum in the last century. We bloom where the winds of fortune plant us."

A serving maid brought a surprisingly hearty tea tray, stacked with sandwiches, shortbread, and little fruit tarts. I'd done justice to my breakfast, but the fresh air and horseback riding had sharpened my appetite.

"Where has St. *Charmant* got off to?" Eulalie mused.

Fanny checked the strength of the tea. "Your bad manners chased him off, Eulie. I swear you are becoming eccentric at an early age."

"I am," Eulalie said, helping herself to a sandwich. "It's time we went a-reaving in 'dear auld Glasgow toon,' Fan. If we both start on Lachlan now, he might give us some pin money by the time snow flies."

I put a sandwich of beef and what looked like slightly melted brie on my plate. "Why does Lachlan need to be importuned for pin money?" I could not imagine asking an English friend such a question.

"Mama made him guardian of my funds until I turned five-and-twenty," Fanny said, selecting a cheddar and ham sandwich for herself. "That was more than a year ago, and the moment has never been right to remind him to pass the reins to me. He has been managing Leland House for years, as both steward and then husband to Mama. I'd feel as if I were disrespecting Mama's memory if I took on the ledgers."

I nibbled my sandwich as St. Sevier rejoined us. A woman unwilling to ask her step-father to yield her the coin she was due might expect a husband to see to that detail for her. In the absence of a husband, why provoke the confrontation? Family members often indulged one another in such compromises. Witness, I had married where my father had told me to and had never given a serious thought to gainsaying him—more's the pity.

St. Sevier was his usual good-natured self, even as he demolished every crumb of the tea tray. Mrs. MacDuie herself brought us over a fresh pot, and the smile she and St. Sevier exchanged included an element of bonhomie at variance with Fanny's report.

We concluded our meal, and St. Sevier assisted the ladies back into the gig. As he and I waited for our horses to be brought around, I took his arm and directed him to the shade of an oak still in the pinkish phase of leafing out.

"So what did you learn?" I asked.

"I learned that it is always good to hear one's mother tongue when far from home." He walked with me a little farther from the stables. "The letters come up on the Perth stage. Madame noticed them for their lack of a return address, which means the postage is paid by the sender rather than the receiver."

"That makes these letters a bit unusual, and the posting inn in Perth might recall them for that reason."

"*If* they come from Perth. Stirling is like the center of a wheel and only a few stops from Perth. By way of Dunfermline and the ferry across the Firth of Forth, Edinburgh isn't much farther. The letters might not originate from Perth at all."

The hostler led my mare over to the ladies' mounting block. St. Sevier checked her girths, and I climbed aboard. He arranged my skirts while I took up the reins, a gentlemanly courtesy nobody had performed for me in ages.

The notion struck me then that Freddie hadn't been a particularly terrible husband. He'd had his strengths—a quick sense of humor, keen political insight that he regularly shared with me, a kind of loyalty that did not include fidelity, and an insistence that my settlements be generous.

St. Sevier was simply a wonderful fellow. *Most* husbands would pale in comparison to him, as would most bachelors. He swung into the saddle with an athlete's grace, and then we were ambling out of the innyard.

"What else did you learn here?" I asked, for some instinct insisted that he hadn't told me all.

"I stepped around back," St. Sevier said, "and who should I see disappearing into the stable but our own dear Donnie. Madame MacDuie noted that Iain occasionally takes the mail up to Leland House if he's out and about in this direction. Donnie seems to make trips intended exclusively to fetch the mail."

"Oh dear."

"Precisely," St. Sevier said. "Is Donnie intercepting letters, opening them, and replacing them with his own prose? Is he attempting to locate the missing groom himself? Does he have an innocent reason for frequenting an inn several miles from the village on his own estate?"

"We need to make a trip into Perth," I said as the horses *clip-clopped* down the high street.

"I will make that trip," St. Sevier replied. "You, I think, would spend that time better by inveigling confidences from Donnie."

"I can do both—travel into Perth with you and talk to Donnie."

St. Sevier sent me a look that was equal parts exasperation and affection. He'd be sending me that look frequently, I hoped, and I would doubtless have many occasions to offer the same glance in return.

The gig had stopped on the road ahead of us when we were more than half the distance back to Leland House. A crew of men in laborer's garb, some undressed down to their shirt-sleeves, were clearing a ditch. This was a thankless task that involved scything the weeds down to knee height, wielding a mattock, then pulling the weeds up by the roots.

The alternative was to allow nature to wreak havoc with drainage and court either flooding or parched crops. My father was of the opinion that stagnant water bred foul miasmas as well, and it did seem to be the case that many illnesses spread more quickly in the warmer months, when muddy ditches and stagnant ponds abounded.

"The big fellow on the end is Iain," I said as St. Sevier slowed our horses.

Iain wore only a plain black kilt and heavy work boots with gartered knee-high wool stockings. He shrugged into a billowy white shirt as we approached, but not before I saw a torso, chest, and back sculpted in lean muscles.

"Remind me to parade about naked for your nightly delectation," St. Sevier muttered.

"Believe me, I will."

Iain approached the gig, and for the first time in my memory, he smiled. He made a halfhearted job of tucking his shirt into the waistband of his kilt, while Fanny or Eulalie engaged him in some sort of small talk. He petted the horse's broad flank with a large, dusty hand as I brought my mare nearer the gig.

"Lady Violet," he said, offering me a bow. "St. Sevier. Bonnie day for a trot, aye?"

The smile faded, though the dour Scot did not entirely supplant the charming laddie. Iain's eyes remained friendly, his manner relaxed. He was, I surmised, a man whose happiness required him to be regularly out of doors and exerting himself physically. My brother Felix had some of the same qualities, though his passion was horses.

"Lovely day," St. Sevier said, "but now we've caught up with the gig and its dust. I'll water the horses if nobody objects."

I dismounted with Iain's assistance as the ladies in the gig bid Iain and his crew good day.

"Shall you have a wee sittee-doon?" Iain asked, exaggerating his accent. "The day is too fine to hasten back to Leland House." He gestured to the stone wall next to the road, which I was apparently to use as a bench, as in *sit ye down*.

The culvert passed beneath the road, though the water was little more than a fast-moving rivulet. "That seems like a lot of ditch for not much stream," I said.

"'Tis now, but a month ago, when the snow was still melting in the mountains, that ditch was barely enough. With the hillsides so steep, water develops significant velocity. We get the occasional watershoot with summer storms, too, and the force of the flooding can carry off livestock."

That was more words strung together than I had heard Iain offer, ever.

"I saw serious flooding last year," I said. "The dam irrigating a water meadow burst after a spate of heavy rain. I did not know sheep could swim, but apparently, they can."

"The lanolin in the wool buoys the ewes up, but not so the little ones."

In the distance, St. Sevier led the horses to the river. They had been offered water at the posting inn, but the mare was still interested in sipping and splashing.

"Eulalie claims you would spend your summer in a shepherd's hut if your family allowed it," I said.

"Oh, aye. Sheep don't care which fork I use or despair of my dancing." He ran a hand through unruly dark locks, the gesture conveying a hint of self-consciousness. As would happen when a man worked out of doors, stray bits of grass or tree buds tangled with his hair.

And yet, Iain didn't bear the rank tang of old sweat. If anything, his scent was lightly laced with heather. His nails were clean, as was his shirt.

"Your family loves you, Iain. They simply want to see you happy."

"I am happy," he said. "Out here. Who wouldn't be?"

"Is Donnie happy?"

He grinned. "Poking your wee English nose into family business, Lady Violet?"

"At Fanny's request, yes. Her beau has disappeared, exactly as you said, and she's keen to know what's become of him."

Iain produced a flask from his sporran. "Fancy a nip?"

Fanny and Eulalie would not have declined. "Please."

I'd passed some sort of test, because Iain's braw-bonnie-laddie smile flashed again. "Go easy, milady. The water of life isn't for the faint of heart."

Thanks to Sebastian and my brothers, I had a passing acquaintance with Scottish whisky, though certainly not a fondness for it. I sipped carefully and was pleasantly surprised.

"That is quite smooth."

"We age it at least five years. New whisky will tear your guts out, but put it in a good oak barrel for a few years, and it mellows considerably."

I passed him back his flask, and he took a stout pull. "About Donnie?" I asked.

He capped his flask and put it away. "Our Donald is an otter. Neither fish, nor flesh. A man knows not where to put him."

Something about those words resonated with my distant schoolroom penances. "Are you quoting Shakespeare?"

"Misquoting him. Donnie cannot resign himself to finding a trade, he hasn't the cachet to marry money, and he won't get his hands dirty as I do. He's destined to be a bachelor uncle, and that is a hard fate."

"You mean that."

"I'd not wish idle uselessness on any proper Scotsman or Scotswoman, much less my own siblings."

St. Sevier was letting the horses crop the lush grass on the riverbanks. I had time to probe further, so I took it.

"Would Donnie court Fanny by correspondence?"

Iain considered the crew tearing the weeds from the culvert. "Anything's possible, but I doubt it. Donnie lacks guile, and he's neither subtle nor patient. He can keep his mouth shut when needs must, but I hope my brother would not deceive a lady that way."

"How has Fanny's beau deceived her?"

"He offered marriage and hasn't kept his word. A man like that deserves nothing but contempt." And Iain's contempt would be a dish served very cold.

"And what if he can't marry her? What if harm has befallen him, or matters simply developed beyond what he intended, and now the whole business is out of his control?" I thought of myself, stuck in a marriage to a man I hadn't chosen. No way out, no way to start over.

"Fanny deserves a man who will love her and cherish her," Iain said. "If her beau can't rise to that challenge, for whatever reason, her feelings will be hurt, and that makes him the lowest of curs. If I knew who the blighter was, I'd beat him silly for abusing her trust."

"You're protective of her." I respected him for that.

"She's worth protecting. Talk to Donnie. When he's fibbing, he tends to laugh. Eulalie has the same habit, which made being their older brother a much easier billet growing up."

St. Sevier took charge of the horses and began leading them back to the road. My conversation with Iain hadn't been particularly productive, but I liked him better for seeing him in his element, rather than in Leland House's fancy dining room.

"Will you take Fanny back to England with you if she can't locate her missing groom?" Iain asked, rising.

He extended a hand to me, a bit of mannerliness that belied his comment about living in a shepherd's hut.

"I will invite her south next spring, when London is all awhirl," I said, getting to my feet, "but I suspect that won't be necessary."

"You are confident you'll find this John fellow?"

"I haven't given up hope yet. Bend down."

He sent me a puzzled look, but obliged so I could fluff the chaff and bits of grass from his hair.

"There," I said. "You look less like you were dragged through a hedge backward."

He scrubbed his hands through his hair, as if he suspected I'd put him in worse disarray than he'd already been in.

"You are stubborn and presuming," he said. "No wonder you get on with our Fanny. I'll bid you good day and ask you to make my excuses at luncheon. No man can tether time or tide, and I've yet to find the secret to thwarting Scottish weeds either."

"Quoting more Shakespeare?"

"You blaspheme, my lady. That's our own Rabbie Burns." He offered St. Sevier a wave, took up a long-handled scythe, and resumed his labors. Somebody started a song, one that matched the rhythm of the blades' swings, and the moment etched itself on my mind.

The melody was a lovely, slow ballad, the men were in excellent voice, and the day was exquisite. My lover approached with a smile for me, and I had all I could do not to throw myself into his arms for sheer joy in being alive.

I would not forget my time in Scotland. Indeed, I wasn't sure I'd ever want to leave.

"Donnie, would you favor me with a walk in the garden before we change for supper?" I asked. I'd come upon him after I'd risen from a lovely little nap full of dreams of St. Sevier. In contrast to Hugh, Donnie seemed callow and boyish, though he was nearly as tall as St. Sevier and well-favored in the looks department.

"I would be honored," Donnie said. "Will you need a parasol or bonnet?"

I really ought to have fetched both. A lady's complexion was a certain indicator of her genteel status. I needed to impress nobody with my status, however, and the late afternoon sun would hardly give me freckles in the course of a fifteen-minute stroll.

"I will brave the elements as I am." I waited until we had crossed the terrace and were descending the steps arm in arm before I started my interrogation. "What took you to Glenbennach this morning?"

"Decent ale," he said, though I detected a hitch in his stride. "MacDuie said a party from Leland House had stopped for tea."

That wasn't quite accurate. The party from Leland House had been in the common, enjoying what amounted to a meal, at the same time Donnie had *also* been on the premises, and yet, he had chosen not to join us. He had likely seen Eulalie and Fanny's gig, drawn by a familiar beast from the Leland House stables, and had ignored its significance.

I was reluctant to press him on those matters. The garden had a magical quality at this time of day. The air was perfectly still, and the spring flowers were approaching their glory. I would not have been surprised had a unicorn trotted out from beneath the birches.

"We did not stop for tea," I said, "so much as we took tea to allow Fanny a chance to ask Mrs. MacDuie some questions."

"What's Fan on about now?" Donnie asked, bending to snap off a small, intensely blue iris. I anticipated that he'd pass me the blossom, but I guessed wrong. He stuck the stem through the buttonhole on his lapel, the blue flower complementing his eyes nicely.

"Fanny's acquaintance with her fiancé has been mostly by letter," I said. "Because John has gone missing, she's hoping to find out what became of him by tracing the route of the letters he's sent."

"If he'll treat her so poorly as to propose marriage and disappear, she's better off without him."

We rounded the corner and came upon the walk that paralleled the fruit wall. The head gardener, Evan, was again at work, training branches to follow the wood lattice. He smiled at us and tugged his cap.

"Away with you, Evan," Donnie said. "You've put in a long enough day."

"Thank you kindly, Donald." He gathered up his tools and twine and strode off, something about his walk familiar—or maybe every man swaggered a little when wearing a kilt.

"He called you Donald," I noted. "Is he a relative of some sort?"

"He's a Scotsman. You will have noticed that many of us have the

same last name. Campbell, Stewart, Ferguson, MacDonald, MacKen-
zie, Graham, Kennedy... We tend to use first names more than the
English do in informal address to save ourselves confusion. Lachlan
will be Mr. Leland to Evan only if company is on hand, and here at
Leland House, I am 'our Donnie,' not to be confused with Donnie
MacDuie, Donnie MacInnes, or Donnie Munro."

"There were six Elizabeths at the school I attended with Fanny,"
I said. "We used formal address to keep them organized, but two of
them were Elizabeth Browns. Shall we sit?"

We took the bench under which I'd found the bouquet two
evenings past. Donnie came down eighteen inches to my left, and I
let the silence stretch. Leland House served its own fine summer ale.
A trip to Glenbennach simply to enjoy a pint made no sense at all.

"I'm not clever," Donnie said, "unlike Iain and Eulalie. Eulie
studies languages to pass the time. I can barely recall a word of Latin.
And Iain..."

"We met him coming back from the village. He was clearing a
ditch and appeared happy in his work."

A pair of little brown birds fluttered to the edge of the fountain
some yards away. They made a game out of flying through the spray,
probably playing an avian version of tag.

"Iain could tell you what birds those are—some sort of warbler, I
think—and where they winter. He loves the land, but if we'd had the
money, he would have gone to study art, truly study it, not simply lark
around at museums by day and disport with the *belles de nuit*
otherwise."

One of the little birds flew to the top of the garden wall and
began to sing. It did, indeed, sound like some sort of warbler.

"What were you really doing at the posting inn, Donnie?"

"Sending out letters of inquiry."

I wanted to believe him. "To whom?"

"The hiring agencies in Edinburgh and Glasgow. I can write a
fine hand, my ciphering is reliable, I know a bit of parlor French, and
my manners are adequate. I could be a secretary for some gouty old

baron who forgets where he puts his spectacles. Or a gouty baroness. And if I had to walk her farty little lapdog or listen to the same stories four times a day, that would be fine, because at least I'd be earning a wage."

This recitation had an air of noble martyrdom out of proportion to the topic, or perhaps more subtle Scottish humor was on display. Somewhat crude Scottish humor, though I well knew the type of canine Donnie alluded to.

"You might consider applying to Dunkeld. He employs two secretaries, and I get the impression he is still quite awash in business correspondence."

"I'd be ashamed," Donnie said, "to ask a neighbor for work when I haven't any experience. I'm not a youth right out of the schoolroom, to be getting my start by calling in a family favor."

"If you worked for Dunkeld, you would earn your coin, Donnie. Of that I am certain. Where do you think we should look for Fanny's missing beau?"

"I don't think you should look for him a'tall. He's a blighter and a bounder and deserves a good thrashing at least."

On that point, Iain and Donnie were in agreement. "She's worried about him. She fears he's come to harm."

Donnie scooped up a handful of pebbles and tossed them one by one in the direction of the fountain. They landed in a nearly straight line, like the bouncing of a rock skipped across still water.

"Fan and her beau used to meet in the stables," Donnie said. "I came upon them once, but they were so wrapped up in each other—I am being delicate—that they did not notice me."

"You're sure they didn't see you?"

"They were..." He scooped up another handful of pebbles. "*Engrossed* with each other." Again, the pebbles landed in a straight line. Donnie was an angler, so perhaps the exercise meant nothing.

"Did you notice anything else about him?"

"I noticed thereafter that Fanny occasionally retired early. She'd be reading along in the library while Eulalie beat me at chess, and then Fanny would just declare herself tired—despite the early hour—and march off. She went to meet that bastard, I know it."

The birds took off, disappearing in the direction of the forest.

"Have you any idea who he is?"

"He's well-to-do, I can tell you that. I caught the glint of moonlight on his watch chain. Gardeners and shepherds don't have gold watch chains. Fanny says her John is well-read, and books are too dear for the average farm boy to read more than a few in his whole life. This fellow has means enough that he ought to have made good on his promise to Fanny."

A watch and chain could be inherited from a deceased grandfather, and libraries were common even in rural Scotland. Rural Scotland had produced no less literary genius than Robert Burns, who'd come from humble stock indeed.

As Donnie and I meandered back to the house, I was struck by other revelations from our conversation. Donnie, by his own admission, wrote a fine hand. John wrote a fine hand. Donnie was seeking a means of leaving the shire. John would likely want Fanny to think he had left the shire. Donnie had no means with which to support a wife. John might very well be abandoning Fanny at the altar out of financial embarrassment—despite his gold watch chain.

And there was that habit of tossing pebbles in a line when pondering a thorny subject...

"Donnie, would your schedule leave you free to accompany St. Sevier into Perth in the next day or two?"

"Of course, but Iain and Lachlan both go into town regularly on estate business. Eulalie goes to buy out the shops about once a quarter if she can't talk Fanny into a trip to Glasgow or Edinburgh. Any of them would be happy to take your friend along the next time they go."

Well, that certainly complicated matters. "Will anybody go this week?"

"Iain or Lachlan," he said, pausing at the top of the terrace steps.

"They didn't go last week, so one of them will go this week. I'd ask Iain before approaching Lachlan."

"Why?"

He blushed, even his ears turning pink. "I suspect Lachlan has a special friend in Perth. He's discreet about it, doubtless out of deference to the late Mrs. Leland's memory, but I can't think of any other reason that he'd always go into town without Iain when they both have business there."

"Thank you," I said, my mind whirling. I could think of another reason why Lachlan would want to conduct his business in Perth discreetly, as well as a reason why he'd cry off if he were Fanny's beau.

But in considering Lachlan as the culprit—or missing groom—I was once again faced with the same question that every other suspect had left me with: *Why?*

Why embark on a relationship that could go nowhere?

Why resort to the elaborate subterfuge of clandestine meetings?

Why take such unforgivable advantage of Fanny and then jilt her if she was in fact held dear by her suitor?

The situation was growing more muddled by the day, and I could not wait to discuss my thoughts with St. Sevier—in private.

CHAPTER NINE

At dinner, it was determined that Iain would accompany St. Sevier into Perth in the morning. Everybody at the table save Lachlan knew the nature of his errand, and I set about remedying Lachlan's ignorance after dinner.

I did so by the simple expedient of asking him for a hand of cribbage when the gentlemen had joined the ladies for the day's final cup of tea. The gentlemen, it should be noted, eschewed the pleasures of China black for a wee dram of the aged whisky Iain had treated me to earlier. I was tempted—Eulalie had both tea and whisky—but wanted to keep my wits about me.

"Ladies first," Lachlan said, passing me the deck of cards.

He was offering me the first deal, which in cribbage was an advantage, but I was disinclined to accept his gallantry. I shuffled the deck and cut a knave.

Lachlan turned over a seven and thus won the first crib.

"I played endless hands of cards with Fanny's mother," he said. "She was a lonely widow, trying to observe mourning after spending years watching her spouse fade. Cards with me were a way to pass the time with another adult that did not involve scandalizing the neighborhood with social outings. Then we played more cards when she herself grew ill."

"Do the Scots take mourning as seriously as the English do?" English women. English husbands, when widowed, were expected to remarry posthaste, and those with small children sometimes did so within weeks of the funeral.

"Scottish grieving is different," he said, expertly shuffling the deck. "We are always in mourning as a people. For our independent past, for our sons fallen in service to this or that king, for the vast numbers driven from our shores by unkind fate and crueler landlords. Another death isn't exactly expected, but neither does it surprise us. We grieve, and we get on with the living."

My hand was useless. Six cards that added up to exactly no points at all. "Do you consider remarrying?"

He arranged his cards, suggesting his hand did have some value. "Do you?"

Across the parlor, St. Sevier was reading French poetry to Fanny and Eulalie. Fanny was purely delighted, while Eulalie's expression was one of pained longing. When he turned the page, St. Sevier looked up, caught my eye, smiled, and resumed reading.

"I do not consider remarrying," I said, choosing to discard a king and a seven. "Not yet."

"Like that, is it?" Lachlan tossed two cards into the crib, the third hand of four cards that would go to whoever dealt that round. "Still looking over the possibilities?"

"I am the daughter of an earl, well-fixed, and not hideous. In London, if I so much as ride out with eligible gentlemen, I will have offers enough." I hadn't taken that step. Hadn't declared to polite society in general that I was once again looking for a spouse.

Hadn't wanted to and doubted I ever would.

"A word of advice from a man who has been bereaved for considerably longer than you, my lady: Don't put off indefinitely the business of rejoining the human race. One loses the knack of accommodating another's foibles, loses the heart to compromise and

see the best in a partner. Without the impetus of youthful enthusiasm, the solitary road can seem the more appealing in the short term."

Lachlan had the merest dusting of gray at his temples, and that
he would speak thus—like a septuagenarian uncle who'd tarried too
long at the wars—made me uneasy. A man was never too old to take
a wife. A woman's age began diminishing her prospects the
moment she left the schoolroom. And Lachlan's implication, that
only the married were members of the human race, struck me
as sad.

"I thought your marriage was a love match," I said, beginning the
pegging.

"It very much was, and do you know what daunts me more than
the prospect of never finding another lady to love as I loved my wife?"

"I could not begin to guess."

"The prospect that I will. I watched Mary slip away, growing
weaker and weaker each season, until I had to carry her to the walled
garden if she wanted to feel the sun on her face. She never
complained, never grew bitter. All she asked of me was that I safeguard this place for Fanny, and I have tried to honor that request.
The thought that I might watch another beloved spouse fade from
this world, or force a woman I adore to stand that watch for me... I
don't have it in me."

This was not the conversation I'd wanted to have with Lachlan,
but I suspected it was a conversation I'd needed to have. My
mourning for Freddie had been complicated by guilt—the guilt of a
woman relieved to have her freedom far sooner than she'd anticipated. I had loved Freddie in my way and tried to be in love with him,
but he'd made that impossible.

The longer we'd been married, the less I'd liked him or even
respected him. Perhaps that was an inevitable wearing away of
romance, necessary if a union was to evolve to a deeper relationship. I
would never know.

What I did know was that I was grateful to have been spared the
chasm of loss Lachlan described, though I also realized that part of

what had died with Mary's passing had been Lachlan's courage to dream.

"What of loneliness?" I asked as we counted up cards, and he passed the deck over to me. "What of all the evenings that have no end, the leaden hours of quiet, the unmooring of all things spousal and sweet?" At least when Freddie had been alive, I could still dream of someday becoming a mother.

"I have family around me," Lachlan said. "I have purpose. I have much to be grateful for, but little to offer a wife. I am content."

Did he also have a mistress adding to his contentment? If he did, I could not begrudge him that solace.

"What do you make of Fanny's situation?" I asked, dealing the next hand. I was already trailing by ten points, which did not bode well for my prospects.

"I hope she has had a narrow escape. A man who will jilt the lady who has forsaken all others to earn his favor is no man at all. I wish Fanny hadn't gone so far as to concoct this engagement, but she doubtless hoped to flush him from whatever hedge he's hiding in."

I was too busy choosing my discards to at first catch the nuance in Lachlan's words. "*Concoct* this engagement?"

Lachlan leaned nearer. "The fellow likely broke off the whole business last year—if there ever was a fellow—and Fanny has been sending herself these letters to keep up the pretense of a correspondence. I don't blame her. Our corner of the world has little enough society for a woman with her means, and she was brought up to expect company of better standing than clodhopping gentry. If you'd invite her for a stay in England, I'd take it as a kindness."

Fanny had a lively imagination. Sending herself letters to fabricate a relationship was something she might have done as a schoolgirl. But why keep that relationship secret for years? Why claim it had escalated to an engagement? Why dose herself with rue?

Besides, Donnie had seen the couple in a passionate moment—or claimed to.

"John is real," I said, "or he was real. His handwriting is quite different from Fanny's, and I saw the letter in which he proposed to her. She has not made him up out of whole cloth, Lachlan. Of that, I am certain."

I was also certain to lose the game. By the time Lachlan had amassed ninety points out of the required one hundred and twenty, I was lagging nearly thirty points behind him.

"This John might be a real fellow," Lachlan said, dealing another hand, "but he is no gentleman. To lead a woman on and then dash her hopes is most cruel, and she's better off without him."

"And if he's fallen seriously ill?" I countered. "If he's been unfairly besmirched by scandal and hounded from his home shores? If he's been carted off to gaol on the basis of false accusations? Would you have left your dear wife to fend for herself in such circumstances?"

I could not imagine leaving St. Sevier to deal with serious ill fortune on his own, nor would he abandon me to my woes.

"Fanny isn't anybody's wife," Lachlan said with a touch of asperity, "and as long as she continues to pine for this bounder, she never will be. I rue the day I suggested she amuse herself reading the advertisements, but it's apparently time she resumes the habit. If literary effusions are what make her happy, she can easily find another correspondent."

To my astonishment, my hand turned out to be a twenty-four-point double-double run, with a triple run of fifteen points in my crib. I took a small lead over Lachlan and ended up winning the game. I had not, however, completed the discussion I was determined to have with my host.

"Fanny has asked me to take a hand in locating her errant swain," I said. "What we have learned so far is that the letters come from Perth. That is what occasions St. Sevier's need to accompany Iain into town in the morning."

Lachlan regarded Fanny, who was laughing at St. Sevier's poetry. She was still pale and skinny, but she had taken a little of each course at dinner and seemed to be regaining her spirits. Lachlan's gaze held fondness and something harder to define.

Not longing, precisely, but some element of frustration.

"I will wish your friend the best of luck in Perth," Lachlan said, "but I fear you are being drawn into a drama largely of Fanny's making. A repairing lease in England might be just the thing to take her mind off her troubles."

"I will be happy to entertain her anytime she'd like to revisit England." If we found John, and by some miracle, he was still of a mind to marry Fanny, she would want no part of London.

As it happened, in the morning we did not find John, but the post did bring another letter from him.

My second night in St. Sevier's arms was as remarkable as the first. His mood was sweet and contemplative, and my satisfaction was all the more intense for having been reached on a slowly rising tide of desire.

As he had the previous night, St. Sevier withdrew before finding his own release. While I appreciated the consideration—very much— I still found the moment disconcerting.

He, by contrast, did not. He dealt with the untidy practicalities with brisk good cheer, then took me in his arms and coaxed confidences from me.

In two nights, I had become closer to St. Sevier than I had ever been to my husband. Hugh and I talked about everything, including first kisses—mine from a groom at school, St. Sevier's from the milkmaid who'd come around his aunt and uncle's house every other morning. We discussed wedding nights—mine in the home where I'd eventually serve out my mourning, his in an army tent on the Spanish plain. He recalled a disobliging tree root. I recalled Freddie making me laugh as he'd listed a dozen different naughty terms for his breeding organs.

I did not yet have the confidence to question St. Sevier further about his marriage, but someday—when I was not as easily distracted by tender kisses and clever caresses—I would. I wanted to know the details, and more to the point, I suspected St. Sevier had never shared the tale with anybody else. I had unburdened myself to Hugh in all manner of regards. I owed him the same kindness.

We were in superbly good spirits as we came down to breakfast, though I had already begun to think of how our situation would change upon our return to London. With a great deal of discretion and some luck, we could continue our liaison, but not with the ease with which we'd begun it.

No cuddling up for the duration of an entire night. No lingering over a shared pot of tea on a sunny balcony as the morning sun rose over the beautiful landscape. No going down to breakfast arm in arm, with not even a chambermaid to raise an eyebrow at our familiarity.

St. Sevier filled my plate at the buffet, and for once, Iain was at the table. His attire was that of a proper gentleman rather than a farmer, and he ate with mannerly enthusiasm. Donnie was nowhere in evidence, though Eulalie sat opposite her brother.

"Fan's having a late morning," she said. "Yesterday's excursion tired her."

"Get her off the property again," Iain said. "Put the roses back in her cheeks. Go calling and drag Lachlan and Donnie with you."

"I would like to see Lord Dunkeld's family seat," I said.

St. Sevier took the place beside me. "As would I."

"We're invited to lunch there tomorrow," Eulalie said. "Aunt Bernie and Aunt Maighread have given you time to recover from your travels, and once they have a go at you, the invitations will pour in. Lachlan will mutter and grumble, for he doesn't like the expense of hosting multiple company dinners, but Dunkeld's the ranking title in the neighborhood, so we could hardly ignore him."

"He is also a friend," St. Sevier said, "to Lady Violet and myself. Your willingness to entertain him and his family was much appreciated. I tremble with dread, though, at the thought of more of Uncle Archibald's fish stories."

Iain passed me the butter. "Carry two flasks, fill them both with water. Refill them from the pitcher in the library as you need to. Lachlan gave me and Donnie the same instructions before our first supper there. We survived, though only just. The old marquess was still about. That one could drink Archie under the table and still outdance anybody over crossed swords."

Eulalie launched into an explanation of the sword dances, dirk dances, and an old-fashioned, peculiar sort of two-man dance based on fighting moves. While she spoke, the butler brought in the morning mail on a silver tray, setting it near Iain's elbow.

Eulalie continued tossing out a dizzying list of strange words for dances, instruments, dance moves, and musical forms, and Iain sorted through the mail.

"Somebody had best fetch Fanny," he said, scowling. "I do believe the ruddy blighter has written her again."

"I'm here," Fanny said from the doorway. "And John is not a ruddy blighter. He'll be family, so please don't disparage him."

An odd progression of emotions chased across Iain's features. Consternation, chagrin, resignation, and possibly humor.

"We have company," he said, passing her the letter, "so I will pretend that I don't argue with ladies."

Fanny sank into the chair beside me. "Don't everybody stare at me."

St. Sevier, on my other side, passed the teapot down to me. "You need not read your private correspondence with an audience, Miss MacPherson."

"Read it," Eulalie said. "We'll just winkle the details out of you one way or another if you try to sneak off with it now."

"Do as you please," I said. "Mail is private." And Eulalie was nosier than four older brothers combined.

Fanny passed me the letter. "You read it. Please."

I slit the purple wax seal. The contents were brief.

. . .

My dearest Miss MacPherson,

Please know that I will always hold you in the highest esteem and that our correspondence and friendship will ever be among my heart's most precious treasures. I regret that circumstances prevent me from pursuing our dealings to the conclusion to which we both aspired. I offer you my most abject and sincere apologies. I hope at some future date you can forgive me for this betrayal of our shared dreams and recall me as fondly as I will always recall you.

In loving friendship, I remain your obed serv,

John S. MacDonald

"He's crying off," I said. "He goes about it prettily, but the message is quite clear."

"Well, that's that." Eulalie tossed her table napkin down beside her plate. "Wretched of him, but at least you're free now."

"Let me see it," Fanny said, snatching the letter from me. She scanned the words, but no matter how many times she read them, the meaning would remain as plain and disappointing as ever. "What circumstances?" she muttered. "What dratted circumstances? I'm relieved beyond words that he's not dead, but I will never be free as long as I have no idea why he has turned away from me. My John would not do this without utterly compelling reasons."

Lachlan joined us in the breakfast parlor, his hospitable charm nowhere in evidence. "I take it Fanny's bounder has made the jilting official."

"Uncle, haud yer wheesht." Iain spoke softly, which was fortunate, because I was prepared to admonish mine host regarding the consideration due a woman dealing with a severe shock.

"I'll not be silent," Lachlan retorted. "The whole business has been dodgy from the start, and Fanny deserves a man who'll court her properly or not at all. Pass the teapot. Please."

St. Sevier obliged. "Miss MacPherson, would you favor me with a turn on the terrace?"

Oh, well done. Get her away from meddling family, let her have a moment to gather her wits.

"Of course," she said, rising and passing me the letter. "Iain, Lachlan, good day to you." She spoke woodenly, and when St. Sevier offered her his arm, she appeared to need the support.

"I hope we never learn who he is," Eulalie said. "He's treated Fanny abominably. Uncle, you must see that a little trip to Glasgow or Edinburgh is in order to lift Fanny's spirits."

"Not now," Lachlan muttered. "You cannot solve every fit of boredom or blue devils by spending other people's money, Eulalie. You replaced your entire wardrobe only last spring. No self-respecting Scotswoman is so unthrifty as to toss out new dresses."

This lecture might have been aimed by my father at his younger sons, but it was still more family business than I wanted to be privy to. Besides, fashions changed from year to year, and a lady wanted at least a few frocks that were bang up to the mark in terms of style.

"Lady Violet," Iain said, "I am bound for Perth this morning. Might I make any purchases for you?"

Eulalie rose. "You may buy me more corset strings, the good kind that don't break after a week's use. If we leave it to Lachlan, I'll be popping out of my dresses in front of the neighbors, and Uncle Archie will make another one of his rousing jokes of me."

"Excuse me," Iain said, following Eulalie from the room.

Lachlan ran a hand through his hair. "I'm sorry, Lady Violet. We seem to be at our histrionic finest this morning. You will decamp for England in defense of your wits."

His hand shook slightly as he poured himself a cup of tea. Did Lachlan console himself of a night with more than a wee dram or two?

"I have four brothers," I said. "By now, they would have been shouting. Table linen pitched at an offending sibling, raised voices, and a glass of water dashed in another fellow's face would not be unheard of. Invariably, they got up to their worst behavior when company was on hand. My father despaired of us."

"You are very kind," Lachlan said, "and Fanny is lucky to have you for a friend. Will you truly invite her to London?"

"I absolutely will, but I doubt she'll accept my invitation. Her memories of England are unhappy."

He winced, then took a sip of his tea. "Her mother thought sending her off to school for the best, and I did not interfere between mother and daughter. Perhaps Fanny can make new memories on a visit with you in the south."

For a man who begrudged Eulalie a short excursion to Glasgow, Lachlan seemed most eager to consign Fanny to London. I mentally set that puzzle aside as I excused myself and left Lachlan to finish his meal in solitude.

Other puzzles were filling my head.

Why had Donnie chosen this morning, of all mornings, to absent himself from the breakfast table?

Did the purple wax on today's letter have any significance, when the most recent letters had all been sealed with red wax?

The date revealed that John had resumed making uncrossed sevens after months of crossing them. Why?

And of course, why was John crying off now—*if* the letter had even come from him?

I waited until bedtime to question St. Sevier regarding his trip into Perth. I had spent the day reading the entire body of Fanny's correspondence, including the copies she'd kept of the letters she'd sent. Fanny was once again a withdrawn wraith, though she'd made an effort to partake of both luncheon and supper.

"We didn't learn much," St. Sevier said, unknotting his cravat.

I stepped closer and pushed his hand aside, the better to enjoy the role of valet. I took his watch, neckcloth, sleeve buttons, and signet ring—St. Sevier was technically some sort of *comte*—and then his coat. Hugh had that inherent sense of style that characterizes many a gentleman from the Continent.

His cravat and cuffs sported a bit more lace than the average Englishman's, and his coat was cut to nip in at the waist for a slightly more elegant line than English tailors usually favored. The embroidery on his waistcoat was exquisite without being gaudy.

"Your hooks," he said, turning me by the shoulders when I had him down to breeches and shirt. His fingers were deft, as were the lips he applied to my nape. "I missed you today. Perth is a bustling town. You would have found it interesting."

"What of the coaching inn?" I asked, ignoring a sweet shiver as he left off his plundering and unlaced my stays.

"The letters to Fanny are brought to the inn by one of several urchins, never the same one twice in a row. You are not to lace up so tightly in future. I say this as a physician and as a man who appreciates the female form."

"The letters arrive in relatively clean condition," I said, "which suggests the urchins don't hold on to them for very long. Were you able to talk to any of these children?"

"I was not. The innkeeper related that Perth has its share of downtrodden children, and allowing them to hang about is not good for business." He patted my bum. "Out of your dress, and I will take down your hair."

Men. Even dear, darling men. "Out of your shirt and breeches," I said, "and I will allow you to tend to my hair. What else did you learn?"

"The children provide the coin to prepay the postage, and Fanny's letters are surrendered to them in the same manner. The little ones pay, then they disappear with the letters. It's ingenious, or diabolical."

I could easily have stepped across the sitting room to tend to my ablutions in my own bedroom, but I took a silly little satisfaction from using St. Sevier's soap, toothpowder, brushes, and combs. I even appropriated one of his nightshirts, though it would hang down past my knees. Whether I took these steps to keep my effects separate from his, or to indulge in yet more intimacy, I did not know.

I wiggled free of my dress and stays, glorying in the moment when my body was free of confinement. I shook out the wrinkles in my chemise and considered that St. Sevier was right: I had no reason to lace up so tightly. None.

"I adore watching you wash," St. Sevier said, propping an elbow on the top of the privacy screen. "I like when you watch me using my soap and flannel too. Someday, we shall bathe each other. My estate in Berkshire has a hot spring. You must visit me there, and we will take the waters together by moonlight."

He spoke of the future and probably hoped I did not notice what he was about, except that I did. On the one hand, the thought of cavorting by moonlight like a pair of selkies was hard to put from my imagination. On the other, we were mere days into this phase of our *affaire de coeur*/courtship/dalliance.

I was torn between the urge to rush headlong into greater entanglement and a natural caution that suggested nothing so lovely could possibly last. St. Sevier wanted marriage, and I wasn't confident that our course would conclude at the altar.

"My day was equally unproductive," I said, "though I think we can conclude John does not live in Perth." I wrung out the flannel and draped it over the side of the porcelain basin. "Your turn."

St. Sevier tossed the wash water out the window onto a patch of scythed lawn, then refilled the basin with an ewer kept warm by the hearth. Standing before the fireplace, he pulled his shirt over his head, passed it to me, and stepped out of his breeches.

He doubtless did this for my delectation, and I appreciated the display. "Why are you so fit?"

He started washing his face and shoulders, his movements methodical and probably not intended as flirtatious. St. Sevier, perhaps because he was a physician, did not regard nudity as inherently prurient. He could be naked before a woman and unaroused, a feat I wasn't sure my late husband had ever accomplished.

"I come from sturdy French stock," he said. "I like to ride and fence. I am happy to tramp for miles through either city or country-side. When I am particularly restless, I work off my fidgets with some hard rowing." He paused, the washing cloth in his hand. "Would you like to assist me with my evening toilette, Violet?"

Now he posed polite questions. "I'm enjoying the view."

"You are preoccupied with those damned letters. Might you not consider preoccupying yourself with pleasures to be shared in my bed?"

"You are right that the letters are still on my mind," I said, slip-ping a few pins from my hair. "I read both the copies Fanny kept of her own epistles and John's replies. They often crossed in the mail, particularly in recent months."

He turned, resting one foot on the raised hearth. This afforded me a view of his long, lean back and muscular fundament, and an excellent view it was too.

"You are thinking," St. Sevier said, "that were John a resident of Perth, he'd pick up Fanny's letters the day they arrived and answer them immediately. Instead, he has his minions send a letter each day for four successive days, while Fanny's missives sit unread."

"Something like that. For the first year and a half, the tempo of the whole undertaking was fairly deliberate. Enough time elapsed between letters that each answered the last one sent. About six months ago, that changed."

St. Sevier turned again, having washed both feet, and wrung out the flannel once more. He was slightly aroused, and that his condition caused him neither to strut nor to blush fascinated me. Freddie had regarded his aroused state like some magic potion that would lose effi-cacy if it wasn't used immediately.

St. Sevier's magic potion was composed of self-confidence, genuine regard for me as his lover, patience, and a soupçon of humor.

"You missed a spot," I said as I found the last of my pins. My braid slipped free to swing along my spine as I approached St. Sevier. "An important spot."

He passed me the flannel. "S'il vous plaît, madame."

St. Sevier was a cleaner fellow indeed by the time I finished with him. I was equally well tended and dozing contentedly in his arms when our amatory exertions were complete.

"What?" he murmured, his hands sleepily caressing my back as I sprawled on his chest. "The millwheel that passes for milady's brain has begun spinning again."

"I just realized that at the same time the tempo of the correspondence picked up considerably, the sevens changed. They went from uncrossed to crossed. What do you suppose that means?" Had the color of the wax changed then too?

He shifted, tucking himself over me. "It means you were not sufficiently impressed with my intimate devotions, if you can already set them aside to ponder Fanny's ill-fated beau. I will remedy this sorry state of affairs, and then you will dream only of me."

St. Sevier absolutely did as promised, and my dreams were sweet indeed.

CHAPTER TEN

In Scotland, the term *castle* was applied to everything from grand edifices belonging to wealthy peers, to crumbling ruins overrun by grazing sheep. Similarly, *house*, as in Leland House, could mean a farmhouse with geese in the yard and a roof in need of rethatching, or a magnificent stately home.

I dearly hoped that Dunkeld House was more on the stately side of the continuum.

I need not have worried. We had—in what Fanny termed a fit of misplaced optimism—ridden horseback to Sebastian's home. The bridle paths were about half the distance of the roads, provided one was willing to hop a stile or two.

I was willing—barely. As a girl, I'd been confident on horseback. I was no longer a girl, but my mare was well trained and forgiving. St. Sevier had an excellent seat, as did Fanny and Eulalie. Iain had not joined us for this outing, but Lachlan and Donnie had, and they, too, rode well.

We emerged from the trees at the foot of a gentle slope, and Dunkeld House rose up before us as if sprung from a fairy tale. The façade was whitewashed stone, like Leland House, but unlike Leland House, the impression wasn't one of stolid prosperity.

Dunkeld House should have been called a castle. An asymmetric series of turrets soared over crenellated parapets, and high walls gave a sense of impregnable strength. The edifice's defensive air was belied by a drawbridge lowered over a lush, grassy moat and bright pots of rioting pansies lining the circular drive.

A blue pennant snapped in the breeze from atop the highest tower, and I half expected a herald in surtout and hose to blast word of our arrival on a four-foot-long brass horn. The fountain in the center of the drive sprayed water a good twenty feet in the air, soaking a statue of a buxom, unclad nymph entwined in the arms of a heroically proportioned god.

My father's estate in southern England encompassed thousands of acres, as well as a rambling pile with no less than thirty bedrooms. I knew what upkeep on a major property cost, and Sebastian's home was a very major property.

"Impressive, aye?" Fanny said, her mare falling in step beside mine as the horses walked along the sweeping curve of the driveway. "You can see Loch Tay from the west tower and a fine view of the Highland Line. Fifty inside servants at last count, nearly as many again outside. Dozens would be out of work if Dunkeld left us for his English holdings."

"Then his trip to London last year occasioned some unease?" I asked.

"We wouldn't have blamed him for taking an English bride. Many's the laird who has had to marry expediently." The implication hung in the air that nobody would have been very pleased had Sebastian's marchioness hailed from England either.

We directed our horses past the fountain, and the view from the drive immediately before the drawbridge was breathtaking. Another high tor—not the one Sebastian and I had ridden to—rose up behind the house, a rocky prominence dominating slopes of enormous firs.

Below the house, the valley stretched out in a patchwork of field and forest, the river winding through the whole in long, sinuous curves.

"Good defensive positioning," Fanny observed. "A lookout on the tor would see troops marching twenty miles off. Give him a spyglass, and he'd be able to count cannon and horse easily."

While I had been admiring the fountain and flowerpots, Fanny had been assessing military potential. Perhaps that, in a nutshell, was the difference between a Scotswoman and her English cousin.

We road across the drawbridge, under an enormous raised portcullis, and into a cobbled courtyard. Sebastian stood at the top of a set of steps, looking every inch the kilted laird.

"The reaving party has arrived," he said, assisting me down from my horse. I was the ranking lady in the group, so he would naturally greet me first. He bowed over my hand, then kissed my cheek, doing the same with Eulalie and Fanny.

This was a side of Sebastian I hadn't seen before—expansive, gracious, possibly even friendly. The house was as magnificent inside as its setting and appearance were outside, and Sebastian led us on a tour of the public rooms.

My overall impression was that Leland House, and probably every manor in the shire, was trying in its humble way to imitate the castle on the hill. The weapons hall made Leland House's display look like an upstart broom closet by comparison. The great hall was a genuine soaring relic from medieval days, with a fireplace at least twenty feet wide and six feet high.

"The laird's traditional chamber is up there," Sebastian said, pointing into the vast darkness above the fireplace. "Heated floors all winter long. Quite cozy, though a bit of a climb. Nice views too."

Everything in Dunkeld House was spotless, elegant, and comfortable. The Aubusson carpets were immaculate, the hearths—there were dozens—swept. Anything brass, from candlesticks to andiron ornaments to candle snuffers, drawer pulls, or fireplace fenders, gleamed as did the gilt on the pier glasses and picture frames.

Room by room, my impression of my girlhood friend underwent

revision. My father thought himself an important man. He was an earl, a wealthy landowner, he sat in the Lords. Sebastian held the loftier title, was clearly wealthier, and could have hosted a royal progress without hiring additional staff—and Papa had turned down Sebastian's request to court me.

Turned him down for a few acres of water meadow. *Papa, you fool.*

We enjoyed a meal as lavish as it was scrumptious, joined by the aunties. To the veiled relief of the menfolk, Uncle Archie was off fishing on such a fine day.

"We must walk the parapets," Aunt Bernie declared when the long meal was concluded. "Gets the blood going and clears the cobwebs."

"To the parapets," Aunt Maighread said, pushing her chair back. "Bernie will bring her spyglass, and nobody's secrets will be safe."

"I mostly watch birds up there," Bernie retorted, "though I did see young Master Henry MacMillan walking hand in hand with Miss Jeannie MacReady. I don't believe they've called the banns yet, but I've started embroidering them a table runner."

The walk around the parapets was a good distance, involving many stone steps and frequent pauses to admire the view or be regaled by bits of local history. Neil Gow—the fiddler—had often walked along that stretch of the river *there*. Robert Burns was said to have called on a distant relation who'd rented the farm between *those* trees. An old fortification thought to predate the Romans faced off the side of *that* hill.

Lachlan escorted Aunt Bernie, and Donnie had offered his arm to Aunt Maighread. St. Sevier was playing the gallant for Eulalie and Fanny, and that left me at Sebastian's side.

"Your home is lovely," I said. "I am grateful to my bones that I got to see it. You belong here."

"I'm not sure I do," Sebastian said as the group wandered farther ahead of us along the crenellations. "I wasn't raised here. My parents occupied one of the marquess's tenant farms, albeit a prosperous one, closer to Perth. Then I was sent to England for civilizing, and from there, I was off to war to engage in gratuitous barbarity. Getting my bearings here has taken some time."

We were on a wider part of the walkway, a sort of terrace outside what had been the laird's chamber. The view across the valley was spectacular, and Sebastian, lounging against the stonework, looked all of a piece with the brilliant blue sky and breathtaking landscape.

"You belong here, nonetheless. Would you ever consider offering for Fanny?"

"Don't matchmake, Violet. Besides, Fanny's heart is spoken for, and we've had this discussion."

"He cried off," I said, joining Sebastian at the parapet. "John, or whoever he is, sent her a polite apology, no explanation. She's devasted and still has no idea why."

"Perhaps he cried off because men are bastards?"

I smiled at him. "I know of at least two who defy that description, perhaps three if we count my brother Felix. Shall we join the others?" I had been hoping to meet Sebastian's daughter, but such an introduction would have been unusual and was apparently not to be proffered.

"John cried off, just like that?" Sebastian wrinkled his nose. "Badly done. If he was to cry off, why not do it before the lady has accepted his proposal? Many an epistolary romance goes nowhere."

"You need a wife, Sebastian. A household of this size doesn't run itself, and you have a responsibility to your title."

He stopped abruptly. "I don't give that,"—he snapped his fingers before my face—"for the title, Violet Marie. The title is why I was sent hundreds of miles from my family, why I wasn't with either of my parents when they died, why no female looks at me now as anything other than a 'good catch.' I've given up fishing. I can't stand the thought of treating a lowly creature as the Mayfair hostesses treated me, a trout to be hooked, landed, and filleted for the enjoyment of others."

I took his arm and resumed our progress. "I don't see you as a trout." But he was still angry. For much of his boyhood, he'd been angry to be banished to England, and then he'd been an angry—and ruthlessly competent—soldier.

He grinned, his ire vanishing. "*Mo chridhe*, you never have seen me as the others do, of all the ironies."

I wasn't sure what to say to that, but was spared a reply by Fanny, who'd apparently fallen behind the larger group. She stood gazing out across the countryside, a handkerchief clutched in her hand. She'd been crying, if pink cheeks and red-rimmed eyes were any indication.

"You're mourning lost love," Sebastian said, taking the place beside her and wrapping an arm around her shoulders. "I'm sorry, Fan. I'd thrash him for you if we could find him."

I stood on her other side, vaguely alarmed that she would give in to tears when the hard cobblestones were a good thirty feet below.

She rested her head on Sebastian's shoulder. "I am angry, and worried, and ready to burst, but I don't want to *do* anything."

"It's like that," Sebastian said. "Heartbreak. Bloody awful. Aunt Bernie would tell you to have a wee nip to dull the edge, but don't become a sot. Take long walks, eat periodically even if you aren't hungry. When the laughter finally comes back, don't fight it."

How did Sebastian know that litany, and why was it left to him to offer Fanny the solace her own cousins had not?

"The worst part," Fanny said, "is that all I have is a pile of stupid letters and this handkerchief."

"Take mine," Sebastian said, passing over a square of white linen embroidered along the sides and monogrammed with a crest. "You can get it all damp and wrinkly and preserve your lover's token from further abuse."

Fanny smoothed out her handkerchief on the stone of the balustrade, and I plucked it from her rather than let the breeze snatch it away. She was angry now, but someday, years hence, her memories of John might be the most precious memories she had, for all they were bittersweet.

"You are a dear, Dunkeld," Fanny said, turning to wrap herself in his arms. "Why does everybody claim you are difficult?"

"Because I spent too much time among the English. This must result in a character defect, as we all know. I am in every other way unobjectionable, so my little lapses of manners are blown out of all proportion. Let's rescue the others from the corrupting influence of the aunties, or your menfolk will be seeing who can pee the farthest off the southern walk. The footmen tell me the trick is to catch the rising breeze, though I wouldn't know myself."

Earthy people in this corner of Scotland.

Sebastian had made Fanny smile, and he kept his arm around her shoulders, as a brother might have, for the rest of the walk. He had been a kind boy. That he was a kind man pleased me. Now, when Fanny felt like some varlet's castoff, Sebastian's affection and friendliness would mean worlds to her.

I listened with half an ear to Aunt Maighread's retelling of some lovestruck swain who'd climbed the sheer wall of the house's northern façade to pay court to a chambermaid. All the while, I considered the handkerchief Fanny had been given by her erstwhile fiancé.

The linen was fine, the stitchwork equally so. The border was greenery with purple thistles—the Scottish national flower—and the initials JMS were also picked out in lavender and green, though the lettering was lavished with swirls, serifs, and embellishments.

"What is it?" Sebastian asked as Aunt Maighread got to the part about the couple being discovered by the lady of the house.

St. Sevier watched me from three yards away, his gaze subtly alert.

"The stitching has been altered," I said quietly. "I am not enough of a needlewoman to know what initials first graced this handkerchief, but they were not JMS."

"Ask Aunt Bernie," Sebastian replied. "If anybody can puzzle it out, she can." He moved away and waited politely until Aunt

Maighread brought the story to its happy conclusion—the couple's firstborn had been named Northwall MacFane.

"Shall we repair to the library for a wee dram?" Sebastian asked. "If I'm not mistaken, the breeze is picking up, and the ride home might be a bit chilly."

He wasn't mistaken. I obtained Fanny's permission to leave the handkerchief with Aunt Bernie, and our party barely made it home in time to avoid a frigid soaking.

The rain beat against the dining room windows in a steady roar, interspersed with hard splatters borne on gusting wind. Our meal at Dunkeld House had been substantial, but then too, the day—from breakfast onward—had been trying. Our supper was thus a subdued affair.

Iain excused himself shortly after the fruit and cheese had been laid out. "I haven't yet devised the tally sheets for shearing," he said, bowing to the ladies. "If we're to start on Monday, I'd best be about it."

"You're shearing this early?" I asked after he'd left.

"Not shearing, per se," Lachlan answered. "First, we must retrieve the flocks that have been wandering higher into the hills as spring progresses. They are hardy, our sheep, and wily as the devil. We will spend at least a week rounding them up and washing them and another week sorting and counting them."

"We mark them," Donnie added. "Every owner's flock bears a different sign. Dunkeld will catch sixty of ours, and we'll catch fifty of his, while MacReady will catch twenty of Dunkeld's and ten of ours... The whole business can grow quite complicated. Uncle Archie sorts us out so we move the fewest sheep the shortest distance before shearing."

"The aunties do the actual tallying," Eulalie said. "Archie does the drinking. We hold a gathering, with libation, food, and dancing, when he reviews the numbers. Dunkeld will host the first *ceilidh* this year, and then the shearing will begin."

"You don't have itinerant shearing crews?" I asked. My father hired an extended Basque family for shearing each year and would not have contemplated shearing without them.

"We can," Lachlan replied, "but those crews cost a pretty penny, so we do as much of the work ourselves as possible. Each owner contributes labor, and the shearing moves from flock to flock. Dunkeld has the largest holdings, so he will send the most hands. The job goes more quickly, and then we move on to planting, haying, and so forth."

Enclosures—walling in of previously open common land—had largely obliterated communal grazing in the south of England, and I realized for the first time how much cooperation and productivity had been buried along with that institution. My father's tenants would share the burden of plowing, planting, and harvesting to a modest extent, but I could not imagine a situation where they'd combine resources with all the neighboring estates.

"If a fellow has no sons or laborers to help out with the harder work," Donnie added, "he might send a few sheep to the larger contributors, or provide more of the food and drink along the way. It all works out, or that's the theory."

"The English did us a backhanded favor," Fanny said, running a finger around the rim of her wineglass. "When we stopped fighting each other long enough to fight the English, we realized we make better allies than enemies among ourselves. We still look to our own much more than the English do, meaning no offense."

St. Sevier held out a slice of cheese to her on the end of a cheese knife. "I would concur, having seen some of both England and Scotland, though I would add that harsher weather in Scotland also compels a greater degree of cooperation. You have a shorter growing season up here, and no hour of daylight can be wasted."

This discussion—not quite political, but certainly not trivial—was unusual in my experience because it afforded me an opportunity to broaden my perspective. In theory, the British Isles were a united kingdom. I was learning that, in practice, we were separate cultures, if not separate countries.

I was glad once again that Fanny had invited me to visit her home, though I wished her own situation was turning out more happily.

"You should stay through shearing," Eulalie said. "We're apparently not to have a wedding, but that's no reason for you to hare off back to England. Even Iain has been a bit more sociable since you've arrived."

These observations occasioned a strained silence.

Fanny tossed her napkin down beside her plate. "Excuse me. I will bid you all good night and wish you pleasant dreams." She was gone before the gentlemen could offer her their good-night bows.

"Well done, Eulie," Donnie muttered. "You hurt Fanny's feelings and insulted Iain in two sentences. Keep talking, and I'm sure you can make a disparaging remark about me or Lachlan too."

"We are tired," I said, "and Fanny's situation is troubling. Eulalie, if you would not mind, I will pass on the teapot this evening and seek those dreams Fanny mentioned."

"I'll join the gents for a nightcap, then," Eulalie said. "I am sorry if my honesty offends." She offered her apology stiffly, and I was certain she hadn't meant to insult anybody.

Besides, she had a point. Iain's demeanor had become friendlier the longer St. Sevier and I bided as guests at Leland House, and—alas—Fanny was apparently not to become a wife.

"Plain speaking rarely offends me," I said, rising. "Gentlemen, good night."

St. Sevier was the first on his feet. "I'll light you up, my lady, and seek my bed as well."

If anybody thought it odd that he and I would retire at the same time, they did not remark it. We left the dining room for the dimmer, colder corridor.

"I want to retrieve the letters from the library," I said. "Something has been bothering me."

"You are more tenacious about those damned letters than a ferret on the scent of a rat."

"I am also genuinely tired and looking forward to the arms of... Morpheus."

St. Sevier opened the library door for me. "A lovely fellow, Morpheus."

I sat at the massive desk, which was positioned to catch the fire's heat, though the hearth held only smoldering coals. I'd locked the stack of epistles in a lower drawer and needed a key from under the wax jack to retrieve them.

Somebody had tossed a ledger or journal onto the stack of letters, which did not particularly alarm me. Fanny's family knew what we were about, trying to discover John's identity. The letters did not appear to have been disordered —I'd arranged them by date—and locking them away was more to safeguard them from a mishap than to keep any secrets.

"That's odd," St. Sevier said, picking up the bound volume I'd set on the blotter. "Why keep the wage book in the library? Such ledgers are usually kept in an estate office or study."

"That's last year's book. The date is embossed on the spine."

St. Sevier propped a hip on the edge of the desk and opened the ledger.

"That is none of our business," I said.

"One is curious. I own several properties, and I can tell you that what I pay my help in France varies markedly from what I pay in rural England. My London staff commits daylight robbery on every wage day, and they work no harder than the others do."

"That is probably part of the reason the Scots are so loyal to family. Family will work harder for the common good than for a wage."

He peered at me. "Some family. Other family simply creates mischief. This book is only for outdoor positions."

"May I see that ledger?"

He passed it over. "Who is curious now?"

"I am. I want to look at the handwriting."

He set the book on the blotter, open to a middle page. The first thing I noticed was that whoever had done this accounting hadn't crossed his or her sevens. The second thing I noticed was that the handwriting—what there was of it—resembled John's, but did not match his penmanship exactly.

The style was close, though. The style was very, very close.

The variety of ways the procreative act could be enjoyed astounded me, for I'd thought my husband a worldly and inventive lover. He'd probably regarded himself in a similarly flattering light.

I had the sense St. Sevier was limiting his advances to those avenues I would find least shocking. Had he announced that our next adventure would occur in a rowboat in the middle of Loch Tay or facing each other on horseback, I would have believed him.

On our fourth night as lovers, St. Sevier began my acquaintance with the sheath, instructing me on its care, maintenance, and use and making a great joke of the little red ribbon with which he affixed this accoutrement to his person.

And while the new positions, sheaths, and vocabulary—there were far more than a dozen naughty words to be learned—fascinated me, my greatest pleasure was simply to fall asleep and wake up in St. Sevier's arms.

If anybody had told me a year ago that my urbane, French physician friend was a cuddly man, I would have scoffed, but St. Sevier was exceedingly affectionate, in and out of bed. I had the sense he was lonely in this regard, as I had been. His little touches and casual hugs soothed an ache for us both, though we had yet to discuss this aspect of our dealings.

We took our first cup of morning tea out on the balcony as I sat in St. Sevier's lap, swaddled in a blanket.

"The handwriting preoccupies me," I said after St. Sevier had held the cup to my lips. "Why did I not think to find handwriting samples earlier?"

St. Sevier drank from the cup and set it aside. "Because handwriting can be disguised? Because the handwriting you can find at Leland House belongs to Fanny's family members? Because, as brilliant as you are, you are not omniscient? Because you did think to assess the handwriting as a means of eliminating Dunkeld from suspicion?"

As I'd dozed so peacefully in my lover's arms, a vague suspicion had emerged from the sleepy fog in my brain.

"I must inquire of Fanny exactly how she began this correspondence with John. For a lady with her means to embark on a relationship through a newspaper ad is not the done thing."

"Certainly unusual," St. Sevier said, tucking the blanket more closely around my shoulders. "Not unheard of."

"But risky. She signed her letters with her real name, and the extent of her wealth would have been easy enough to learn. She is the MacPherson heiress. We referred to her thus at school ten years ago, and now she has inherited."

St. Sevier spoke with his lips against my temple. "I want to take you back to bed. You are an ache in my blood, and I will never get enough of you."

I was sitting in his lap. His comment was not mere flirtation, but rather, an expression of present intent.

"I thought my husband unusually lusty. He wasn't, was he?"

"I cannot speak with any authority regarding a man I never met, but I can tell you that with few exceptions, the healthy young male is imbued with a chronic preoccupation relating to the exercise of his animal spirits. We dearly love to fuck, to use the Anglo-Saxon vulgarity. Only more refined sensibilities—consideration for the ladies, unrelenting awareness of what could result from our enthusiasms, the occasional need to eat—prevent most of us from spending the livelong day naked and naughty."

I knew what that vulgar word meant. I'd overheard my brothers and husband use it as a passing profanity not meant for a lady's ears. That St. Sevier would include such a term in our conversation made our dealings somehow more intimate. And when he used it, the effect was humorous and self-deprecating rather than filthy.

I scooted around to straddle his lap. "What man set aside those sensibilities and took advantage of Fanny? I would bet my favorite shawl and bonnet she was ignorant of men prior to her engagement with John."

St. Sevier was quiet for a moment, his cheek resting against my hair. "I hope for her sake this John person intended to speak his vows."

"Which brings us to Fanny's central frustration. Why break it off? Why spend years cultivating her trust and esteem only to cry off?"

"And if we know the who, we will likely know the why. You will snoop about the house collecting handwriting samples, won't you, my lady?"

"Yes."

He kissed me and whispered in my ear, "Then I shall snoop with you."

What a delight to be cozened so flirtatiously. "Will you also pay a call on Aunt Bernie with me?"

"I think not. You will have a more productive chat with her on your own. She will be distracted by my abundant charm."

I was distracted by St. Sevier's abundant charm—and a few of his other abundant attributes—but we were not so late to breakfast as to have the table to ourselves. Donnie was lingering over a pot of tea, and Eulalie a pot of chocolate, though crumb-strewn plates sat before them both.

"Good morning," Donnie said, rising to greet me with a bow. "I've ordered up another glorious Scottish day for your enjoyment.

Eulalie and I thought to dip our rods again, if you'd like to come with us."

"I will pass on that kind offer," I said as St. Sevier held my chair. "I have correspondence to catch up on today, and if the weather holds, I'll poke around a bit more on horseback."

St. Sevier began filling a plate at the sideboard. "I, too, have been remiss in my correspondence. Her ladyship doubtless brought a lap desk among her traveling kit, but I was not so foresighted. Might I impose to the extent of some paper, ink, and wax?"

Clever man. I knew what he was about, as he so casually helped himself to the omelet.

"The library has some supplies," Eulalie said, "but the estate office is always well stocked. Penknives, wax, sand, pounce pot. You'll find it all in Lachlan's desk. He and Iain went out to talk with the shepherds about the sheep counting, and I doubt they'll be back before supper."

What a shame. "A lovely day to be out of doors. Would anybody object if I asked the gardener to cut a bouquet for my sitting room?"

"Certainly not," Eulalie said. "Cousin Evan has an eye for pretty posies, and he will be delighted to know they brighten your day."

St. Sevier placed the plate of eggs and ham before me. He'd chosen the right portion sizes and set a single croissant to the side so it did not touch either the omelet or the meat.

His version of courtship was approaching virtuosic heights.

"Cousin Evan?" I asked, murmuring my thanks to St. Sevier. "He's a relation?" I had asked Donnie that question directly, though Donnie appeared to find the sugar bowl fascinating now.

"Not a cousin in the English sense," Eulalie said. "Lachlan's step-uncle was a rascal with the means to indulge his wandering eye. Evan's papa was a by-blow, and thus he's acknowledged as family, but he prefers to keep to a station consistent with his origins."

"He need not," Donnie muttered. "We saw him educated. He never went without, but he prefers the dirt and the digging."

Donnie clearly resented his cousin's industry.

"The gardens benefit from Evan's choices," I said as St. Sevier took the place beside me, even as Eulalie's disclosure created a cascade of questions in my mind.

Why had Donnie obscured Evan's family connection? By-blows were a fact of life at all levels of society. I suspected my father had his share, and I was supporting my late husband's illegitimate daughter.

Would a quasi-step-cousin consigned to manual labor aspire to become Fanny's lover? Would he have the education and ambition to maintain a drawn-out correspondence with her? Had Evan filled out the wage book I'd found in the library last night, and was it coincidence that his handwriting bore such a close resemblance to that of Fanny's prodigal fiancé?

"Your eggs will get cold," St. Sevier said, setting the teapot by my plate, though he had to know that my millwheel was once again spinning.

"I'm off to round up my rod and tackle," Donnie said, his good cheer coming across a bit forced. He went jaunting on his way, leaving Eulalie frowning at the dregs of her chocolate.

"Evan is a reproach to the idle ornaments in the family," she said, "who are two in number, myself among them. Donnie feels the comparison with Evan keenly."

The eggs were quite good, the ham delicious. "Finding a direction in life for somebody with only a gentleman's education is difficult," I said. "A god-father or great uncle comes in handy at such a time, and I gather Donnie has neither?"

Eulalie made a face. "Lachlan is as close as we come—an uncle, of sorts. He feeds us and clothes us, and he relies on Iain, but Donnie and I... We are a burden on the exchequer."

"If Fanny comes to London to visit me," I said, "you must come too. Lachlan cannot have you all to himself forever." And Fanny would very likely not feel comfortable traveling without a female companion.

Though I did not particularly want company at my London

home. I wanted freedom and flexibility after two years of being nearly imprisoned in that house by the strictures of mourning.

Eulalie excused herself shortly thereafter, claiming a need to change into properly ancient fishing attire, and I contemplated the information we'd gleaned over breakfast.

"You suspect Evan," St. Sevier said.

"And Donnie."

He passed me the butter and the jam pot. "We will have a busy day, but be careful, Violet. Somebody is guarding a secret, and you mean to expose it."

"I suspect," I said, finishing my tea, "we will find multiple secrets at the bottom of this mess and more than one person guarding them."

CHAPTER ELEVEN

Fanny declined to accompany me on my visit to Aunt Bernie, and because I knew the way and would pass directly from Leland House to Dunkeld land, I did not take a groom. The day held fair, and when the breeze died, the sun had some power.

To ride alone was a rare joy, one I might have indulged in on my father's estate, but certainly not in London. As I cantered past greening meadows and contented sheep, then through the quieter patches of pine forest, I realized that returning to London held an element of dread for me.

I had been unhappy in London. First had come the tension and drama of my court presentation, then the additional tension and drama of my initial social Season. A lady swooning in a hot ballroom because her corset had been laced too tightly had become the subject of vicious rumors. A young man led on by unworthy friends had been ruined and hounded off to the Continent after a single night of gambling.

Years later, these were the memories that stayed with me. Candlelit ballrooms, pretty dresses, sedate outings to the park...

Those all faded beneath the weight of the terrible imperative to find a husband. And then had come my marriage.

But if I did not dwell in London, where would I live, and what would St. Sevier think of this preference on my part? What did it say about how I envisioned my future with him, for I was not ready to end our delightful affair for the sake of fresh air and blue skies?

He was courting me, but this time I—not my meddlesome father —would have the final say.

I cantered my mare over the last stile and we emerged onto the Dunkeld House driveway. This, too, was a memory I would keep— the castle ramparts soaring against the bright blue sky, the stately firs rising on the hill behind the majestic edifice, the magnificent pines imbuing the air with a subtle tang. The blue pennant snapping in the wind—the laird was in residence—and the spray of the fountain creating a rainbow over the drawbridge.

Whether I was moved by the grandeur of the view or something more personal, a tear trickled down my cheek. I would leave Sebastian here in his castle and possibly never see him again. At a time in my life when loneliness makes many girls foolish, he had been my friend.

Another tear followed the first, and I realized that even the privacy to cry had been in short supply in London. I could remedy that much on my return, at the very least. I wiped my cheeks with the back of my riding glove and urged my mare up the drive. A groom appeared to take my horse, and before I could knock on the massive front door, it swung open.

"Why were you crying?" Sebastian, looking severely handsome in a kilt, posed the question while drawing me by the hand into his home.

"Don't you employ a butler, Dunkeld?"

"You call me Dunkeld to vex me. If St. Sevier is causing you tears, I'll pound him into so much French dust."

"What makes you think he won't pound you into so much Scottish dust?"

Sebastian grinned and passed me a handkerchief. "He probably would, and then we'd have a wee dram or three and teach each other some drinking songs and be the despair of our womenfolk."

"You are doubtless already the despair of your womenfolk. I am here to call on Aunt Bernie."

"Rude of you not to call on me, too, but that's the English for you. No social instincts. Come, we'll find Auntie in her parlor with her familiars."

He led me past the grand display of weaponry, past gleaming armor, down sunlit corridors, and up spiral stone steps.

We emerged into another sunny corridor, and I was struck by the difference between this ancient castle and Leland House.

"Somebody built this place with an eye toward using every available sunbeam," I said. "Leland House seems quite commodious until I compare it with your home." *Most* of Leland House.

"Leland House might have begun life as a defensive dwelling, but Dunkeld House, higher on the hill, defined itself as such for centuries. I think, too, the various marchionesses realized that they would spend most of their time here in the wilds, so to speak. They exercised what civilizing influence they could, and that meant,"—he lowered his voice as if conveying a family secret—"windows."

Sebastian moved with a kind of energy and purpose that was unique to him, also a contrast with some of the denizens of Leland House. Iain applied himself with purpose to his various tasks, but the rest of the family seemed to drift about. Even Evan the gardener was never in a hurry.

Sebastian stopped beside an arched plank door. "Will you tell me what this call is about, Violet?"

"How do I look?" The real question was, *Do I look as if I've been crying?*

Sebastian gazed at me, assessing. "You look as if Scotland is agreeing with you. You've roses in your cheeks and a sparkle in your eye. I might even detect a few freckles attempting to enhance your pallid English complexion." He brushed a callused thumb over my cheek. "Why the tears, Violet?"

The last question was put quietly, no banter or teasing.

"I don't know. Homesickness, but not for London."

He crossed the corridor to sit in a sunny window seat. "The Welshmen under my command had a word—*hiraeth*. We have similar terms in Scottish Gaelic and Irish. *Hiraeth* means longing of the heart, fond regret, something hard to express in English. Profound love and heartrending loss, all in one word."

"Perhaps that's it," I said, joining him on the window seat. "I was not a happy wife, but now I see Fanny, wifehood snatched away from her, and I am desperate to learn the reason why she's been so ill-used."

"She's not carrying, is she?"

"She might have been," I said, which revealed a confidence, but Sebastian would hardly judge Fanny for following her heart. "She dosed herself with rue to a dangerous degree in an effort to prevent conception."

"I hope St. Sevier put a stop to that?"

"He was very stern with her. She seems to be doing better, physically."

"A Scotswoman thwarted in love is a ferocious creature. What does Aunt Bernie have to add to this conundrum?"

I explained about the stitching on John's handkerchief.

"Somebody is playing a deep game," he said. "Whoever this fellow is, he has much explaining to do. If there's a clue in the stitchery on his kercher, Aunt Bernie will find it. No couple on Dunkeld land goes to housekeeping without some token of her skill with a needle."

We found Hibernia in the company of two enormous long-haired black cats, one perched beside her on her sofa, one sprawled across the top of the sofa back.

"Oh, my dear Lady Violet," Aunt Bernie said, hopping to her

feet. "What a joy to see you. Sebastian, send the footman for some tea and leave us to our gossip."

"No tea," I said. "Thank you just the same."

"You're more interested in gossip," Aunt Bernie replied. "Run along, my boy, and then you will escort her ladyship back down the hill when she departs." This was not a suggestion.

Sebastian bowed and withdrew, tossing a wink at me over his shoulder.

"He is different around you," Aunt Bernie said. "More like his old self. He recalls however vaguely that he was a shy young lad once with a hidden streak of mischief. Come sit, for yonder handkerchief is an interesting puzzle."

I took the place beside her and soon found a cat climbing over my shoulder to ensconce himself in my lap.

"Pollux likes you," Aunt Bernie said, "and he's the more stand-offish of the two. Castor is a shameless flirt."

Pollux must have weighed two stone, and half of that was his luxurious coat. "He's quite impressive." And thank heavens I was wearing a riding habit, which would not show the feline hair it was doubtless collecting.

"Polly," Aunt said, glowering at the cat. "Get off Lady Violet this instant."

The cat stretched in my lap, his enormous black plume of a tail pointing skyward while his front claws dug into my skirt, then he ambled across the sofa to resume his perch on the back.

"You have been greeted properly," Aunt Bernie said, taking the place beside me. "Now, about this handkerchief. Somebody went to a lot of trouble to alter a lovely bit of stitching. Look here."

She spread the handkerchief out on my lap, a fetching bit of embroidery. The green and purple threads were not exactly mascu-line colors, but punctuated with gold here and there, the effect was lovely.

"What do you see?" Aunt asked.

"Thistles, greenery, initials. JSM, but it's a monogram, so the M is central and larger."

"And the M doesn't help us one bit, because half of Scotland is MacSomebody. The S might stand for Stuart—the other half of Scotland—but it could be Swinburne, Smith, who knows? Look at the J, though."

I peered at it closely. "There are two different colors of thread involved, slightly different shades of lavender."

She turned the cloth over and smoothed it out again. "Use this." She passed me a quizzing glass.

"The first letter was initially something other than a J, wasn't it?" The script of the J, unlike the S or the M, was very flourishy and ornate, and the upright stroke was an infinitesimally darker hue than the whorls and curlicues forming the letter into a capital J.

"It was not a J, and because that little straight part is the same thread as the other initials, we also know this fellow's real name doesn't start with any letter that curves out to the left. Not C, G, O, Q, or S, and we can probably eliminate A, V, W, X, Y, and Z as well, because of the angle of the upright portion."

"That still leaves more than half the alphabet." The letters E, for Evan, and D, for Donnie, for example. Even L, for Lachlan, was a possibility, but not—I was ashamed of myself for the relief I felt—S, for Sebastian.

Though what about E for Eulalie? Particularly Eulalie MacKellan?

"Would Eulalie concoct this whole campaign for some reason?" I asked, smoothing my fingers over the knots and threads on the back of the handkerchief. "Could she have undertaken the correspondence and then induced some fellow to take on the trysting part?"

"That's a cruel lark," Aunt Bernie said, "but Eulalie is bored and clever. If Fanny remained preoccupied with an imaginary suitor, the field is left clear for Eulalie."

That motive would explain much. "Does Eulalie have the skill with a needle to create this monogram?"

"Easily. Lachlan doesn't allow his family much in the way of frolic. Needlework helps pass the time and beautifies the hall."

I thought back to Eulalie's attire, which in general was more refined than Fanny's. "Are you familiar with the Leland House head gardener, Evan?"

"I knew his father, and yes, I do mean in the scandalous sense. Lively lot of fellows on that side of the family. Evan is a good sort. He keeps the grounds in fine trim and has no reason to ruin Fanny. The family would turn him out on his ear if he cut up like that, and nobody would hire him once the details became known."

My father would doubtless get on well with Aunt Bernie.

"What if Evan loved Fanny, and Eulalie learned of that love?" My mind was tumbling over itself with snippets of fact and memory: Donnie noting that Evan had been educated—by the same tutors who'd taught Donnie and Iain? Evan in the garden passing Fanny a bouquet of daffodils, which traditionally symbolized new beginnings. Fanny's swain lurking in the garden, meeting her in the garden, and dodging away from her in the garden.

Then too, Evan had a closely trimmed beard, such as a man might shave off and then regrow in a matter of days.

"If Evan loved Fanny," Aunt Bernie said, "and she loved him, there would be no impediment to her marrying him. Her mother took an unconventional husband both times. A penniless artist the first time, her land steward the second time. A woman with wealth has that prerogative."

"But Evan is illegitimate, which makes him a different order of mésalliance altogether."

Aunt Bernie looked unconvinced. "Fanny has no title, has no connection to a title. This is Perthshire, not Mayfair. She's getting on, as brides go, and hasn't had offers. A marriage to Evan would be a nine days' wonder."

"Then why wouldn't Evan simply declare himself?"

The cat at Bernie's side rose and strolled across both of our laps to touch noses with his brother and then hop to the floor. English cats would not be permitted to behave with such rudeness... except they would act thus anyway. Cats knew of no nationality save citizenship in the kingdom of felines, and I envied them that.

"If Evan learned that Fanny would reject him once Fanny learned his true identity,"

Aunt Bernie said, "then he's better off keeping his mouth shut and not losing his post, isn't he? Fanny might have made a chance comment about a gardener's dirty hands, or servants getting above themselves, or some offhand remark that dashed Evan's hopes. If he keeps silent, he's left the field, kept his job, and nobody's the wiser."

My head was swimming with speculations and what-ifs. What if Eulalie had embarked on the correspondence to keep Fanny from noticing the local swains, Evan had learned of Eulalie's ploy, and Evan had taken over the letter-writing? What if Evan had embarked on the correspondence, Eulalie had learned of it, and Eulalie had forced him to break it off?

"Sebastian mentioned the Welsh tongue to me," I said slowly, thinking aloud. "Isn't the name Evan the Welsh equivalent of John?"

Aunt Bernie folded up the little handkerchief and passed it to me. "In Scots, Evan means right-handed, and in the Gaelic, it connotes a young warrior, but I believe you are correct. The Welsh translate Evan to John, and Evan's grandmama was Welsh."

Oh dear. *Oh drat and damnation.* "I must return to Leland House. You have been very helpful, Aunt Bernie." I rose and curt-seyed my farewell, sparing a pat for each of the splendid kitties before departing.

On the way down the hill, I acquainted Sebastian with the secrets the handkerchief had revealed. Half of the alphabet was out of contention, but I was now suspicious of Evan and Donnie, and especially of Eulalie and Evan. The handsome gamekeeper—Septimus MacFarlane—was also out of contention, but only just.

"I don't see Eulalie as having that degree of slyness," Sebastian said. "She's forthright to a fault. If you stay long enough to attend the shearing *ceilidh*, you'll see that Eulalie has no problem outshining Fanny and nearly every other young lady at our local gatherings."

Then why wasn't Eulalie married?

"Whom do you suspect?" I asked as the track turned to border an ancient orchard.

"Evan might be your man," Sebastian said, drawing his horse to a halt. "He has had the opportunity to play the entire charade—letters and trysts—and a good reason to be deceptive about his identity. I agree with Aunt Bernie that he's not an exact fit, though. Shall we race to the end of the orchard?"

My mare was a perfect lady, and I was a perfect lady. Or maybe I had been a perfect lady for too long.

"On three," I said, reverting to old custom with an old friend. I, of course, bolted forward on two, as did Sebastian. His larger mount should have beaten us, but my mare was game, tenacious, and lighter of frame. We reached the end of the orchard with the horses matching each other stride for stride, though I would have sworn my mare was pulling ahead.

"Now we must walk them the rest of the way, or Lachlan's head stable lad will turn me over his knee," Sebastian said, patting his gelding soundly on the neck. "Well done, Hannibal."

I offered my mare similar praise, though she was clearly game to stretch her legs again. "Is Lachlan's head lad so venerable that he had the honor of paddling your little bum years ago?"

"MacDougal is that protective of his horseflesh, and yes, he's venerable. He can tell stories on Aunt Bernie and Aunt Maighread that predate the Flood. Even Uncle Archie moderates his fish stories when MacDougal is in the audience."

I liked that everybody in the neighborhood knew everybody else, and class distinctions were blurred by shared history and an extended version of family and—at least for form's sake—disdain for the

English. The Scots had a grasp of nationality that I never sensed among my English relations and acquaintances.

"Would MacDougal know if somebody was trysting in the stables?" I asked.

"You will doubtless ask him, and his answer may require translation. He understands English far better than he speaks it, or so he'd have us believe."

"Can you do that translating?"

Sebastian hesitated. "I can, but might you spare the old boy the embarrassment, Violet? Confront Evan, and if he confesses all, you have solved the mystery."

I was about to retort that Evan would be a fool to admit fault and lose his job when we came around a bend in the track and were assailed by raised voices. Farther down the hill, in a clearing visible through the pines, two men were engaged in a heated argument.

"Lachlan and Iain," I muttered. "What are they shouting about?"

"It's Gaelic," Sebastian said. "I can't make it out at this distance. Something to do with sheep and slaughter and..." He fell silent, brows knit. "Innocent lambs?"

"They were to meet with the shepherds this morning," I said, though the topic was to be shearing, not slaughter.

"We aren't meant to overhear this," Sebastian said, nudging his horse forward. "Lachlan has played the role of steward at Leland House for more than twenty years. He knows what he's about, but times are changing, and agricultural science isn't what it was twenty years ago."

"Let me guess: He's lord of the manor when it suits his whim and expert steward when he'd rather wear the expert-steward hat. He won't get his hands dirty clearing a ditch, but he also won't listen to Iain when it's time to try a strain of new wheat."

Sebastian cocked his head. "Sounds about right."

"My father does the same thing, particularly with Mitchell. Expects Mitchell to have both a prospective peer's initiative and a toady's deference, and to know from moment to moment which of his lordship's whims to gratify first. I don't always like my oldest brother, but I don't envy him either."

We rode into the Leland House stable yard some minutes later. Sebastian greeted the wizened groom in the Scottish tongue and swung down to help me from my mare.

"I almost forgot," he said as I unhooked my knee from the horn. "Congratulations on becoming an auntie again. Felix sent me a pigeon. Your brother is nearly incoherent with joy at the birth of his son. If Felix was delighted to be married, fatherhood has put him into celestial transports."

I slid to the ground in the middle of this recitation. "And Katie? Is she well?" Felix's wife had first struck me as a pale, retiring little cipher, but my opinion of her had improved vastly upon further acquaintance.

"Right as a trivet. They named the boy James Evander and asked me to be godfather."

I hugged Sebastian hard, joy and relief waltzing in my heart. "I was worried, for Katie, for the baby, for Felix. I was so worried."

"I know, *mo chridhe*, I know."

He hugged me back, and given the news, I needed Sebastian's arms around me. He'd gone to war with Felix, and he and Felix had kept each other safe. Sebastian's generous offer to lease out one of his English estates to Felix was one of the reasons Felix's fledging horse-breeding business was off on a good foot. In this regard, Sebastian was family, or closer than family, for I could not imagine sharing such a moment with my oldest brother.

"And a son," I said, stepping back as a stable boy led my mare away. "Mitchell will be beside himself."

"Mitchell thanked him," Sebastian said, smiling. "Seems there's now renewed enthusiasm on the part of the viscountess for her husband's company."

Mitchell, in line for my father's earldom, had only girl children—thus far. "One can hardly imagine such a thing. I am simply glad for Katie and Felix." Also envious. Married less than a year and already the parents of a healthy baby. Of course, they had anticipated their vows, as many couples did, but still... a healthy baby.

"I am glad as well," Sebastian said, "though it means another trip south this summer. One must make the acquaintance of one's first godchild, after all."

"Mitchell would stand in for you at the christening."

Sebastian scoffed. "As if I would allow a mere courtesy lord to take the place of a genuine Scottish marquess when our wee Jamie is making his first appearance in polite society. You English and your love affair with expedience will be the ruination of the species."

"Walk me to the terrace," I said, reluctant to part with him. Sebastian had delivered good news to me, and we'd raced to a draw at the orchard. I would rather tarry in his company than return to the intrigues waiting in the house.

He winged his arm. "How much longer will you stay?"

"I rely on St. Sevier's escort, so the decision is not entirely mine. I would like to tarry until this shearing celebration, or whatever it is."

"You should bide at least that long, Violet. We'll get out the swords once the whisky starts flowing. You'll seldom see the sword dances outside of Scotland."

We ambled along a flagstone walkway, circling around toward the back of the house. "Does the whisky ever stop flowing?"

"Only long enough to brew a pot of tea or pick a fight. Speaking of which..." Sebastian halted a dozen yards from the garden's side door.

Another pair of irate voices reached us as we stood outside the high wall. This argument was happening with the sort of controlled exasperation evident when emotion was nearly outdistancing the need for discretion.

"That's Donnie," I said, but again, the language was unfamiliar to me.

"We should make ourselves known." Sebastian marched forward and opened the garden door. "Come along, my lady, I'm sure the family will want to hear your brother's happy news."

He'd raised his voice, such that the argument within the garden abruptly ceased. I did not know what I expected, but it wasn't Donnie and Evan, both of them holding bouquets of flowers and looking as if they'd rather be engaged in a round of fisticuffs.

The warring parties pasted on smiles before we got within six feet of them.

"For my lady," Evan said, offering me a bunch of purple irises. "My lord." He bowed in our general direction.

"MacKellan, good day." Sebastian peered about as if he were the royal inspector of rural gardens. "Your beds are two weeks ahead of ours at Dunkeld House."

"We're down the hill from your lordship's property, and our garden walls are higher. If I might return to my labors." He sent Donnie an unfathomable look and strode off, kilt swinging.

"Best put those in water," Donnie said. "Evan gets offended if we don't cherish his bouquets. I was taken to task for appropriating a few posies, if you can believe that."

I couldn't, not entirely. "Your yellow tulips will go nicely with these irises, or did you want the tulips for yourself?"

Donnie looked a bit sheepish. "The tulips are for you, my lady. You mentioned at breakfast that you'd like some flowers for your sitting room, and these struck me as cheerful and abundant. Evan is more jealous of this garden than a mama cat with one kitten, though. I ought to have asked his permission."

I took the tulips from him and added them to the irises. "The garden is lovely, but you're right about the tulips. They bloom in abundance here. We should enjoy them in the house as well. Dunkeld, come along, and we'll find a vase for these."

Sebastian very likely did not want to *come along*, but I couldn't interrogate him about Donnie and Evan's altercation while Donnie hovered at my elbow.

"How was the fishing?" I asked Donnie when Sebastian merely sent me an obdurate look.

"Nothing was biting for me," Donnie said, "though Eulalie and MacFarlane were having better luck. Trout at supper would be my guess. Eulalie has more patience than I do, or MacFarlane shows her the better places to cast her line."

I hoped for Fanny's sake that Donnie was not her errant fiancé. He was grumbling about his sister and the gamekeeper having better luck with the fish, and if I was to believe him, he'd argued with the gardener over a few purloined posies. I felt sorry for him, and I hoped Fanny's swain wasn't pitiable.

Disgraceful, perhaps, but not pitiful.

"Does Evan's family connection make him so forthright?" I put the question to Donnie as Evan pushed a wheelbarrow full of weeds through the gate at the foot of the garden. "For a gardener, he was certainly offering you an emphatic opinion."

Donnie began walking with us toward the house. "Evan is one of those people who holds his tongue over the big issues, but can let fly over a triviality. His path hasn't been easy. He had the same tutors as Iain, Eulalie, and me, but at sixteen, he was sent out to apprentice to a gardener, which is old to apprentice in nearly any trade."

"He appears to have taken to the post," I said. "This garden is a work of art."

"Lachlan won't let him change much," Donnie said. "Mrs. Leland laid out the beds, and they've stayed the same since her death. The whole space is a memorial garden of sorts, and that frustrates Evan. He gets his revenge by wreaking havoc elsewhere."

"Havoc?" As in dallying with Mrs. Leland's daughter?

"You know, potted camellias in the alehouse windows, hanging baskets in the folly, a bed of roses beside MacFarlane's cottage. Evan's hand is obvious in the unlikely places he exercises his authority."

"Her ladyship will think we're eccentric, Donnie," Sebastian said as we climbed the terrace steps. "Turning rosebushes into gestures of defiance."

"We are eccentric," Donnie said. "No denyin' that. Your own aunt Maighread claims to have the sight. How eccentric is that?"

"The sight is how we explain an excellent ear for gossip and a mind given to logical deductions, mixed with a few nips from the flask." Sebastian stopped at the top of the steps. "St. Sevier, good day."

St. Sevier bowed. "Dunkeld, the pleasure is mine."

Whenever he and Sebastian met, I had the sense the available air had been reduced by half. Tension sprang between them, though they were never overtly hostile. They were merely *masculine* with each other, even fraternal, and occasionally friendly as yearling colts are friendly.

The snorting, pawing, rearing, and prancing were subtle, but detectable nonetheless.

"Let's put these in the library," I said, striding for the French doors. "I'll take a few blooms up to my sitting room before luncheon."

All three men followed me into the library, though it was Sebastian who produced a vase from the bottom of the sideboard.

"I'll excuse myself," Donnie said. "Fishing attire isn't exactly suitable for luncheon."

"Before you go," I called over my shoulder, "I have a question for you, Donnie. I found last year's wage book stashed among Fanny's letters. Should it be returned to the estate office?"

"If it was the outdoor wage book, that stays here in the library," Donnie said. "Evan prefers not to have to use the estate office when Lachlan and Iain both already do. Just leave the book where you found it. Not as if wages are any great secret on this estate."

He left, closing the door behind him.

"He always sounds as if he's complaining," St. Sevier remarked. "I find that unusual in a Scot."

"We grouse," Sebastian said, passing me a pitcher of water. "We grumble, we philosophize, and we drink, but we don't complain— unlike the French."

I poured water into the vase and began adding stems, one by one.

"My lord is correct," St. Sevier said. "The French have a talent for a well-wrought lament, and we have the courage to name the sorrows and foibles others pretend don't exist. Hence the great works of Molière, Diderot, Voltaire—"

"I need a penknife," I said. "And Donnie has confirmed that the wage book is an example of Evan's penmanship. I want to see samples of Donnie's and Lachlan's writing too."

"Aren't you forgetting somebody?" St. Sevier asked, rummaging in the desk drawer as Sebastian passed me a short knife from a garter scabbard worn immediately below his knee.

"Eulalie," I said. "I have a nagging sense that she's caught up in this intrigue somehow." I trimmed iris and tulip stems with Sebastian's knife until I had an arrangement that pleased me. Symmetric, balanced, pretty.

"That will never do," St. Sevier said, approaching my bouquet. "You have made these innocent flowers too woefully English."

Sebastian eyed his knife, which was still in my hand. "Where would you like us to bury you, St. Sevier? Here in Scotland, where Violet gutted you, back in France, or on one of your English properties?"

St. Sevier began nudging flowers this way and that. "Any fool can see some greenery is needed, some element of the unexpected. I will raid the garden, and you two will look over the documents I happened upon in the estate office while tending to my correspondence. Lachlan's handwriting was everywhere, but Donnie's wasn't as easy to find. I put them both in the drawer with Miss MacPherson's letters, and I can retrieve a sample of Miss Eulalie's handwriting from the herbal."

He sent the bouquet one last pitying look and sauntered out through the French doors.

"He would have made a fine Scotsman," Sebastian said. "You are never to tell him I said that."

"He doubtless thinks you would have made a fine Frenchman,

whereas you would both fail utterly as Englishmen, God be thanked. Let's have a look at the handwriting samples, shall we?"

Sebastian remained by the sideboard, considering the flowers, while I set out one of John's recent letters, the wage book, and a list of tenants and rents owed. The final sample was a somewhat crumpled draft, complete with marginalia and editorial notes, of an inquiry to an Edinburgh hiring agency.

"St. Sevier raided Donnie's dustbin," I said. "That was enterprising of him."

"He's enterprising, all right," Sebastian muttered. "Do you recall what yellow tulips signify?"

I glanced up, regarding the arrangement in its plain white bisque vase. "Yellow tulips symbolize doomed love."

"Do you suppose Donnie knows that?"

I almost dreaded to look at the handwriting on the draft inquiry. "I hope not. Come have a look at these penmanship examples."

He crossed to the desk and peered over my right shoulder.

CHAPTER TWELVE

While Sebastian and I compared penmanship samples from Evan, Donnie, Lachlan, and Eulalie, St. Sevier fussed with the flowers on the sideboard.

"They all write much alike," I said, scowling. "Lachlan's hand is somewhat different, but the other three..."

"They likely had the same tutors," Sebastian pointed out. "And Eulalie never went off to finishing school. She's added a few flourishes to her capital letters, but those could easily be dropped to impersonate a man's penmanship."

In the alternative, she could easily *add* flourishes to the stitching on a handkerchief.

St. Sevier set his floral creation on the reading table, and I had to admit, he'd done far more with a few sprigs of lavender, some ferns, and the flowers than I had with my simple bouquet.

"Is it too fussy?" he asked, walking around the table. "Too French?"

"Those are Scottish flowers," Sebastian retorted. "You cannot make them French by adding Scottish greenery and putting them in a Scottish vase in a Scottish library."

"But I," St. Sevier said with all the dignity in the world, "am French, and thus the work of my hands will have the inimitable imprimatur of Frenchness. The bouquet wants contrast, something vivid and unexpected. Ah—I have it. Violet, your stock, please."

"My stock?"

He gestured to his throat. "I believe that is how you refer to an equestrienne's neckwear, *non?*"

The scarlet silk knotted at my collar complemented my dark blue habit. I untied the scarf and passed it over, though I felt a trifle undressed without it.

St. Sevier arranged the length of silk around the vase in an off-center bow, and the result was lovely. Unexpected and vivid, as he'd said, and delightful.

"*Et voilà tout,*" he said. "Now I can turn my powers of divination to the handwriting."

He ambled to the desk and looked over my shoulder. "None of the men cross their sevens. The recent letters have all the sevens crossed. I should look again in the herbal to see if I can find an example of Eulalie's handwriting that includes numbers."

Sebastian stepped away. "How did you see that so quickly? I could have stared at these pages all afternoon and not seen that."

St. Sevier grinned. "It's quite simple, Dunkeld. I stared at them for most of the morning."

"But does that help us?" I muttered, trying to will the pages to reveal a solution to me. "Anybody can affect a crossed seven, and for a time, John wasn't crossing his." I had the sense I was missing something obvious and important, as obvious as the red bow on St. Sevier's flower arrangement.

"Each author has some qualities in common with John," St. Sevier said, taking a quizzing glass from the drawer and holding it over John's latest epistle. "And they are all close enough to his penmanship that imitating his style would not be difficult."

"We're forgetting something," I said, accepting the quizzing glass from St. Sevier.

"I'm forgetting an appointment with my Glasgow land steward," Sebastian said. "He has traveled some distance to await my pleasure. I will leave you two to your sleuthing. Violet, congratulations again on becoming an auntie."

"How many land stewards do you have?" I asked, rising from the desk.

"Four—in Scotland." Sebastian looked self-conscious about this. "And two house stewards. The lot of them bicker like old women, so I must constantly sort them out."

"Invite Archie to share a meal with you and this steward," I suggested. "Your man won't set foot out of Glasgow again for a year."

"An inspired suggestion," Sebastian murmured. "And the Edinburgh stewards are due to come through next week, and my fellow from Inverness the week after—"

"*That's it*," I said, snapping my fingers. "The steward. We forgot Iain. He is tall, Scottish, dark-haired, and travels into Perth regularly. If he was educated by the same tutors as Donnie, Evan, and Eulalie, then his handwriting ought to be in the same style as John's."

"John's handwriting is little more than schoolboy copperplate," Sebastian countered. "Besides, Iain is just not... He's too..."

"He's *Iain*," St. Sevier said. "Happy to sleep in a shepherd's hut and the only person around here who actually puts in a day's work. He doesn't need to attract the notice of an heiress, unlike Donnie, and he hasn't any of Evan's legitimacy issues."

"But does he cross his sevens?" I asked.

"You are being stubborn," St. Sevier said, smiling at me. "Admit it. Iain could court Miss MacPherson openly, exactly as Lachlan courted her mother."

"Her mother was a widow. Widows have more latitude than ladies who've never been married, and as long as Lachlan is around, Iain is only a sort of under-steward." I was arguing for form's sake. I did not want John to be Iain. I liked Iain, and of all Fanny's relations, he was the easiest to respect. His first conversation with me had shown him to be interested in Fanny's happiness, and I could not say the same for his siblings.

"I might have a note from Iain," Sebastian said. "Something about herding dogs or covering a mare with my stud. I'll have a look tonight."

"Please do," I said, "and thank you for escorting me down the hill."

He crossed the room, kissed my cheek, bowed to St. Sevier, and left through the French doors.

"When Dunkeld departs," St. Sevier said, gaze on the French doors, "one feels as if a storm has moved out to sea. He was clearly jealous of my talent with the bouquet."

"Clearly," I said, thinking back to a little tuzzy-muzzy of violets and forget-me-nots. "He was also intent on escaping before I could ask him what Donnie and Evan were arguing about. They were bickering like a pair of old men trying to recall a cricket match twenty years past."

"Not old women?"

"Old women don't bicker. They just get even."

St. Sevier closed the distance between us. "You are an auntie again. Has Katie come safely through her travail?" He slipped his arms around me, and I went gratefully into his embrace.

"She and Felix have a son. James Evander, and Dunkeld will be the godfather. Mother and baby are thriving. I expect I'll get the news from Katie or Aunt Charlotte any day."

He stroked my hair. "Do you want children, Violet?"

I was reminded of his earlier claim, about the French having the courage to name sorrows others tried to ignore. I did not know if the entire nationality could boast of that trait, but Hugh St. Sevier certainly could.

"I did want children," I said, "and my life would be very different now were I a mother. Freddie left a daughter. I've met her and her mother—I support them, in fact. Sophie Renfrew isn't educated, wealthy, or well connected, but when her daughter calls her Mama, she has a trove of joy I can only dream of."

Having a child, a male child especially, would have somehow compensated for my many inadequacies as a wife. Snuggled in Hugh's arms, I realized that part of my hesitance to remarry was because I did not want to disappoint another husband as I had disappointed Freddie—nor did I want to *be* disappointed.

I was reminded of Lachlan's comment about not wanting to watch another spouse die, nor force a wife to watch his own demise. Lachlan had chosen the safer path, at least to appearances, but had he also chosen sorrow over joy?

Hugh was not Freddie, and I was not a seventeen-year-old girl too cowed by paternal authority to question my father's choice. I stayed in St. Sevier's arms for another moment, savoring the sheer pleasure of his embrace.

"Do you want children?" I asked when I stepped back.

"I do," he said, no hesitation. "I became a physician with a view toward someday practicing as an accoucheur and children's doctor. Medical men were needed on the battlefields, so off I went, but I would adore having children of my own to love and nurture."

Englishmen—the ones in my family—talked of *securing the succession* or *siring the heir and spare*. Even Freddie had wanted children to somehow add to his consequence and imbue his wealth with dynastic dimensions.

St. Sevier wanted children *to love and nurture*. "You are a good, dear man," I said. "Any child would be lucky to have you as a father."

I had not answered his question: Did I want children *now*? The subject required thought, because I had given St. Sevier permission to court me, and he was informing me that children figured prominently in his marital aspirations.

In my marriage, I had expected that children would come along. When, after a year of Freddie's relentless husbandly enthusiasms, I had not conceived, I'd accepted that conception was not simply an inevitable result of marriage.

"I am of a certainty, a good, dear man," St. Sevier said. "Also skilled at arranging flowers. Is there a but?"

I considered my bright red stock, which now added a bold flourish to an unusual bouquet. "But I am not certain I can bear children. I have lost two, need I remind you."

He cupped my cheek against a warm palm. "I am not withdrawing my request to pay you my addresses, Violet. I would adore my own children, but there are many children in the world already who need love and care. Let's steal a moment upstairs, shall we? You cannot intend to come to lunch in your riding habit, and I adore being your lady's maid."

I let him change the subject, though he had given me much to think about. When he had divested me of my habit, we made love swiftly and silently, and I realized anew how much I longed never to see London again.

And also how dear Hugh St. Sevier had become to me.

Luncheon was a subdued affair, with only Donnie, St. Sevier, Fanny, and myself at the table. I was in good appetite, though, and aglow with Felix and Katie's good news. My father would be particularly pleased, though he had objected the loudest to Felix and Katie's union. Everybody had objected, come to that, but Katie and Felix had been certain of their love.

How I envied them the clarity of their sentiments.

When St. Sevier muttered something about needing more time with his correspondence, I suggested a postprandial walk to Fanny. The day remained fair, and I could waft about indoors to my heart's content in London. I wanted to spend as much of my Scottish holiday in the fresh air as possible.

"Where shall we go?" Fanny asked as we gathered up shawls and bonnets.

"Anywhere but the garden," I said. "Donnie and Evan were spatting out there earlier today, and I've a mind to stretch my legs rather than daunder along."

"Let's walk to the belvedere," Fanny suggested. "The tower has a lovely view of the river, and the way is mostly level."

"Perfect." For I was mindful that Fanny had yet to regain the vigor she'd had at school.

Fanny directed me to a path through the woods that traveled on a barely perceptible upward incline. The scent of the firs was thick in the air, our footfalls were muffled by the carpet of pine needles, and the only sound was the wind soughing through the trees.

The springy layer of pine needles gave my step a peculiar buoyance, and I was happy to be once again stretching my legs.

"I've been meaning to ask you something," I said as we strode along. "How exactly did your correspondence with John begin?"

"Slowly," Fanny said, her smile wan. "I waited days and sometimes weeks for his early letters, but they were long, well-thought-out, and interesting. I would take my time replying, making draft after draft. John did not seem inclined to delve into personal matters at first."

"Do you recall the advertisement you responded to, or was there more than one?"

"I recall it quite clearly and still have it. I'd scoffed at the notion of matchmaking by mail, though it's common enough in certain circles. Eulalie took to reading the ads aloud in the parlor of an evening, for amusement while we waited for the gentlemen to join us. Lachlan had mentioned exactly that diversion more than once, though I suspect he's also read those advertisements for his own purposes. Eulalie came across one posting..."

Something moved in the undergrowth yards away. Something much larger than a squirrel.

"Deer," Fanny said, pointing to a retreating pair of russet flanks. "The mamas hide their babies in the woods and hedgerows when it's time to go off and graze."

We passed from beneath the trees to an open meadow. Wildflowers dotted tufts of grass, an array of violets, yellow cowslips, rusty sheep sorrel, and heartsease. The meadow was the antithesis of the tidy, tended walled garden and, in its way, more beautiful for being nature as God made her. Near the top of the hill sat a round stone structure that rose to a height of three stories.

"The aunties claim there was a tower house here, and those stones were used to build the belvedere. What you see now was built in the time of James VI, so it's actually rather new."

New meant the belvedere was thus a little over two centuries old and had probably done duty as both a watchtower and a folly in its early life. Nearly one hundred and fifty years of bloody religious and political strife had followed the union of the thrones, and present-day repercussions were far from benign.

"What was special about the advertisement John posted?" I asked as we turned our steps uphill.

"Everything," Fanny said. "If I sat down to write out my fondest desires as they related to a potential mate, they would be embodied in that advertisement. John sought a lady of refined education with a lively sense of humor, good Scots vigor, an interest in letters and languages, and a proper sense of her place in the world.

"She had to be of mature years," Fanny went on, "but willing to entertain the notion of starting a family if matters progressed in such a sanguine direction. She must not be dependent on shallow socializing or the blandishments of the shops for her entertainments. Her loyalty had to be to Scotland, without any ambition to leave our pulchritudinous shores for foreign climes. He used words like that—sanguine, pulchritudinous, blandishments. The advertisement wasn't the usual pathetic list edited for brevity in the interest of economy. John was willing to pay to see his wishes stated in full. I liked that."

"And Eulalie brought the advert to your attention?"

"More than once. She knew he was right for me."

Fanny extracted a key from a crevice in the drystone wall encircling the tower. The structure was gray granite, and the sole door appeared to have been fashioned from a single enormous plank. The lock gave easily, and Fanny tucked the key into a pocket.

"Up we go. The view is worth the climb, I promise. We used to play here as children, before I was sent away. After I was made to attend school, on summer holidays I'd take a picnic and a book to the top. Those were happy hours."

The steps circled to the right, and an iron handrail was bolted to the wall. Fanny had left the door open, but no windows pierced the structure until we'd climbed at least twenty feet. The going was dim, dank, and chilly.

"I have been wondering about something," I said as we spiraled ever upward into the gloom. "Why isn't Eulalie married? She's pretty, lively, and apparently well-liked. If she urged you to find a spouse among the advertising bachelors, why hasn't she followed the same route?"

Fanny paused on the steps above me. We were nearing the top, and sunlight filtered over her shoulder.

"And look where I am now," she said. "Mortified, two years older, and wondering what is wrong with me that a man who seemed my perfect match cries off at the altar."

"Nothing is wrong with you," I said as we resumed climbing, "and nothing is wrong with Eulalie either. Does she have any suitors at all? Cousins who call when you and she make your shopping trips to Edinburgh? Local swains with whom she stands up for the waltzes?" She'd certainly not been shy with St. Sevier.

"We're barely waltzing here, my lady. In some ways, Scotland has embraced progress like a long-lost son. In other ways, we're still reusing the stones quarried by the Picts, and determined to thwart any change."

England had the same quality, at least in the shires. London was a temple to progress—also to dirt, stink, crowding, noise, despair, depravity, and foul air.

"Fanny, have you ever wondered why Eulalie, who longs for more Society, hasn't found a beau?"

We emerged onto the top of the tower. The walls encircling the space came to about rib-height, meaning the surrounding countryside fell away in a lovely panorama. One side of this circular terrace was roofed, though open, and along that portion of the wall, a wooden bench had been fashioned. A little cisternlike structure collected rainwater from the roofing into what looked like a birdbath, with a sloped spout to send the overflow cascading down the side of the tower.

"Ospreys nested up here my first summer back from school," Fanny said, gaze on the mountains rising across the horizon. "I was furious, but Lachlan was adamant that I not disturb them. My mother agreed, and even though I can grasp now that they were right, at the time, I felt as if they were keeping me from coming that last little bit home. He wasn't my father, but he was telling me what to do, and my mother was abetting him. I was sorely aggrieved, but not enough to look forward to resuming my studies in England."

"Ospreys eat fish, don't they?" And they were big, impressive birds who migrated north from Africa. That was the sum of my knowledge regarding them.

"They do," Fanny said, bracing her elbows on the mossy parapet. "Hence the proximity of the river appealed to them."

The river was close in one sense—at the foot of the slope on which the tower perched—but many, many feet below us. I had never been afraid of heights, and scenery like this simply wasn't to be found in England.

I joined Fanny at the wall. "What will you do, Fanny, if John turns out to be some stable hand or laborer on Leland House property?"

"I don't care what his station is, Violet. I care very much that he has humiliated me by breaking matters off after..."

"After stealing your heart?"

"He had my heart months ago. I should not have given him my virtue."

Frank talk indeed, though I detested the terminology. A woman was no less virtuous for having been with a man, and no more virtuous for eschewing that pleasure.

"I disagree, Fanny. Sooner or later, you will meet somebody else, and you will be wiser and less gullible for your experiences with John. When I married, I was completely dependent on my husband's good offices to explain to me how to go on regarding our intimate dealings. The longer I look back on that situation, the more I loathe it."

"You sound like Miss Davenport," she said, referring to the literature teacher who'd instructed the oldest girls at our finishing school.

"Miss Davenport was right. Young ladies need to arm themselves with education, the better to choose carefully in which men to repose their trust. Miss Davenport likely meant the education available from books, but I posit that we need all manner of education—including the education to be found trysting with the occasional swain."

"You weren't happy with Mr. Belmaine?"

"Not after the first year, and Mr. Belmaine was not happy with me. Our marriage was a plot hatched by the elders to which neither one of us felt free to object. Freddie and I both tried, but we did not suit. I could not give him children, he could not give up his entertainments. We were growing increasingly distant. Had I any experience of men, of how to stand up for myself with a man, I might have spared both myself and Freddie difficult years."

Fanny slipped an arm around my middle. "I am very glad you came to visit, Violet. You are still you, still honest and dear." She squeezed me in a half hug, then straightened and pulled away. "What on earth?"

On the path along the river, a couple had emerged from the trees —and they *were* a couple. Her arm was twined around his waist, his arm rested around her shoulders. Their pace was meandering until they stopped and indulged in a most passionate kiss.

"I suppose that answers that," Fanny said. "Eulalie has a beau."

"Apparently so." And he was tall, dark-haired, and kilted. "Do we investigate further?"

"I'm not sure I want to," Fanny said. "But this does explain why Eulalie hasn't attached any followers."

"If you're wondering whether the shearing is any great marvel worth biding in Scotland for another fortnight, I'm afraid you will be disappointed. May I join you?"

Lachlan Leland gestured to the bench I occupied. I had retreated to the Leland House conservatory, which in midspring was a rather untidy place. Some of the hardier plants had been returned to their outdoor settings, while many others remained, all in a jumble, still housed within the glass walls.

My father's estate had a similar feature, but I had never seen Papa's conservatory in this much disarray. Tools had not been put away, but merely stashed in buckets. Ferns sat next to potted lemon trees, and rows of seedlings marched unlabeled along the windowsill.

Evan either prioritized his attention to the walled garden, or he needed more under-gardeners.

And yet, the conservatory was peaceful, full of light, away from the breeze, and conducive to quiet contemplation.

I set aside my embroidery. "Please do join me. We have our shearing rituals in the south, including an informal assembly to mark its conclusion, but most of the major landowners use itinerant crews, so I'm sure the English celebration is tamer than its Scottish cousin."

Lachlan smiled, and I was reminded that he was yet a handsome man and probably would be into great old age. I could see why Mary MacPherson had been smitten with her steward and wondered again why Lachlan had not remarried.

He sat back, entirely at ease in his kilt and hose. "I thought the defining ambition for every English aristocrat was to make a splash during the London Season. I know Fanny would be greatly diverted to see some of that spectacle, and Eulalie would positively adore you for hosting them if you saw fit to be that gracious. Donnie would happily escort the ladies south, and he's the picture of the braw, bonnie laddie in his kilt."

Lachlan was striving for a jovial tone, but the message was less than hospitable. I was to gather up his relations and take them south in time to catch the final weeks of the London Season.

"Are you trying to get rid of me, Lachlan?" I would have to depart within the week to meet the schedule under discussion.

"Yes." He leavened that admission with a smile. "It's more accurate to say I'm trying to arrange a diversion for the younger members of the household without having to take the time myself to travel south for what amounts to a lark. Mary was thrifty, and she thus would not approve of a come out for Fanny. Fanny lacks the social standing to be presented at court—her father was only nominally a gentleman—and her mother was mindful of that as well."

"For a woman who expired years ago, Fanny's mother yet casts a long shadow over her daughter's life." Not the most gracious thing I could have said, but Mary MacPherson *Leland* should have grasped that London Society would overlook a lack of perfect breeding in any heiress.

That lack of breeding would have been tacitly expected, in fact, because it would mean a husband connected to a distinguished lineage could bring the "more valuable" asset to the union. Such was the arrogance of the upper ten thousand.

"Mary had four babies," Lachlan said. "Two with each husband. Only Fanny, the eldest, survived past infancy. Mary was perhaps too protective of Fanny, with the result that a perfectly lovely young lady has been denied some of the frolics to which she was entitled."

From that perspective, I understood Lachlan's position. By virtue of my station, I was uniquely situated to host Fanny for the remainder of the Season. She was unlikely to have another such opportunity, ever, and Eulalie less likely still. As for Donnie, London hostesses would adore showing him off in his Scottish finery.

"What makes you think Fanny wants to come south with me?" I asked. "She's had rather a difficult time lately."

Lachlan rested an arm along the back of the bench, looking for all the world like the lord of the manor at his ease. English gentlemen did not tend to sprawl like that, and I hadn't seen the tendency in St. Sevier either.

"She won't want to go," Lachlan said. "She'll want to stay here and pine for this mysterious John fellow, who could well be a creation of her own fertile imagination. You probably think me backward, because I don't entertain more, host shooting parties, a hunt ball, or more than the occasional neighborly dinner, but think of Fanny."

"Fanny isn't exactly reclusive," I said. "She's as sociable as the next person, regardless of her love of reading."

"Fanny would be the hostess for each of these events," Lachlan replied. "At every dinner, ball, or hunt breakfast, she'd be the lady of the manor, watching other women on the arms of their husbands and beaus, watching others announce their engagements or await impending births. Of all the young ladies she went to school with, you are the only one with whom she still corresponds."

Because, I surmised, the rest had husbands—and children.

"Have you discussed this with Fanny?" I would resent my family imposing a lot of social obligations on me, but Lachlan's conclusion that Fanny would be pained by the role of hostess depended on assumptions I could not entirely credit.

"I don't have to force the admission from her," he said. "I see how she behaves at the occasional informal supper. I'm spending her money to wine and dine the local gentry, appropriating time she would rather spend with Lord Byron, or distracting her from her dreams of true love with her fickle correspondent. Every dinner we host means several evenings wasted in reciprocal pursuits and more rubbing Fanny's nose in what she doesn't have. Mary would want me to save the coin and leave Fanny in peace."

I folded up my embroidery and returned it to my workbasket. "I admire your loyalty to Mary's memory, Lachlan, but that money is Fanny's now. Rather than importune me to take Fanny south—where she will see nothing but young ladies on the arms of charming swains

—you ought to discuss with her the running of her property. She's intelligent, and she loves this place. I can assure you that death stalks even healthy men in their prime, and Fanny should not assume you will manage Leland House for her indefinitely."

He might have taken offense at that plain speaking, but instead, he offered me another smile, more mischievous and somehow sadder than the perfunctory version he'd shown me earlier.

"Iain has the place in hand," he said. "His family was set to send him off to art school, of all the daft notions. I saw the real potential in him, the love of the land, the ability to do what's needed without fussing. He would not come here without his siblings also being given a home, and so I promised his mama I'd take them all in. Iain isn't quite the expert he believes himself to be, but he's come along, and when I'm gone, he'll do well enough."

And Iain was supposed to content himself with the status of lackey until Lachlan stuck his spoon in the wall some thirty or forty years hence. I wondered what Iain thought of that plan.

"I will make a bargain with you," I said. "You and Iain sit down with Fanny and explain to her every expenditure needed to run this property, along with all the income it generates. Review the current wage books and ledgers with her and encourage her to supervise their maintenance. When you and Iain have completed that task, I will emphatically encourage her and Eulalie to visit me in the south, if not now, then in the autumn, when the Little Season starts up."

Lachlan looked out over the hodgepodge of plants, pots, wheelbarrows, and tools in the conservatory.

"And Donnie?"

"He will be welcome to come south as well."

Lachlan rose and extended a hand to me. I thought he was offering to help me to my feet, but when I gave him my hand, he shook it.

"Iain hasn't the time right now to pore over ledgers and tallies with Fanny, but I can take that on—assuming she's willing to be bored witless for half a day."

I rose and dropped his hand. "Lachlan, who do you think Fanny's correspondent is?"

He picked up my workbasket and started for the conservatory doors. "I have my suspicions, Lady Violet, but I can tell you most sincerely I wish I had not goaded Eulalie into reading Fanny the damned adverts over the teapot."

I laced my arm through his, trying to hide my surprise. "You instigated Eulalie's reading of those advertisements?"

"And may I be consigned to the arctic winter for my folly. Mary and I met, so to speak, because of the advertisements in the Edinburgh newspapers. I was her steward, she was widowed but past first mourning, and I would see her in the garden or out on the terrace reading those advertisements. When she began to make a list, I lost my temper with my employer."

We stopped before the doors that joined the conservatory to the ground floor of Leland House proper.

"This is clearly a fond memory," I said.

"The fondest. I observed to her that she was daft to consider the merits of strangers from Edinburgh when a man who worshipped the tea cups she drank from stood right before her. I was a much bolder fellow in my youth. I marvel at that younger man's arrogance."

He held the door for me.

"You were in love," I said. "This affliction has yet to befall me, though I understand it can compromise all sense. I do believe Fanny is in love with her John."

"You think he exists."

"I know he does." Fanny would not poison herself for the sake of a phantom of her own creation—would she? Donnie had seen the couple cavorting, or so he'd claimed.

"If John does exist, there's something or someone he loves more than he cares for Fanny," Lachlan said, closing the conservatory door. "Why else would he serve her such a cruel turn?"

"Perhaps he had no choice."

We had reached the main corridor of the public part of the house.

The magnificent library was two doors down, the company parlors across from that, the music room adjoined to the parlors. The corridor itself was tastefully appointed with the usual landscapes, pier glasses, and plaid touches I was coming to regard as normal.

Lachlan looked around at all the elegance on display, his expression bleak. "We all have choices, Lady Violet, and I hope Fanny chooses to make a jaunt south with you. God knows she's overdue for a change of air."

He passed me my embroidery basket, bowed, and stalked away.

CHAPTER THIRTEEN

Dinner that evening was subdued, despite excellent fare. Iain said little, and I wondered if his altercation with Lachlan was to blame. But then, Iain was not by nature garrulous—something to like about him. When it came time for the ladies to withdraw, I maneuvered such that Iain was my escort from the dining room.

"I left my workbasket in the music room," I said, a convenient truth. "Might we fetch it?"

"Of course." If he thought it inane that I requisition his escort to trot down the corridor to retrieve my embroidery, he was either too tired or too gentlemanly to remark it.

"I wanted to ask you about something, two things really," I said when he'd requisitioned a lamp from the corridor sconces to bring some light into the music room. "The first is somewhat delicate."

"Out with it, my lady. I'm not much given to delicacy myself."

I did not agree, but men must have their conceits. "Earlier today, Dunkeld and I came across Donnie and Evan having an argument in the garden. They sounded quite wroth with each other."

"They are family of a sort," Iain said, holding the carrying candle up while I peered about the room. "Family will argue."

"They weren't merely bickering, Iain. What does the term *làmh chlì* mean?" My workbasket sat beneath the piano, though I thought I'd left it beside the sofa.

"*Làmh chlì* refers to the left hand, or being left-handed. *Làmh dheas* would refer to the right hand. If they were arguing in the Gaelic, then guests were not meant to overhear."

He was chiding me, which I deserved. "I am concerned that they know something relevant to Fanny's situation. Lachlan is all but harrying me back to England, ostensibly so I can share the blandishments of a London Season with Fanny, Eulalie, and Donnie. I cannot imagine Fanny or Donnie give two figs for the usual Mayfair nonsense, and Eulalie might have reasons for wanting to remain here in Perthshire." A tall, dark-haired, kilted reason. "Something is afoot here, Iain. Something untoward."

In the flickering shadows, he was once again the taciturn, forbidding stranger I'd met on my ramble home from the village.

"I had not taken you for a fanciful creature, Lady Violet. Family members will argue. Lachlan feels Fanny's unhappiness keenly, and I'm sure he's simply looking to divert her from a faithless suitor."

He preceded me into the corridor, giving me the choice of joining him or looking like a fool by remaining in an unlit parlor.

"Why doesn't Lachlan divert Fanny by explaining to her the workings of her own property?" I asked, taking Iain's arm. "I struck a bargain with Lachlan: I will invite Fanny, Eulalie, and Donnie—and you, too, for that matter—to visit me in London, if Lachlan will sit down with Fanny and review Leland House's ledgers and finances with her. I asked that you be included in that meeting, but Lachlan said you were too busy."

Iain set the carrying candle on a sconce. "You are meddling."

"You are not too busy to go over a ledger or two with Fanny, are you?"

He dropped my arm, took me by the wrist, and pulled me into the library. "What did Lachlan tell you?"

"Unhand me, Iain." He hadn't hurt me, but I was reminded that he was a sizable fellow and sometimes short on charm.

He dropped my wrist and paced away to the hearth. A desultory peat fire cast his features in harsh shadows, and I was reminded that he, too, had been arguing with family earlier today.

"I am sorry," he said, "but Lachlan exerts an authority to which he no longer has any claim. I steward this property for Fanny and to keep a roof over the heads of my siblings. Lachlan plays at being lord of the manor, but from a certain perspective, he's our dowager. Mary left him a competence, and he could live comfortably on it anywhere in Scotland, but he chooses to remain here. You are Fanny's guest, and he should not have spoken to you of leaving, much less dragging my siblings south with you."

"Will you review the ledgers with Fanny?" This had become important to me. My aunties had made sure I knew how to manage a household budget, and Freddie had maundered on about his investments often enough that I had a grasp of how to handle my funds.

Fanny was an heiress. Somebody—Lachlan, the family solicitors, her mother's relations—should have explained her finances to her.

Iain sent me a glance, a little haunted, a little annoyed. "Shearing approaches. Let her meet with Lachlan, and then perhaps I'll have a talk with her."

"You think Lachlan will spin her a Banbury tale?" I joined him by the fire because the library was chilly, and I did not want us to be overheard. "'Oh, what a tangled web we weave,' and all that Shakespearean family intrigue?"

"That's not Shakespeare," Iain said, his smile fleeting. "It's Scott, from *Marmion*, and we are hardly on a par with his debauched nuns, scheming lords, and unjustly exiled knights."

"A lonely heiress, a secretive admirer, family squabbles in the gardens and forests, a meddling English lady... Scott might disagree with you."

"You overheard Lachlan and me airing our opinions?"

"Dunkeld and I did. We did not overhear specifics." Because

Sebastian was too much of a gentleman to make a proper job of eavesdropping. Even as a boy, he'd been more of a stickler for etiquette than I was.

"Lachlan and I butt heads regularly," Iain said, pushing away from the mantel. "I'm sorry you came upon us behaving like that, but it's nothing unusual. You came here for a wedding and instead find we excel at bickering."

"You should hear my father and brothers when their tempers flare. Papa dearly loves to have the last word, and the trait breeds true in the male line."

"One doesn't think of the English even raising their voices," Iain said, crossing the library to hold the door for me. "But then, they did somehow manage to sustain war with France for more than a century, embark on more than thirty years of civil war, indulge in a spot of regicide, then more civil war... I suppose one must not mistake English manners for genuine civility."

"You are correct," I said as we approached the family parlor. "I can be very well mannered, but I will not rest until I discover who has played Fanny false, and why."

His expression was bleak in the dim lamplight. "She might be better off not knowing, my lady."

"Men prescribe ignorance as the better course for women when knowledge will leave those same men looking less consequential."

He arched a dark brow at me, more of his dour Scots posturing. "Is that a quote from some radical English philosopher?"

"That's an observation from Lady Violet Belmaine. Would you mind making my excuses to your womenfolk? The day has been fatiguing, and I am ready to seek my bed."

"Sleep well, my lady." He bowed and left me standing in the corridor.

I liked Iain. He put me in mind of Sebastian, with his nimble mind, robust physique, and unexpected humor. I did not envy him the position of de facto under-steward. He had more responsibility than authority, with one foot in the family parlor and one foot in a weed-choked culvert. No wonder he sought the peace and quiet of a shepherd's hut.

I sought the peace and quiet of my bedroom, but was surprised to find St. Sevier already abovestairs and changed into a dressing gown. He reclined on the sofa in our shared sitting room, his feet bare, nothing on under his dressing gown but silk pajama trousers.

"You have retrieved your embroidery," he said, rising. "I concluded you had a hidden reason for dragging young Iain off to the shadows, but my suspicions were in error." He kissed me. "I've been wanting to do that since this morning."

I set aside my workbasket and wrapped my arms around St. Sevier's waist. "How can I miss you when I see you at every meal, sleep with you, and wake with you? And yet, I do."

He draped an arm around my shoulders and guided me not to the sofa, but to his bedroom. "You are unhappy with yourself, because you would rather forget me between sightings. You want me to be like a tea cake. A treat, far from necessary. Pleasant and even luscious, but forgettable. It's fortunate for Frederick Belmaine that he has gone to his dubious reward, else I should have words with him."

"Freddie was a symptom." This was a new insight, one that shifted some blame from Freddie to my general upbringing, and to my father specifically. This insight was a result of seeing how Fanny's family treated her and how she deferred to her step-father regarding wealth and property that belonged to her alone.

"Freddie was what I was supposed to meekly accept and even love. I vexed him exceedingly when I reproached him for being something he could not be." Could not or would not? I would never know.

"Here is what I can be," St. Sevier said, taking my hands. "I can be devoted, faithful, passionate, and patient. What I would like *you* to be is undressed."

"We are in accord." I turned so he could undo my hooks. I was settling into the seductive comfort of an evening routine with St. Sevier. He knew exactly how to ease me out of my clothing and into an amorous mood.

"Were you happy with your wife?" I asked when I was in my dressing gown and slippers, and St. Sevier was brushing my hair.

"We were never happy. In the months of our marriage, we were ecstatic, furious, rapturous, enraged, giddy, sullen... anything and everything but happy. We were also young and stupid. She played games to make me jealous. I pretended indifference to hurt her back. Truly, one ought not to marry until age thirty at least, for the combination of youth and *amour* is ridiculous."

"I am not yet thirty."

"Ah, but you will never allow love to make you ridiculous, *mon coeur.*"

And St. Sevier, having endured a tempestuous union, probably appreciated me in part because I was somewhat reserved and hesitant in my romantic aspirations.

"What happened to her?" I asked.

"A French patrol, or so I am to believe. She left me in the dark of night, and the general conclusion about the camp was that she tried to make her way to the coast in the company of English deserters. Much desertion happened in both directions, depending on which army had the better rations from week to week. Sorting true deserters from spies, double deserters, or brigands was difficult. I do not know where my late spouse is buried, or the specifics of her death, but I keep her in my prayers."

He braided my hair, and I turned to rest my forehead against his hip. "I am sorry for your loss. You are a sweet man. I am coming to care for you more deeply than I am comfortable with."

"Sweet fellow that I am, I rejoice to hear of your discomfort. Come to bed with me, Violet, and I will show you how thoroughly I am coming to care for you too."

He knew better than to speak to me of love, but the word lingered in the air nonetheless.

I straightened and stood. "I did talk to Iain, and he confirmed that he and Lachlan are often acrimonious." My change of subject was so maladroit as to provoke St. Sevier into smiling at me.

"I happened by the herbal yet again on my way upstairs," he said. "I found a whole ledger book kept in Eulalie's hand, and, Violet?"

"Hmm?" I was busy unknotting St. Sevier's dressing gown and running my hand over the silken bulge below his waist.

"Eulalie crosses her sevens."

St. Sevier's amorous skills the previous evening had distracted me from the puzzles in my mind, doubtless the only reason I fell asleep, but I awoke with the certainty that I was missing a pattern, missing the significance of some fact already in evidence.

I also awoke in St. Sevier's arms.

And that, too, deserved some reflection.

I liked sleeping with St. Sevier. I hadn't necessarily enjoyed sleeping in my husband's bed. Freddie and I had had separate bedrooms connected by our dressing closets, but I had developed the habit of sleeping in his bed most of the time, the better to protect my privacy.

Freddie knew, when I took to my own bed, that I was either indisposed or in a temper with him. He did not impose himself on me in those instances, and why should he have? He'd had other sources of erotic gratification besides his tame and boring wife, and—I hoped— he cared for me enough to respect my moods.

The sun was not yet up, though birds were singing outside the window St. Sevier had cracked open the previous night.

"Did you dream of crossed sevens?" he asked, wrapping himself around me spoon-fashion.

What had I dreamed of? A wisp of something... "I dreamed of purple hyacinths, which is odd."

"A spring flower. I haven't seen any in Evan's garden." St. Sevier gathered me against his heat. We slept without clothing, not only because I enjoyed undressing my lover, but also because sleeping skin to skin appealed to me.

I was becoming a wanton widow.

How *lovely.* "I've seen many other purple flowers here," I replied. "Maybe the irises put me in mind of the hyacinths. They are often planted as a progression. When the hyacinths finish, the irises begin."

St. Sevier had a way of squeezing me—my neck, my shoulders, my fundament, my calves—that was unexpectedly pleasurable. His touch was unhurried, and the last thing from an erotic overture, but I adored these caresses from him.

"What do purple hyacinths symbolize?" he asked, gripping my bum quite firmly.

"Regret." And that, for some reason, was significant. Who had expressed regret over Fanny's situation?

Not Donnie.

Not Evan.

Not Eulalie, though I'd entertained the notion that Eulalie had been Fanny's correspondent. Two girls at school had been some variety of smitten with each other, and more than once, I'd heard bedroom doors opening and closing late at night in the dormitory wing. One didn't speak of those things, or so I'd believed, until Freddie had told me entire brothels existed to cater to such inclinations.

But then, Eulalie apparently had a swain.

"Lachlan regrets Fanny's situation," I said. "That's part of the reason he's so keen to send her to London. He must feel that he's failed her, or failed her mother's memory."

St. Sevier paused to untangle my braid from the pillows. "How could he be failing her? The estate thrives, she has family about, she's well regarded by the neighbors, and Iain appears ready to take over should anything happen to Lachlan."

"Why is it," I said, sitting up, the better to organize my thoughts, "I've never seen but the one head gardener in the walled garden or anywhere else on the estate?"

"The walled garden is private." St. Sevier replied, heaving a sigh and pillowing his head in my lap. "It makes sense to me that a head gardener would maintain it, particularly if Evan is family."

St. Sevier would not press and tease and wheedle until I consented to an interlude. He would instead find a dozen ways to casually touch me throughout the morning, drop any number of subtle hints into our conversations, and make me regret not starting the day with an amatory frolic.

And I would treasure him for his tactics and lavishly reward his patience—later. Some obvious-in-hindsight realization was beating at the windows of my mind like a starling inadvertently trapped in a glass house.

"The conservatory is a mess," I muttered, stroking Hugh's silky hair. "I know spring is a busy time, but it's as if everything is stashed in there all willy-nilly."

"We aren't all as compulsively tidy as the English," St Sevier replied.

"You are." I winnowed my fingers through his hair, which was growing a trifle long. "You are quite tidy."

"My staff is tidy. I am well groomed, though I love it when you disarrange me."

"I will disarrange you again soon," I said, "but at the moment, I feel as if Lachlan is herding me toward the door just as I'm about to find all the answers Fanny needs."

St. Sevier took my hand and kissed my fingers. "Almost as if Lachlan has something to hide—perhaps an untoward interest in his step-daughter?"

"For Fanny's sake, I hope not. Donnie suspects Lachlan has a special friend in Perth. That is hardly a matter to be hidden. Discretion is in order, surely, but not subterfuge. Fanny would not order Lachlan from the property at gunpoint because he indulges in such a liaison."

"Lachlan might be ashamed of that arrangement, or think his family would tacitly censure him for it."

"Donnie clearly doesn't." I scooted out from under St. Sevier and climbed off the bed. "Fanny became lovers with her intended. I cannot see Lachlan involving himself with his step-daughter in so distasteful a manner." But then, why keep the meetings so clandestine?

St. Sevier shifted to sit on the edge of the bed. He was tousled, rumpled, naked, and delectable—also somewhat in a state of readiness for procreation—but what drew me to him more than his great masculine pulchritude was the way he smiled at me. Another man would have been annoyed at my mental peregrinations. St. Sevier was amused and admiring. He stood and held my dressing gown for me.

"If Lachlan had never married Fanny's mother," he said, "an attraction between him and Fanny would be unremarkable. He's not that much older than she, he loves this property, he knows her family, and he cares for her."

I leaned into St. Sevier, loving his scent and warmth. He was well-groomed, even fastidious, and also a glorious sight in the altogether.

"But Lachlan *was* married to Fanny's mother," I said, "and if anything, Fanny's attitude toward him was one of resentment. She never called him 'my step-father' at school. He was always 'my mother's husband,' or even 'my mother's current husband.'"

And Lachlan had twice put forth the theory that Fanny had written the letters to herself. Who did Lachlan protect with that theory, besides, possibly, himself?

"Let's have our tea on the balcony, shall we?" St. Sevier said, stepping back. "I'll join you out there in a moment."

He yawned, scratched, and otherwise made a production out of shrugging into his dressing gown, but I suspected he would use that moment to deal with his animal urges.

"Tea can wait five minutes," I said, unbelting the dressing gown I'd just put on and climbing back onto the bed.

St. Sevier looked down at his masculine splendor, his expression aggrieved. "Five minutes, Violet? *Five minutes.*"

"Ten?" I countered.

The tea was cold by the time we drank it, and neither one of us minded that a bit.

The letters seduced me into spending my morning in the library. I read them all, start to finish, putting both Fanny's and John's epistles in the order in which they would have been written. I peered at John's handwriting through a quizzing glass, comparing his consonants and vowels to those penned by Lachlan, Donnie, Evan, and Eulalie.

The similarities were a testament to ubiquitous education in standard schoolroom copperplate penmanship. The differences were slight and many, and nobody's hand was absolutely consistent with itself, though John's came close.

Toward the end of the previous year, John had begun crossing his sevens. No other shift in the penmanship was as marked or consistent. In one letter, he'd been nattering on about a recently published young poet named Keats—born in 1795, seven uncrossed—and in the next, Dante's Seventh Circle of Hell—styled 7th by John and crossed —was populated exclusively with English generals, owing to their prowess with violence off the battlefield.

His dates reflected the same shift. Once he started crossing sevens, he did not uncross them until the final letter in which he'd cried off—dated, fortuitously enough, April 17. I set aside the last six months of letters and read them again, though this time I noticed other differences.

A warmer tone had crept into the language—*my dear, my dearest, most esteemed lady*. The closings shifted from *I remain, your most obedient servant* to *yours, eternally* and *ever thine*.

Thine. I did not know whether to be amused, appalled, or envious. It was as if Fanny's suitor had emerged from some cocoon of gentlemanly restraint into the tenderheartedness of a truly smitten swain six months ago. He'd then proposed, been accepted, consummated the union—and scarpered.

Or been chased off. Why?

"St. Sevier said I'd find you here." Sebastian strode into the library. He wore riding attire, which disappointed me slightly. I did so fancy the sight of him in his kilt.

"My lord." I rose and curtseyed. "A pleasure to see you. Shall I ring for a tray?"

"No tray. I cannot tarry, but I wanted you to see this." He withdrew a folded piece of paper from his pocket. "Iain's handwriting, listing his estimates of the crews needed from each landowner for washing and shearing."

Sevens, sevens, please let there be... I unfolded the paper and was greeted with abundant examples of every numeral. Eight men from that farm, six or seven from the other. A dozen from Dunkeld, provided seven of those were talented shearers, and five adept at handling the pens and the washing.

And Iain most definitely crossed each and every seven.

I sank into my seat at the reading table. "Could Fanny have had two admirers?"

"She could have had twenty." Sebastian propped a hip on the corner of the table. "Why?"

"'Why?' is the question that plagues me the most." I peered around at the kilted laddies and bonnie lassies on the walls, abruptly homesick for the cabbage roses suffusing my personal parlor in London. "Do you ever tire of plaid?"

"Yes. But tartan cloth is attractive and lightweight for how much warmth it yields. Even wet, wool will keep the wearer warm. God knows the damned stuff never wears out either, and if we can grow one crop in any and every corner of Scotland, it's sheep."

"Wool is cheap in Scotland?"

Sebastian humored me, despite whatever hurry he was in, and took the chair opposite mine at the table. "In England, you can grow the breeds that generate the best-quality wool—the Spanish merinos do well in England, for example. Until the last century, few breeds were hardy enough to thrive through Scottish Highland winters, but that changed. We now have breeds that could likely teach reindeer a thing or two about survival, but the wool is coarse, mostly fit for carpets."

"And that kind of wool isn't very lucrative?"

Sebastian crossed an ankle over a knee. "Violet, what badger hole are you digging at?"

"I have been troubled primarily by one question: Why would a man who writes letters like these,"—I brandished John's recent epistles—"inveigle Fanny into sharing her favors and then cry off? The words and the actions are inconsistent. The man who wrote these letters is in love, Sebastian. He's smitten, arse over teakettle. I suspect he never planned for that to happen, but it did, and he proposed in good faith."

"What has wool to do with this?"

"Not wool, but maybe wool money. Can you join us for dinner?" I wanted Sebastian on hand when I aired my theories, not only because he was my friend, but also because he was the ranking title in the shire. If he wasn't the justice of the peace at the moment, he was as good as.

"My evening is spoken for. Aunt Hibernia wanted you to have this." He passed over John's handkerchief, and I realized I had the last clue I needed to test my theory.

"When can you spare me an hour?" I asked. "The family will behave better if you're on hand when I reveal the truth of Fanny's situation."

"You are in possession of the truth now?"

I studied the handkerchief, my fingers itching to get to work on it. "I soon will be. I'd like Evan to be present as well."

Sebastian's gaze took in the letters stacked neatly on the table, the portraits beaming plaid good cheer on all and sundry, and my apparently grim expression.

"You've figured out that part too, Violet?"

"I believe I have, though not all of the whys. I have enough of them to start a very lively discussion."

He muttered something in the local tongue. "I will regret this, but I will be free this afternoon. I intended to confer with Iain about his list. We can start the sheep washing earlier if we use a pond on my land rather than the river. Name a time."

"Come by at three. You're off to have lunch with your factor again?"

"With some god-daughter-at-six-removes Aunt Bernie has unearthed." He stood, glowered at the couple whose portrait hung over the mantel. "Auntie is determined to see me wed to a bonnie Scottish lady, and this one just happened to be traveling through the shire with her parents."

"Wear your kilt," I said, rising. "She'll propose to you before the second bottle of wine has been opened."

"That's what I'm afraid of. She's doubtless a lovely person, but, Violet, she's seventeen. She has never met me before, but she would have kissed my hoary old uncle on the location of his choice to become his marchioness."

I took Sebastian by his broad and muscular shoulders. *"Don't settle.* Don't capitulate because her papa thinks to dangle a water meadow before your handsome eyes. Don't give in to the family's expectations while telling yourself it won't be so bad. For her and for you, it will not be so good, Sebastian, and you deserve better than that."

He took my hand and clasped it between his two larger, callused palms. "I sometimes want it to be over, the choosing and rejecting, the speculation. Tell me again not to settle."

I grabbed him by the hair at his nape and shook. *"Do not settle.* Marry in haste and regret it for the rest of your days and nights, Sebastian. You'll watch that regret affect your children and even your grandchildren. Better the title go to a cousin than you make yourself and your marchioness quietly miserable in the name of duty."

He smiled, bowed over my hand, and made for the door. "Thank you for the excellent advice. I will not wear my kilt at lunch, and I will tell Uncle Archie that our guests love a good story."

He blew me a kiss, and then I was once more alone with the letters. I locked them into a desk drawer, took up the handkerchief, and repaired to the sitting room I shared with St. Sevier. Once there, I located my workbasket and took it and the handkerchief out to the balcony, where the light would be ample.

The work was slow, but because I knew what pattern I expected to emerge, I made progress. By the time the lunch bell sounded, I had restored the monogram to its original state and thus was nearly certain of the identity of the man Fanny had met in the stable.

That did not mean, however, that I had revealed the identity of the letters' initial author.

CHAPTER FOURTEEN

I had quietly asked Fanny and Eulalie at lunch to make themselves available to me at three in the family parlor. Donnie received a similar discreet invitation from St. Sevier, as did—separately—Lachlan and Evan.

The difficult case was Iain, who on a fine Scottish afternoon had a dozen tasks to be about on the estate. I told him Fanny had some questions for him about the property and its running, and he agreed to meet with her at the appointed time and place.

Donnie and Evan arrived together, both looking uncomfortable.

Sebastian arrived on the dot of three, looking somewhat harried, but he winked at me as he made his bow, and I breathed a sigh of relief. The Dunkeld laird had not settled—not yet.

Lachlan was the last to join us, and he stopped short on the threshold. "And what are we about?" he asked, surveying the assemblage. "Has some portentous news arrived?"

"In a way," I replied, "yes. If you'd please have a seat."

He ambled over to the windows that overlooked the garden. "I'll stand."

Evan had also declined to take a seat, which in his case was more understandable. Family he might be, of a sort, but he was also the head gardener—perhaps the only gardener. Sebastian stood as well, propping an elbow on the mantel and looking utterly bored.

St. Sevier had taken one wing chair and Iain the other, while Fanny and Eulalie occupied a love seat.

"Lady Violet," Sebastian said, "I believe you have the floor."

Now that the moment was upon me, I hesitated. I had no reason to believe anybody had acted out of ill will, no reason to accuse anybody of a crime. But bad decisions had been made and trust betrayed nonetheless.

"I came to Scotland," I said, "intent on sharing in my friend Fanny MacPherson's nuptial joy. I still hope to have that honor. This is my first trip to Scotland, so when Monsieur St. Sevier and I—who are neither related nor married nor engaged—were given a family suite for our accommodations, I thought that was simply Scottish hospitality, and the rooms are lovely."

"You are quite welcome to them," Lachlan said, "but I will not be lectured to in my own home. If the company will excuse me—"

Sebastian shifted to stand before him. "Lady Violet asked you here for reasons, Leland. Do stay."

The tone was polite, the expression dead calm.

"Be quick about whatever you have to say," Lachlan retorted. "Some of us have other places to be."

Iain, I noted, who had a dozen other places to be, was not chafing as Lachlan was, and Donnie and Evan were exchanging glances at a great rate—and not guilty glances either.

"Leland House is struggling," I said. "What I first took for examples of Scottish thrift—a closed-off and nearly empty guest wing, a reticence to permit the ladies much in the way of shopping, a single overworked gardener whose efforts are mostly limited to one walled space—are instead evidence of finances in bad repair."

Eulalie took Fanny's hand. "I knew it. I knew we were rolled up. Lachlan Leland, you have much to answer for."

Iain glowered at her. "Leave him alone. Since the war ended, everybody's struggling, and matters here were not exactly well run by the previous laird. He married money, but he never had the knack of making money. Lachlan has given us a home and a place to be a family."

"But that's not all Lachlan has done," I countered. "He enticed Fanny into correspondence with a man who did not exist. He wrote an advertisement as if penned by Fanny's ideal suitor, and he maintained the correspondence over a period of many months."

Fanny looked sick. "Lachlan? Lachlan wrote all those letters?"

She was doubtless thinking Lachlan had met her in the stable, too, which was not the case. "He did not write all of them, Fanny. He stopped sometime last year, when I suspect Iain caught him either mailing letters to you or drafting them."

"Both," Iain said. "I found the discarded drafts in the estate-office dustbin, but I did not want to believe Lachlan had written them. I thought perhaps Donnie would undertake such a subterfuge. He had the time, and based on what I'd found, the correspondence had been mostly philosophical and literary. Anybody with access to a decent library and the current newspapers could have written those letters. Then I caught Lachlan retrieving mail from a flower girl in Perth. On another occasion, he'd passed two missives and a coin to a boy hanging about the stable at the posting inn."

Fanny looked ready to cry. "But why? Why lie to me like that? Why pretend an affection that isn't real?"

The affection was real. I was betting my friendship with Fanny on it. "Lachlan did not want you to marry," I said. "The settlement negotiations would have revealed the state of your finances, which I suspect are not in robust good health."

The entire room looked to Lachlan. I watched as he sorted and discarded options. Defiance, indignation, cajolery... To his credit, he chose the truth.

"Your mother's illness meant her solicitors were not as well managed as they should have been. They would not deal with me, and during her lifetime, her trusts did not contemplate my involvement. Her fortune was substantial when she died, but my ability to manage so much money for you was wanting. By the time I realized the solicitors had turned from bleeding the coffers to outright pillage, the fortune was further reduced."

Fanny had dropped Eulalie's hand. "Is there any fortune at all, Lachlan?"

He gazed across the parlor at nothing in particular, looking abruptly aged. "Yes, but not the sum your mother bequeathed to you. Barely half that, in fact, and I was determined... That is... I sought..." He muttered something in Gaelic.

"You thought to buy yourself time to replenish Fanny's fortune," I said, "from which you had borrowed liberally and without permission. You distracted Fanny with an imaginary suitor. A clever strategy, but something went badly awry."

"Everything went badly awry," Lachlan replied. "From flooding to foot rot. The army was the biggest consumer of wool, and with the Corsican buttoned up, the market has crumbled. Every country with a blade of grass is now raising its own sheep, from the Americas to the Antipodes, and they raise a finer grade of wool than we can manage here at Leland House."

"So you tricked me into a correspondence based on a romantic premise?" Fanny asked. "You manipulated me and lied to me, abused my trust and my funds?"

Lachlan's gaze pleaded for understanding. "I wrote to you of books, Fanny. Your mother loved books. You and I shared opinions about politics, as your mother and I often discussed politics. Nothing in my letters to you encouraged any sharing of intimate sentiments, and I vowed that should you demand to meet John S. MacDonald, I would break it off. I never meant to hurt you, only to amuse you for a time until matters could be sorted out."

Fanny rose and crossed the parlor, and I knew her objective as if it had sprung from my own mind. She slapped Lachlan hard across the cheek, then backhanded him as well. Her blows left his cheeks bright red, though he looked, if anything, relieved.

"You betrayed me," she said. "You betrayed my mother's trust in you. I don't care about the money, Lachlan. I care about the lies. You did not break it off, not at all."

"He did," I said, "but somebody else took up the pen in his stead. Iain, what have you to say for yourself?"

I passed him the handkerchief, from which I'd picked free the extra stitching that had turned a capital *I* into a flourishy *J*.

Fanny rounded on him. "Iain? *You?*"

He rose, a braw, bonnie laddie at a complete loss. "Yes. Me. An under-steward with no prospects, save hard work and more hard work, but I was working for *you*, Fanny, and I was happy."

They stared at each other, and I sensed Fanny was comparing Iain, in his work boots and plain black kilt, with the dashing swain she'd met in the stable.

"I do not understand," she said, subsiding back onto the sofa. "I don't understand anything."

"Neither do I," Eulalie said, "and it's not my fortune that was stolen."

"Not stolen," Lachlan said. "Borrowed, and borrowed in good cause. Ask Dunkeld. The markets have been awful, the weather disobliging, and nobody is thriving. I've made every possible economy, sold off some of the treasures Mary so loved, pared the staff down to old retainers, to the extent I could. It hasn't been enough, but I've reason to hope I can yet turn the business around."

"We'll get to the money later," I said. "Iain owes Fanny and his family an explanation."

"I confronted Lachlan," Iain said. "I told him if he sent Fanny one more letter, I'd start asking questions at the bank. I see the ledgers and wage books. I know what the price of wool has been lately. I had my suspicions about how Leland House was making up the shortfall."

Fanny plucked at the tassels of a pillow embroidered with what I knew to be an offer in Gaelic of ten thousand welcomes.

"I am listening, Iain," she said.

"I took up the correspondence," Iain said softly. "Last year. I never meant to do anything other than maintain the exchange Lachlan had started, to give you a private joy, but then... Your mother married her steward, and I have long esteemed you. Writing to you was so easy. I could share everything—the frustrations, fears, hopes, my whole heart. I could not stop."

Fanny was looking at him as if unsure who he was. "Then I asked you to meet me."

Donnie, Evan, and Eulalie were clearly fascinated with this convoluted tale, while St. Sevier was trying to look politely inter-ested, and Sebastian was studying his watch.

"Did you alter the embroidery on your handkerchief?" I asked Iain. "The stitchery was very well done."

He nodded. "I wanted Fanny to have something of mine. Some-thing real. If I'd given her a sketch, she might have suspected my true identity. I sketched the embroidery out first, then used needle and thread to alter the monogram."

"So much for art school," Eulalie muttered.

"Just because a man can sketch or paint doesn't mean he wants to go to art school," Iain retorted. "I met Fanny when she was on holiday from school, and when Lachlan offered me the post here, I was over-joyed to take it. I thought eventually, perhaps in time, if Fanny devel-oped no other attachments, I might be more than a distant family connection and employee to her."

I thought again about tangled webs and how quickly Iain had corrected me regarding Shakespeare, Burns, and Scott.

I thought of the surprisingly soft texture of his hair when I'd brushed the grass and dust from it at the culvert.

Of how easily I'd overlooked that the name Iain was one of many cognates for John.

No one fact or observation had declared Iain to be Fanny's suitor, but his expression now confirmed his regard for her.

"So what happened?" Eulalie asked. "You became Fanny's secret admirer, and she accepted your proposal, but you aren't John MacDonald."

"The name is not mine," Iain said, "but the sentiments John MacDonald has penned over the last eight months are straight from my heart. I have overstepped and mis-stepped, but my heart has remained Fanny's and always will."

"A nice speech," Donnie observed, "but Fan isn't looking very impressed."

"You broke it off," Fanny said. "You broke it off after... proposing to me, Iain. You say you care for me, but you broke it off."

Lachlan spoke up. "I did that. I at first did not realize that Iain had resumed the correspondence I'd dropped. When I found out, matters between you and him had progressed to the untenable posture of an engagement. I sent that last letter and told Iain I would take certain steps if he interfered again."

Evan strode across the room to within three steps of Lachlan. "Take the damned steps," Evan said, his voice flat with disgust. "Sack me, sack Iain, send Donnie away. We'll manage. I do the work of three men for the wages of a boy because I consider Leland House my home, but I've yet contrived to put a bit by. I know my trade, Donnie has a gentleman's education, Iain would be an asset to any estate. We'll manage."

Gone was the agreeable gardener. In his place was a family member at the end of his patience. Clearly, Lachlan had threatened to banish Evan—at least—if Iain refused to cry off.

"You were waiting for Donnie in the garden," I said slowly. "You had no idea that Fanny and Iain were occasionally trysting, and you and Donnie took up the same signals..."

Lovers had doubtless been pitching pebbles at windows since the invention of glass, but I truly had not foreseen that Donnie and Evan were entangled.

"Lachlan threatened to have Evan arrested for theft," Iain said. "I didn't think he'd do it, because we're family of a sort, and everybody knows Evan would never steal from his own. Still, I could not trust Lachlan. I would never have forgiven myself if I'd caused Evan, who has worked tirelessly for years, to be banished. I told myself I could resume my letters to Fanny when matters had settled down, concoct some excuse, repair the damage..."

"Why not simply tell me the truth?" Fanny asked. "Why not simply tell me that my fortune is half gone—a fortune I never wanted —and that I've attracted the notice of a family connection? Why all this drama and deception?"

Lachlan spoke first. "I never felt good enough for Mary, and I was determined to do right by her daughter. The first time I borrowed from the trust, I told myself it would be the only time, the last time, and quickly repaid. We're years past that promise, and I haven't repaid it. I was never much of a step-father to you, Fanny, but I thought I could remedy that as trustee of your funds. I was trying to safeguard your legacy, but my real motivation was simply pride. For what it's worth, I am sorry."

I understood why Mary Leland had fallen for her steward. Lachlan was a good man, though he'd made bad decisions.

"I understand what it is to feel you don't fit in," Fanny said, "to feel you are inhabiting a role you never chose. That is exactly what I endured at that idiot school to which Mama consigned me. I was always watching from the corner of my eye to monitor others' reactions to me, always afraid of speaking too loudly, or too boldly, or too seriously—too much like a Scot. I don't care about the money, Lachlan. Being the MacPherson heiress has been nothing but a blasted lot of bother."

St. Sevier had the courage to pose the question I could not. "What of being John MacDonald's fiancé?" he said. "Nothing but bother there too?"

He'd injected just the right balance of insouciance and curiosity into his query, though the moment was far from light.

Iain rose, crossed the parlor, and sank to one knee before Fanny. "I am sorry. I am abjectly, deeply sorry. I should never have lied to you, but I thought if you could see me as somebody other than the grouchy fellow Lachlan dragged up from Edinburgh to wrangle a lot of stinking sheep, you might like me a little."

He took her hand, and I must confess, the picture they made, with Fanny hanging on his every word, Iain on bended knee, and emotions of every stripe at springtide, moved me. However misguided and convoluted the path, Iain and Fanny had arrived to a profoundly romantic moment.

She touched his hair, then drew a finger along his eyebrow. "You are not grouchy, you are often tired and frustrated. You told me that. I am frustrated, too, to be of no use to anybody, to be idle, to be an ornament with a fortune attached. I told you that."

Iain bowed his head over her hand. "And I said to you, without your fortune, you are yet my treasure. I meant that, Fanny. I truly, truly... Please don't send me away. I'll go if you insist, but all I ask is that you not..."

St. Sevier was smiling slightly, while Sebastian scowled at the carpet. Evan had speared Donnie with a look, and Eulalie was agog. Lachlan, I surmised, saw a younger version of himself in Iain, a supplicant for the hand of the fair maid.

"Leave us, please," Fanny said. "Iain and I have matters to discuss in private."

I surmised the discussion would happen after a deal of kissing and a few passionate declarations—a few *more* passionate declarations. Sebastian all but bolted for the door, though St. Sevier paused long enough to whisper in my ear.

"Well done, my lady. I have suspected you harbor the heart of a romantic."

"Don't be ridiculous."

He kissed my cheek, the blighter, then escorted me from the room.

When I closed the parlor door behind me, Iain had shifted to sit beside Fanny, their hands still linked, their heads close together. His posture struck me as protective as well as penitent, and I hoped for both their sakes that Fanny could accept his apologies.

The lot of us filed out into the corridor, milling about until Sebastian spoke up.

"To the library," he said, "where we will all partake of a medicinal dram—or three."

Sebastian and St. Sevier played hosts, with Sebastian pouring drinks and St. Sevier handing them out. The whisky—the smoothest I'd ever encountered—did have a restorative effect on my humors.

"I'm puzzled about something," I said, taking my drink to a window seat.

"I'm nigh barmy," Donnie said. "My family is a lot of slyboots."

"You are a slyboots too," I countered. "You were not sending out inquiries at the posting inn, Donnie. You would no more leave Leland House voluntarily than you would burn down Evan's garden. I see that now. What were you about?"

"Tell her," Evan said. "She'll just nose about at the posting inn and figure it out for herself."

"Thank you," I replied, lifting my glass in Evan's direction. "I plan to do just that."

Donnie smiled and saluted me in return. "I was peddling the whisky. We have barrels and barrels of it, from when Mary's father was alive. She thought our water of life had medicinal properties and accounted the whisky as the reason her father and grandfather lived to great old age. I have talked the posting inn into both serving and selling our whisky, thus making us a bit of coin."

Sebastian took another sip of his drink. "Do you have plans to sell it elsewhere? Archie favors your aged whisky, and he considers himself an unparalleled connoisseur of the grape and the grain. He calls it storytelling whisky."

"Donnie has plans," Evan said when Donnie remained silent. "The posting inn is just the start, a place to begin getting the word out. The larger posting inns—Stirling, Perth, Edinburgh—come next, then down the Great North Road. Leland House whisky is finer than anything else on the market, suitable for sipping, suitable even for discriminating ladies. If we could get a few cases to the better gentle-men's clubs in London..."

Clubs such as a Scottish marquess might frequent... "I would be happy to serve this to my guests in London," I said, not that I had many guests.

St. Sevier took the place beside me. "I lack Uncle Archie's discriminating palate, but I find this whisky quite enjoyable as well. I have family in Paris. I will send them a case as a souvenir of my Scot-tish travels, if you are willing to part with a few bottles?"

"You'll pay for them," Sebastian said. "I won't have my neighbors giving away a quantity of fine libation to any old passing Frenchman trying to impress his relatives."

Evan sent Donnie an I-told-you-so look tinged with humor and something else, something hopeful and private that I wasn't meant to notice.

Though I did. I also noticed Eulalie's wistful expression and knew that she, at least, would never censure Donnie and Evan for a love much of society would view askance.

"I keep telling you," Lachlan said, "the best whisky in the world won't sell itself. You will need money to get your product to the market, to make proper labels and buy fancy bottles. You will need somebody to keep account of the places selling your goods, to make sure they don't water it or change the label to a competitor's. You can't just pass around a few flasks and expect a fortune to result."

Eulalie peered at him over the rim of her glass. "You are jealous because Donnie thought this up and has put wheels in motion, while you remain stuck in the past worshipping at the grave of a woman who would neither respect nor encourage your unnatural grief."

Sebastian's brows rose. St. Sevier had found some fascinating prophecy to study in the bottom of his whisky glass.

"Lachlan makes good points," Evan said. "He simply makes them as if they are a reason to give up, rather than a reason to go carefully. We will start small—we have already started small—and the results have been encouraging."

Lachlan went to the window and spoke with his back to the room. "I don't worship at Mary's grave, but I do respect her memory. She married me—her steward—and told all of society to go to blazes. She was not given a long life, but what life she had she lived bravely. I felt I owed it to Fanny to stay on here and try to put the place on sound footing. I failed Fanny and Leland House, and I'm sorry."

Eulalie took the place at his side. "You took us in when you brought Iain here. I'm grateful for that, Lachlan. Had you not, I might never have met Septimus."

He scowled at her. "MacFarlane?"

The gamekeeper was tall, dark-haired, and Scottish, and Eulalie had claimed to be out fishing the day I'd seen her with her swain.

"I'm having his baby," Eulalie said, "which might explain why the whisky isn't sitting as easily as usual."

And explained why compromising herself with a wealthy French physician might have figured in her plans. Ye gods, this family was full of schemes.

"You will want to avoid strong spirits and strictly limit your wine and ale too," St. Sevier said. "The midwives will tell you that drinking ale every day will result in a smaller baby and thus an easier birth, but you must ignore that advice. The nature of a lady's travail depends on several factors besides the size of the child, and an infant stunted by the mother's—"

"St. Sevier," I murmured quietly. "Later."

Donnie was on his feet. "You are having MacFarlane's baby, Eulie? You aren't saying that merely to shock us?"

"Are you shocked?" she asked, sounding hopeful.

"I am," Lachlan said. "I thought I was the only family member who'd stoop to subterfuge and scheming, and I find Donnie is selling whisky, Iain has compromised my step-daughter, and now you take up with the gamekeeper."

"So maybe it's time you start walking out with that widow in Perth," Donnie muttered. "Eulalie, tell us the truth. What are you and MacFarlane about?"

She looked down at her still-flat tummy. "About two months along? Fanny confided to me earlier this year that John had proposed. I realized that if she married, I would have no place at Leland House other than as a poor relation. I groused about this to MacFarlane, and as it turns out, I do have a place—at his side."

And in his bed, apparently.

Lachlan watched her, his expression hard to read. "You're sure?"

Eulalie's chin came up. "I will raise his babies in the gamekeeper's cottage, learn to roast partridges and boil porridge, and make him the best wife I can. Septimus loves his job, and he loves me. He feared he'd lose his post if we began walking out, and I could not promise him he wouldn't."

"So you conceived a child instead," Lachlan said, "giving your family the choice of consigning you to ruin or teaching you how to boil oats." He was quiet for a moment, studying the garden Mary had designed and treasured. "Mary would approve. If it means anything, you have my blessing. You, too, Donnie. Tell me what I can do to assist with the whisky—and whatever else—and I'll do it, assuming Fanny doesn't have me arrested."

Whatever else must surely encompass Evan's role in the family.

"Fanny won't turn you over to the law," I said. "She's loyal, though she might appreciate your removing to Perth in the foreseeable future. You will have to explain to her the financial workings here—to her and to Iain, to the extent he doesn't already grasp them—and the situation will want patience." Perhaps years and years of patience, which was the nature of families.

"When you make that explanation," Sebastian said, "you might point out that to have preserved half her fortune was probably greater success than most landed families have seen in recent years. We all hated the Corsican, but we are learning that he had his uses in terms of thriving markets and profitable prices."

The war had made many fortunes, and peacetime had ruined many more. That much was true. That Sebastian—who'd seen the human cost of those thriving markets and profits—would offer this observation was a great kindness.

I was about to ask Sebastian for a turn in the garden, the better to encourage him to invest in Donnie's whisky venture, when Fanny and Iain joined us in the library.

"We have an announcement," Fanny said, turning an adoring gaze on Iain.

His expression was no less besotted. "Fanny has agreed to become my wife, and we would like to invite you all to attend the ceremony."

"Felicitations," Lachlan said, adding some toast or other in the Highland language. "Donnie, a wee dram for the happy couple, and I see that Evan's glass has somehow also grown empty."

Eulalie shouldered her way to Fanny's side, hugging her and laughing. Donnie slapped Iain's back, and I felt at once a part of the family's joy and removed from it.

St. Sevier slipped an arm around my waist. "You made this possible with your meddling English ways. I hope you are pleased with yourself."

I was pleased with Fanny and Iain, with Donnie and Evan, and even with Eulalie and her lusty gamekeeper. I was pleased that Lachlan also seemed to have a way forward, if the lady in Perth held his genuine regard, and I was very pleased not to have to return to England so soon after arriving in Scotland.

I was also aware of the temptation to take St. Sevier by the hand and drag him to our private suite, where I would give him permission to announce yet one more engagement. We could be married in Scotland, where the laws were much kinder to engaged couples, and take a long wedding journey through the Scottish countryside as summer approached.

I allowed myself to consider that fantasy for a moment, to enjoy it even, but I also saw Sebastian across the library, sipping his drink, and pretending to ignore St. Sevier's arm about my waist.

Don't settle. I looked at Sebastian, and the words simply popped into my head. *Don't settle.*

My liaison with St. Sevier was in its infancy, and we were enjoying a fairy-tale idyll in rural Perthshire. I had no idea how our dealings would change once time, daily life in England, and family considerations came to bear on us. I had no idea who St. Sevier's relations were, where they lived, or how he got on with them, and my family had hardly made a good first impression on St. Sevier.

No impromptu announcements, then, not from me.

Not yet.

But perhaps one day in the not-too-distant future.

And perhaps not.

But that is a tale best told on another day.

TO MY DEAR READERS

There's much to be said for that fresh Scottish air! I had the best fun ever writing this tale, putting Violet and St. Sevier among the kilted laddies and bonnie lassies, and the beautiful scenery of central Scotland. Lordy, I'm homesick for Scotland myself, and no matter how much shortbread I dunk in my single malt, it's just not the same as being there. Maybe soon...

Until then, we can accompany Violet and St. Sevier south, to gorgeous landscapes and domestic intrigues in the Lake District. An excerpt from Book Four, ***Lady Violet Enjoys a Frolic*** is included below. I've published the first six Lady Violet mysteries all at once (December release in the webstore, February at the major retailers, and you can read about the other stories on my web site's ***Lady Violet series page***. I expect to add to the series soon, probably a trilogy because six more books would take a while to publish.

If you'd like to stay up to date on all my releases, discounts, and pre-orders, following me on **Bookbub** is probably the easiest way to do that. I also have a **Deals** page on my website, which I update about monthly, and that lists any sales, early releases, or freebie, especially those happening on the **web store**. If you're inclined toward

newsletters, I publish one about every month or so, and I promise that unsubscribing is easy, and I will never sell, spam, or swap your addie.

However you prefer to keep in touch, I wish you always...

Happy reading!
Grace Burrowes

Read on for an excerpt from ***Lady Violet Enjoys a Frolic***!

LADY VIOLET ENJOYS A FROLIC— EXCERPT

Lady Violet, escorted by the estimable Hugh St. Sevier, has journeyed from Scotland to the Lake District where she and Hugh are visiting some of his old army comrades.

Had anybody told me that my host, Damien, Lord Rutland, had charm to eclipse even the vast stores St. Sevier claimed, I would not have believed them. His lordship was no boy, his blue eyes having crow's feet, his countenance being a trifle weathered. His physique was trim and muscular, though he lacked a few inches of St. Sevier's height, and the barest thread of silver graced his temples.

His smile was nonetheless the warmest, friendliest, merriest specimen I had encountered in many a year. Faint echoes of my late husband's insouciance echoed in that smile, as did the ability to create an instant conspiracy of two against all the world's seriousness and woe.

"Lady Violet will want a tour of the gardens, I hope," his lordship said, tucking my hand over his arm and escorting me up the two dozen terraced steps leading to a wide front portico. "You may rest your weary bones, St. Sevier, for I intend to take her ladyship captive."

St. Sevier merely cocked his head, silently asking me if I was willing to *be* captured.

How well he knew me, already. "St. Sevier will find his way to your library, my lord, and plunder all of your botanical pamphlets and medical treatises. I will accompany you on a tour of the garden, the better to abet your truancy from correspondence, ledgers, and other duties." Also to *move* after hours of drowsing in the coach.

"You have found me out," his lordship said, patting my knuckles. "I do adore a discerning woman."

He ushered us into the house, though *house* was too modest a term for the vast edifice his lordship called home. Our steps echoed in a soaring circular foyer, and afternoon light poured in through tall windows and a central skylight. White marble floors, alabaster statuary, and portraits in gilt frames all added to a sense of grandeur.

Having grown up in a rambling country house, all I could think was that in winter, the foyer would be an icehouse, and white floors showed every speck of dirt.

We commended St. Sevier into the keeping of a pretty, mob-capped housekeeper whose smile was genuinely cheerful. Perhaps the crisp northern air made the locals happy, just as London's smoke made the capital's denizens ill.

St. Sevier sent me a wink over his shoulder, and I was abandoned into Lord Rutland's keeping. I should not have minded that I had no idea where Hugh would sleep or how to find him, but two years of mourning had left me with nervous tendencies, and thus I admitted to slight anxiety as I saw him disappear up a majestic curving staircase.

"Away with us," Lord Rutland said, taking my hand and replacing it on his arm. "A soldier learns to treasure the fine weather, because the other kind inevitably comes around at the most inconvenient moment. The gardens are just beginning to bloom, and Athena and I are insufferably proud of them."

"Do you miss army life?" I asked as he led me into a corridor that opened off the foyer. An abundance of windows—one might say an extravagance of windows—filled even this part of the house with sunlight and warmth. The corridor begged for green plants and for the occasional napping cat, but instead held more art.

"I miss army life probably in the same way you miss the Season you made your come out. You have memories of that time gilded with a fond, inaccurate patina. You made great friendships that you will treasure into old age, and yet, you would not wish that same ordeal on anybody you cared for."

He'd got the last part right.

"Tell me, Lady Violet, how does my friend St. Sevier honestly fare?"

The question took me somewhat aback, for I was not Hugh's wife, ;;or even his official intended, that my counsel on the subject of his wellbeing should have been sought.

"He is well," I said, which was true. Hugh enjoyed roaring good physical health and impressive animal spirits. "As far as I know, Monsieur is happily settled into civilian life."

"His situation was difficult." Lord Rutland ushered me through another door onto a sprawling back terrace. "He served well, despite all, and his facility with the French language was abundantly useful. Welcome to my garden, Lady Violet."

I stepped out into the sunlight and was immediately aware of the scent of the forest rising up behind the house.

Forests in southern England tended to roll placidly along next to farmland, tamed in antiquity and put in service to civilization. Many had been reduced to mere home wood status, providing fuel, game, and timber for a specific estate.

In contrast to that sylvan domesticity, Rutland Wood manor was enthroned before high hills blanketed with tall conifers. The forest remained primeval here, dense, dark, and imposing, despite the grand gleaming manor seated on its border. Oaks and other hardwoods lined paths to the stables and outbuildings, but I had no doubt that given a few generations of freedom, the mountain forest would swallow every evidence of civilization.

Perhaps Rutland enjoyed the challenge of keeping nature battled into submission, for the struggle would be endless. His gardens were not safe from the mountain's encroachment, for all they were exquisite. Formal parterres were lined with brilliant beds of tulips in a repeating pattern of red, yellow, and white. A few precocious irises —alternating beds of purple and white—lined up along the central walkway, and faded daffodils had been subdued into tidy bundles along the peripheries.

"How delightful," I said, resisting the urge to shake free of my escort and wander at will. His lordship would march me up and down the rows, I was certain. We'd move sedately and smiling all the while, but we'd travel the route of his choosing at the pace he set.

"Athena loves her garden," Lord Rutland said, "and I love Athena, hence we indulge our gardeners."

A profession of husbandly devotion ought to have charmed me. I instead found it a trifle gauche. A man should *show* the world he loved his lady rather than bandy the words so genially before a near stranger. Freddie had been full of adoring words as he'd slipped out the door to cavort with his mistresses.

Or perhaps a devoted husband ought to do both—make the professions and perform the devoted deeds. I was hardly a qualified judge of marital romance.

"Your garden reminds me of one facet of London life that pales compared to rural splendors," I said. "And how I adore the scent of the forest. I'm put in mind of my recent stay in Perthshire."

Though in central Scotland, the forest had a more stately quality, perhaps because the pines were enormous and thus spaced more widely.

"Did you enjoy your time up north?" Lord Rutland asked, leading me down the steps.

"Very much. The people are quite friendly, the scenery breathtaking. I did not want to leave."

St. Sevier had escorted me north to attend a friend's wedding, and he and I had got more than we bargained for in terms of prenuptial intrigue. I had also seen, for the first time, the ancestral home of Sebastian MacHeath, Marquess of Dunkeld. Sebastian had been a dear acquaintance of my youth, but military service and misunderstandings had parted us.

I had only recently begun to rebuild my friendship with the marquess, and I hoped in future to continue with the project.

"I did not want to leave Rutland Wood," my host said, starting me down a path along a south-facing fruit wall. "But my family has had military connections for generations, back to the original baronies and probably to Roman days. I could not fail my heritage, and I wasn't about to let old Boney threaten all of this."

Boney's hopes of invading England had been dashed when Nelson had dispatched the French fleet at Trafalgar in 1805. British troops had not been sent to the Iberian Peninsula until several years later, and I was still hazy regarding the precise motivation for their deployment. Stopping the Corsican fiend had been the rhetoric of the day, but regaining access to Continental markets had likely been the true agenda.

I did not raise that question with my escort, knowing how military men could wax lyrical about battles, campaigns, and marches. My brother Felix had served, and from him, I'd gained a realistic and ugly picture of war.

"Your wife has a military background, does she not?" I asked.

"Born in an officer's tent while her papa was on maneuvers," Rutland said, bending to snap off a fading daffodil and toss it into the opposite lavender border. "Athena knows military history better than Oxford dons know their Latin, and she's the equal of Wellington for planning a campaign. I sometimes think she married me so she could divert herself with the management of a regiment of inside servants and another battalion out of doors. We did not expect you quite so early in the day, and she will be mortified to have missed your arrival."

"The coach made good time," I replied. "For which a toll will doubtless be exacted when we continue south."

"Then you must bide with us a while and fortify yourself for the looming ordeal," Rutland said, his hand over mine on his arm. "We see little company here, except in high summer when the hillwalkers swarm the surrounds. They appear for a few weeks, like summer roses, and then decamp for the south for another year. We are always glad to see them arrive and equally glad to see them go."

"Are your neighbors sociable?" I asked as we turned the corner at the foot of the garden.

"Oh, very, and I have created a sort of old soldiers' regiment at the Wood as well. My erstwhile quartermaster, Thomas MacNeil, is my senior steward. Garth Jones, a former aide-de-camp, leases out the largest tenant property from us. Be warned: Athena will insist on taking you calling at Spruce Manor. I also employ Patrick O'Dea as my botanist and surveyor, another former aide-de-camp. We and our ladies form a very congenial company, and enlisted men who served under us have also found employment on the estate."

Rutland was proud of his congenial company, as if he'd carved out a circle of civilization in some foreign wilderness. Perhaps that instinct, to create a sense of home from a shared flask and stories around a campfire, was one of the military's strongest and best qualities.

"I very much appreciate your hospitality," I said as we passed a bed of yellow tulips. A lone red specimen bloomed near the center of the bed, which I found whimsical. Life was like that—unexpected at times, refusing to follow the ordained pattern. "No traveling coach appeals after about the third day on English roads."

"Excuse me," Rutland said, peeling free of my hand. "Somebody has been lax." He produced a penknife and sliced off the red tulip, pitching it into a hedge before I could claim it. "With twelve under-gardeners and more than a dozen apprentices to oversee, discipline is sometimes wanting."

A horticultural staff that size would also be responsible for the kitchen gardens, apothecary garden, scent garden, and conservatory —on a large estate, much depended on the competence and diligence of the gardeners—but still... My father was an earl, and his seat was not nearly this impressive.

"We have been discovered," Rutland said, taking my arm again. "My darling wife approaches, and she will steal you away from me." He *twinkled* at me, as if he and I shared a luscious little secret, and then turned the same affable, boyish smile on the lady coming down the gravel walkway.

She was smiling as well, her skirts swishing as she marched along.

"You must be Lady Violet," she said. "Rutland, you are very naughty to whisk our guest off into the garden before she has been offered tea and a chance to refresh herself. My lady, good day. I would ask my husband to make the introductions, but we aren't particularly formal here at the Wood. I am Athena, Lady Rutland. My lord, be off with you. We ladies must get acquainted."

Clearly, I was in the presence of the general's daughter.

"I have my orders." Lord Rutland bowed to me and kissed his wife's cheek, though so casual was his aim that his lips grazed the corner of her mouth. She bore this affectionate display with good cheer—I had the sense her ladyship did everything with good cheer— and then took my arm with the same proprietary air her husband had displayed toward me.

"Come along, my lady. I have a tray on the way to the conservatory, and when we have drained the pot, we will find Monsieur St. Sevier and demand that he escort us on a tour of the house. You will meet the others at dinner, but I must have you to myself for a little while first."

Rutland beamed at me, saluted with two fingers, and strode off. Perhaps he enjoyed springing his wife on their guests, or perhaps the fault lay with St. Sevier, of the wistful smile.

In any case, Athena, Lady Rutland, was quite the most beautiful woman I had ever beheld.

Order your copy of ***Lady Violet Enjoys a Frolic***!

Made in the USA
Middletown, DE
02 September 2022